Ulterior Motives

*Also by Terri Blackstock
in Large Print:*

Blind Trust
Evidence of Mercy
When Dreams Cross
Broken Wings
Justifiable Means

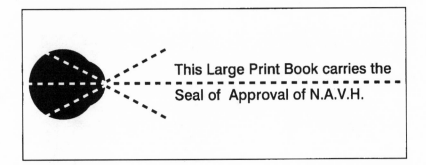
This Large Print Book carries the
Seal of Approval of N.A.V.H.

Ulterior Motives

Terri Blackstock

Thorndike Press • Thorndike, Maine

Published in 1998 by arrangement with Zondervan Publishing House.

Thorndike Large Print® Christian Mystery Series.

The tree indicium is a trademark of Thorndike Press.

The text of this Large Print edition is unabridged. Other aspects of the book may vary from the original edition.

Set in 16 pt. Plantin by Al Chase.

Printed in the United States on permanent paper.

Library of Congress Cataloging in Publication Data

Blackstock, Terri, 1957–
   Ulterior motives / Terri Blackstock.
      p. cm. — (Sun-coast chronicles)
    ISBN 0-7862-1556-9 (lg. print : hc : alk. paper)
    1. Large type books. 2. Kidnapping — Fiction. I. Title.
II. Series: Blackstock, Terri, 1957– Sun coast chronicles.
[PS3552.L34285U4 1998]
  813′.54—dc21   98-27480

*This book and all those to follow it
are lovingly dedicated to
The Nazarene*

Acknowledgments

I could not have written this book if I had not known what it is to be a mother or a step-mother. So I'd like to thank my children for the invaluable material they've given me.

My thanks to Michelle, my firstborn, who is so much like me that it makes her angry sometimes. But unlike me, Michelle has extraordinary gifts. She can sing like an angel, and write like a poet, and think like a philosopher. She feels things deeply, has compassion and encouragement for those who hurt, and is never afraid to share the good news with those who are lost. I can't wait to see what God does with her!

My thanks to Marie, my baby who's not a baby anymore, who has probably been used of God more than anyone else to teach me about gentleness and patience. Her sensitive side sometimes requires more care than the average child, but I suspect that that is one of God's special gifts that he intends to use in his time. She has other gifts, as well. She is an organizer and planner, and rarely forgets anything, and her fertile imagination is as well-developed as her sense of humor. She is a friend to many, even at her young age. I know God has special plans for her, too.

My thanks to Lindsey, my stepson, who is both peacemaker and jester. He has the special gift of bringing harmony wherever he goes, making people laugh, putting them at ease. He sees people through special eyes, not as others see them, but as God sees them. I see God working in him already, preparing him for something big!

None of these children has had the privilege of sailing through life without jostles or bruises. No child of divorce has that privilege. But I firmly believe that God will use each jostle, each bruise, for good in these children. He's making them into precious instruments already.

Thanks, guys, for giving me all of the emotions I needed to write this book!

CHAPTER ONE

He had never killed before, but it hadn't been as difficult as he'd imagined. It was a simple thing, really. The element of surprise, along with the right weapon and the adrenaline pumping through him in amazing jolts, had made it all happen rather quickly. There had been no noise, no hopeless pleading for mercy. He hadn't even had to look in his friend's eyes as he'd pulled the trigger.

With one foot on either side of the body, he bent down and probed his victim's pockets with his gloved hands. Loose change spilled out onto the floor, along with a set of keys. He took the keys and stepped away from the body, leaving it where it had dropped.

Hurrying up the stairs of the elegant art gallery — the walls accented with paintings from known and unknown artists — he reached the office. The door was locked, and he fumbled for the right key and opened it. The pungent scent of paint dominated the small studio, along with the smell of mineral oil. Canvases lay propped against the wall in varying stages of progress; in the back corner sat several framed paintings waiting to be exhibited downstairs and possibly sold. Some old, cracked, and damaged paintings by well-known artists sat in stretchers awaiting restoration so that they could be sold at European auctions for thousands of dollars.

But none of these things were what interested him.

On the other side of the studio was another door, and he unlocked it and went in. It was the office from which Dubose, who now lay dead on the floor of the gallery, had conducted his business with important clients, and as always, it was immaculate and tasteful, with antique Chippendale chairs in the corners and a Louis XIV desk at the center of the room, a throne-like leather chair behind it. On the polished desk sat a small banker's lamp, a desk diary, a Rolodex, and a calculator. Behind it, on the lavish credenza, was an eight-volume set of the *Dictionary of Painters and Sculptors*, widely known in art circles as the definitive resource on lost and stolen art across the world.

He pulled the chain on the lamp, lighting a circle beneath it, then opened the desk diary and turned to this week. There it was, written beneath tomorrow's date — the name and number of the man Dubose had kept so secret. The man Dubose was to have met with tomorrow. He tore off the page, folded it neatly, and slid it into his coat pocket. To-morrow he would contact the man and take over the deal himself. He needed only one thing more, and he knew exactly where to find it.

He unlocked the small doorway at the rear of Dubose's office that led up to the attic. He turned on the yellow lights that lit the top floor of the building. Slowly, carefully, he made his way up the stairs.

The attic smelled of dust, and the floor creaked beneath his feet as he stepped between boxes, over stacked antique frames, past discarded sculptures and paintings. What he wanted was in a corner of the attic — in a long wooden box built into the top corner, in which Dubose had stored what they'd worked together to hide for so many years. He opened the panel and reached inside.

It was gone.

Shock and fear made his heart race, his skin turn cold. He pulled a box over to step up and look inside. The compartment was empty.

Rage exploded like lava inside him, and he whirled around, scanning the contents of the attic. Where could it be?

He sank to the dusty planks beneath him and slid his gloved hands through his hair.

Someone had taken it. But who? Had Dubose realized that he was going to be double-crossed by his partner? Surely not; he'd played it too carefully. Dubose hadn't known what was coming.

He felt himself growing dizzy with fury as he rose. He steadied himself on the rail as he made his way back down the stairs, through the office and studio and back down to the gallery. The body still lay facedown in a pool of blood. He had acted too quickly, he thought. He should have made sure he had what he wanted before he pulled the trigger. Now it was too late for Dubose to tell him where it was.

He would have to figure it out for himself.

Already, he had a good idea, and he would find it no matter what it required. It was his, and he had earned it. No one else was going to reap the profits of his labor.

He didn't care who else had to die.

CHAPTER TWO

Christy Robinson stretched as tall as her six-year-old body would allow and reached for the bottom branch of her favorite back-yard tree. She could touch it with the tips of her fingers, but that wasn't good enough to pull her up.

"Use the ladder," her mother called from the screened porch of their home. "That's why I had it built."

Christy backed up from the tree and eyed the ladder that went up the tree's trunk to the tree house nestled in the branches. "No, ladders are for wimps," she called back to her mother. "Watch this, Mommy! Are you watching?"

Sharon came outside onto the patio and leaned back against the apricot stucco of her huge Florida home. She was dressed in a blue business suit and high heels, and her short auburn hair rustled in the wind that was a little too cool even for February in St. Clair, Florida.

Satisfied that she had her mother's full attention, the little girl got a running start and leaped high to grab onto the branch.

She swung for a moment, then flipped until her feet came up between her arms. She wrapped her legs over the branch and hung upside-down, looking at her mother as her face slowly turned crimson and her foot-long cotton-colored hair flopped beneath her. "See? Told you I could reach."

"If you hurt yourself I'll kill you!" Sharon said, moving closer as if to catch her as the child righted herself and began climbing farther up. "I knew Jake was putting the tree house too high."

"No, Mommy," Christy said as she made her careful way higher. "It's perfect. Just right. Mr. Jake said I had to get used to heights if I'm gonna jump out of airplanes when I grow up."

"Over my dead body!" Sharon returned. "I need to have a little talk with Jake about putting these ideas into your head."

"They're my ideas!" Christy said. "I put them into *his* head."

Sharon tried not to be nervous as her daughter — who looked tiny so high up — reached the tree house and took the last step to the top of the ladder that went into the entrance hole at the center of the tree house's floor. Christy had insisted on the hatch in the floor, rather than a front door, and Jake had built it exactly to her specifications.

"The kid knows what she wants," he'd

told Sharon. "Might as well do it her way, if she's the one who's going to use it."

When she was satisfied that Christy was safely inside, Sharon called up, "I have to go in and finish some paperwork, honey! Don't climb down until I get back here. I'll leave the window open so I can hear you."

Christy stuck her face in the square doorway. "Okay, Mommy. I'll call you when I get through making my guitar."

A guitar? Sharon thought with a smile. There was no telling what the child was making it out of. She had spent the past week collecting tissue boxes, drink cans, milk cartons, paper towel rolls, rubber bands, and heaven knew what else. All of them had been carried up in a backpack and stored like little treasures inside the tree house.

Still smiling, Sharon went back inside the huge house and looked through the front windows for any sign of her sixteen-year-old, Jenny. Sharon had told her to come straight home from school to baby-sit Christy so that Sharon could make it to the closing of the house on Lewis Street. She was only a few minutes late, but it worried Sharon nonetheless.

She went into her study and made some necessary revisions on her paperwork, frequently glancing out her open window to keep an eye on Christy. Then she loaded the papers into her briefcase, took it into the den, and set it in a chair next to a small Queen Anne table covered with framed pictures in a variety of sizes and shapes. The pictures told part of the story of their family. Sharon and her two daughters graced the table in elegant antique frames, their faces representing different ages and eras of their lives. The girls' father was conspicuously absent in the pictures on this table. But upstairs, in the children's private domain, one could find the whole story. Sharon and the two girls — Jenny and Christy — and their father and his new wife Anne, and the two young children that new family had produced, half-sisters to Jenny and Christy.

It was a tangled web, this modern family with all its branches and extensions, and she would have moved heaven and earth to stop it from becoming this way. But that decision had been taken out of her hands. Marriage was sacred to her, and divorce had never been an option. But her husband had not held the same sentiments.

She heard a car pull into the driveway, and rushed to the kitchen to look out the window.

Sixteen-year-old Jenny, who wore her

prettiness with uncertainty, got out of her little car and headed for the door. Though her blonde hair was recently brushed and her makeup was flawlessly applied — no doubt she'd touched it up in the bathroom during her study hall — Sharon could see by the look on Jenny's face that something was wrong.

Sharon opened the door. "Hi, honey."

"Hi."

Sharon noted the despondence in Jenny's voice — and remembered that her moods were sometimes sincere, sometimes practiced. One never knew if Jenny's crises were really crises or just part of the daily drama that was the life of a teenager.

"Sorry I'm late," she said. "I had a note on my windshield from a friend in trouble, and I had to go help."

"That's okay. I'm not late — yet." Sharon rushed back into the den and grabbed her briefcase, then returned to the kitchen. Her daughter had not yet kicked off her shoes and gone to the refrigerator, her usual routine upon arriving home, which meant that something was on her mind. "Something wrong, honey?"

Jenny plopped into a chair, her long blonde hair falling into her face as she covered it dramatically with her hands. "Oh,

Mom, it's just awful! This friend of mine —
someone I care a lot about — is in trouble,
and I've been trying to help. I really need to
get back there. I can take Christy with me.
It's just — I have to go. Mom, they're in
such a mess!"

These were real tears, Sharon noted with
surprise. She set her briefcase down and
stood next to Jenny, pulling her close.
"Honey, tell me. Who needs you?"

The words burst out: "Mom, these friends
of mine, they're married and have these precious little kids, and yesterday he got fired
from his job for no reason at all. And to
make matters worse, they got evicted from
their house and last night they spent the
night in their car — their *whole family*. They
didn't have any money, so they ate food that
people had thrown away behind a fast-food
restaurant."

"That's awful," Sharon said. "Who are
they? Someone you know from church?"

"No. Not from church. They're friends
from Westhaven."

Westhaven was an artsy area on the west
side of St. Clair. It was the area where Ben
lived — Sharon's ex-husband and Jenny and
Christy's father. Since her children had an
entire life in Westhaven on alternate weekends that she knew little about, the explana-

tion didn't surprise her.

"Mom, can you picture those little kids sleeping in the backseat of their car?" Jenny cried. "It's not fair."

Sharon's own eyes began to well. "No, it's not. Where are they now? Can you get in touch with them?"

Jenny sniffed and looked up at her. "Yes, I know where they are."

"Then go get them and bring them back here. At least we can give them a place to sleep and some food until they get on their feet. We have plenty of room."

Jenny hesitated, but her wet eyes were hopeful. "Mom, are you sure?"

"Of course. When I bought this house, I promised myself that I'd never turn away anyone in need. I would never deliberately let some poor family sleep out on the street when we have five bedrooms. Besides, it wouldn't be the first time we've taken somebody in."

"But you don't even know who they are."

"It doesn't matter who they are. They're welcome here."

A tentative smile broke through Jenny's tears.

"What are you waiting for?" Sharon asked, getting up and heading for the refrigerator to see if she needed to make a trip to the store before their guests arrived. "Go get them. My closing won't take long. I'll hurry home, change the sheets in the guest rooms, and cook something nice for supper. Don't worry about Christy. I'll take her with me."

But Jenny kept sitting there, staring, as if she had something else to say but didn't quite know how to say it. "Mom?"

Sharon checked the pantry, distracted. "Hmm?"

"There's one more thing you should know."

"All right," Sharon said. "Shoot."

"This family . . . it's Dad and Anne and the kids."

Sharon felt the blood draining from her face. Slowly, she turned to face her daughter. "Is this a joke, Jenny?"

Jenny didn't look amused. Tears filled her eyes again, and she wiped her face as it reddened. "It's no joke, Mom. Mr. Dubose fired Daddy yesterday, just out of the blue, and took all his credit cards that the gallery had given him. Daddy was living in the apartment provided by the gallery, and Mr. Dubose told him to get out last night. They had no place to go, and Mr. Dubose refused to give Daddy his last paycheck or the paintings he still had in the studio."

"And your father didn't have any savings?

Any money in his wallet?"

Jenny closed her eyes. "Mom, you know Daddy's never been good with money. He's an artist, not a banker. The gallery took care of things for him so he could paint."

"Well, what did he do to get fired?" Sharon spouted.

"Nothing!" Jenny shouted back. "He has no idea what happened."

"Right," Sharon bit out. "Just like he had no idea how Anne got pregnant while he was still married to me. Life is a big mystery to your father."

"Mom!" Jenny cried.

Sharon leaned over the kitchen counter, angry at herself for breaking her cardinal rule not to put Ben down in front of his children. She let out a ragged sigh. "I'm sorry. I shouldn't have said that."

Jenny sank down into a chair. "Mom, you offered to let them stay here. You said it didn't matter who it was."

Sharon swung around. "That was before I knew it was them! You lied to me, Jenny! You set me up!"

"I did not lie!" Jenny cried. "I just didn't tell you who they were! I knew you would refuse to help if you knew, and I wanted you to see how hypocritical that is!"

"Your father lost his job and his home, and

21

now *I'm* a hypocrite? How do you figure that?"

"Because you'd help anyone else! The Golden Rule applies to everybody but Daddy, doesn't it, Mom? 'Doing unto the least of these' is great — unless the least of these is Daddy."

"Jenny, you can't be serious! It's crazy to think that I, of all people, would take him in, with that woman who destroyed my family, and those children that she loves to flaunt in my face!"

"Mom, I've seen you spend entire weekends working at shelters with winos and runaways. I've seen you go to prisons and teach Bible classes to inmates. If you'd do it for them, why not for my father?"

"One very good reason," Sharon said coldly. "Because he brought every bit of this on himself. He's irresponsible, and it's catching up with him!"

"But Emily and Bobby are my sister and brother! They don't deserve to eat out of a garbage dump or sleep in a car."

"They're your *half*-sister and brother. There's a big difference."

"They're my *sister* and *brother,* Mom, whether you like it or not. And if they were in the same predicament and didn't belong to Daddy, you'd be one of the first people I know to help them." She tilted her head pleadingly. "Please, Mom. Won't you let them stay here just for a few days? We have all this room — five bedrooms — and they have nothing!"

The thought of inviting the man who had cheated on her and betrayed her, not to mention the woman who had wrecked their marriage, to sleep in her home was repulsive. It had taken Sharon five years to lose the pain, to learn not to grieve each time the kids went to spend their alternate weekends with their father. When she saw Anne, Sharon no longer seethed with hatred for this woman who had seduced her husband, then delightfully announced that she was having his child. Yes, she had grown beyond the misery. But this . . .

"They *cannot* stay here," Sharon said, setting her hands on her hips. "You can put a guilt trip on me for this if you want to, and blame me for everything, and convince yourself that this is all my fault, but I can't take that man and that woman into my home. I can't do it! It's too much to ask."

The crushing disappointment on Jenny's face made Sharon feel about an inch tall, and she found herself getting angry about her daughter's grief.

"Mom, what are they gonna do? This is

my father, and my family, and I love them! Little Bobby's getting sick, and there they are out in their car. And it's cold —"

"Bobby's sick? Whatsa matter with him?" Christy stood in the doorway holding a makeshift guitar made of a tissue box with rubber bands for strings and a paper towel roll for the neck. The whole thing glistened with transparent tape.

"Christy, I told you not to come down without me!"

Christy looked apologetic. "I wanted to surprise you with my guitar." She strummed it, making a discordant sound, and danced a little. Ordinarily, Sharon and Jenny would both have laughed, but neither was able to at the moment.

Christy stopped dancing and looked up at her sister's red, wet face. "What's wrong, Jenny? What did you say about Bobby being sick?"

Jenny seized the moment to get her clout-carrying little sister involved. "He doesn't have a place to live! Neither do Daddy or Anne or Emily," she blurted. "And we have this huge house, but Mom won't let them stay here."

"Oh, for heaven's sake . . ."

The little blonde girl came farther into the kitchen, her huge eyes full of distress. "Why

24

can't they stay here, Mommy?"

"Because!" Sharon glared at Jenny for dragging the child into this. "Jenny, you're not playing fair."

"Neither are you!" Jenny's face was growing redder as the tears came faster, and though Sharon knew she was, indeed, being manipulated, she also knew that it wasn't an act. Jenny was seriously tormented by her father's plight. "Mom, how would you feel if your father were out on the street? I know you hate Daddy and Anne, but think about the kids. Christy and Emily are close, Mom, really close — and right now Emily hasn't had a bath in two days, she hasn't slept in a bed, she hasn't eaten a full meal. Mom, she's only five years old! She shouldn't have to face this. And the baby just cries all the time. They need to take him to the doctor, but they don't have any money! Mom, just forget how you feel about him, and do this for *me*. Please!"

Sharon looked from Jenny's pleading eyes to those big blue eyes of her younger child, staring up at her with disbelief that she couldn't help her father when he was so obviously in need. She grabbed her purse and yanked out her wallet. "I'll give them some money for a hotel and food. That's all I can do."

"Really, Mom?" Jenny asked. "You'd do that? Because that would help. He'd probably even like it better."

Sharon breathed a laugh. "I'll bet he would." She jerked the money out of her billfold and began to count it. When she looked up again, she saw the hurt looks on her daughters' faces.

She took a deep breath, trying to calm down, hating herself for the feelings coursing through her. "No matter what you think, Jenny, I don't hate your father. I never wanted to see him destitute. I'll give him as much as I can." She handed her the stack of bills. "I have $150. I just went to the bank today. Give it all to him."

A smile broke through Jenny's tears. "Thank you, Mom. This means so much."

Sharon decided not to reply to that, so she leaned over and kissed Christy on the cheek. "Go get your shoes on. You and Jenny are going to take the money to Daddy while I go to my appointment."

Christy hugged her fiercely. "Bye, Mommy."

Deep love rose inside her for the small child she had raised virtually alone. "You be good, okay? And when you get back, no tree climbing. That tree is off-limits unless I'm home."

"Okay. Can I take my guitar to show Daddy?"

"Of course. Maybe you can play it for him and cheer him up."

She hugged Jenny and felt the extra squeeze her daughter gave her.

"We'll see you tonight, Mom."

"Yeah," Sharon said. She got her briefcase and headed for her car.

CHAPTER THREE

Tony Danks stooped near the body. It had been found by a cleaning woman who had called the police, frightened out of her wits. Her 911 call had been almost incoherent. From the looks of things, the man had probably been dead since yesterday. Tony studied the change lying on the floor, as if it had fallen out of the victim's pocket. Something didn't ring true. Change didn't just jump out of pockets like that. He pulled out his notepad and jotted down the possibility that this had been a robbery, even though his wallet looked undisturbed in his back pocket.

Squatting beside the body, he reached into the pockets himself and found only a pair of keys. Probably the keys to the gallery, he thought. He took them out and dropped them into an evidence bag in case they were needed later.

He looked up at the photographer. "Did you get a shot of this change lying here?"

"Yeah," the cop said. "You can go ahead and tag it."

With rubber-gloved hands, Tony began to pick up the bloody change and drop it into a bag of its own. He came to a gold money clip with the initials BLR. "Hey, Jack? What did you say the victim's name is?" he asked the cop who'd been the first to arrive on the scene.

"Louis Dubose."

"Hmm," he said, and dropped the money clip into another bag. "The initials on this say BLR."

"Maybe he's our killer," the photographer said. "Maybe it fell out of his pocket."

Tony was skeptical. "If so, there were an awful lot of things falling out of pockets."

He got another bag and pulled the hairs from the victim's fingers. "On the other hand, there was probably a struggle before the killer shot him in the back. Who knows?" He carefully tagged the hairs. They would be sent to the lab today and would probably go far in helping them to identify the killer.

He stood up. "So what's the story on that apartment at the back?"

Jack checked his notes. "According to the cleaning woman, some artist named Ben Robinson lived back there until yesterday. Looks like he moved out in a rush. Left all the furniture behind, but no clothes or personal items."

"Ben Robinson," Tony repeated. "BLR. I'd say he's the first person we need to question."

"If we can find him."

"We'll find him," Tony assured him.

The front door opened and Larry Millsaps, Tony's partner, came in brandishing a bag. "You'll never guess what I found in the dumpster out behind the gallery."

"What?" Tony asked.

"The murder weapon. A .22."

"Did you run a check on it?"

"Yeah. It's registered to a Ben Robinson. At this address."

Tony looked back around the gallery, where other cops were videotaping, fingerprinting, photographing. "What do you bet that our Ben Robinson has long blonde hair?"

"Did you find some?"

"Yep. That and a money clip with his initials. Looks like he was in a hurry to leave, too. Didn't stick around long enough to clean up."

"I'd say it's time to make an arrest," Larry said.

"I'm right behind you," Tony told him.

CHAPTER FOUR

Bobby was sound asleep when Ben Robinson checked his family into the inexpensive motel room, carrying the bags of food they had picked up at the nearby fast-food restaurant. Ben laid the six-month-old baby down on one of the double beds, covered him with the blanket he was wrapped in, and felt his head. "I think his fever has gone down," he told Anne, who was ushering Christy and Emily in. "The Tylenol helped."

Jenny sat down next to him, careful not to disturb the sleeping baby. "The least Mr. Dubose could have done was give you his crib."

Anne set the bag of two-liter drinks on the table. "He said all the furniture belonged to the gallery," she said in a weary monotone.

"It did belong to the gallery," Ben said, his tone reflecting hers.

"Yeah, well, we should have seen this coming," Anne went on. "When you depend on other people, you wind up out in the street, sleeping in your car."

"Mommy, can I eat now?" Emily asked.

"Sure, sweetheart." Anne's tone softened as she looked down at the five-year-old, a couple of inches shorter than Christy, and with shorter hair, although in color it was identical to Christy's. It was obvious to anyone that they were sisters, even though they did have different mothers. She dug into the bag for Emily's burger. "Christy, here's one for you."

Christy looked questioningly at Jenny.

"I told you we don't need anything," Jenny said. "Christy and I can eat at home. You need to save your money."

"I could tell she was hungry," Anne said with a half-smile. "Besides, it wouldn't be fair for her to sit there and watch us eat and not have anything herself. Here, Chris. Your drink is in the box."

Christy smiled and went to get it.

Jenny got up from the bed and went to her father, who stood leaning against the wall, his pale eyes distant and dismal. His usually clean blonde hair was oily because he hadn't had the chance to shower since yesterday, and he had it pulled back in a ponytail, a look that her mother found disgusting, but all her friends considered cool. He was unshaven, and she noticed the tired lines under his eyes. Without those lines, he could have passed for her older brother, rather than her forty-year-old father.

She slid her arms around him from behind

and laid her head against his back. At six feet, he was almost a head taller than she. "Daddy, are you okay?"

He pretended to snap out of it, and smiled. "Yeah. I was just thinking. Somehow I've got to get all my paintings out of the gallery. They're my livelihood. If I could sell them, or at least take them to another gallery . . ."

"Have you tried calling Mr. Dubose again?" Jenny asked. "Maybe he's cooled off by now, and he'll talk."

"I tried," Ben said. "There's still no answer. Besides, he had nothing to cool off from. I didn't do anything to prompt it."

"Are you *sure?*" Anne asked again, as she'd asked a thousand times since yesterday. "Ben, *think*. A man doesn't fire you from your job and evict you from your home the same afternoon, if you haven't done anything. If you could apologize, maybe —"

He stiffened. "Anne, how many times do I have to tell you? There's nothing to apologize for! When are you gonna believe me?"

She held up a hand to stem the argument, and breathing a deep sigh, turned back to the children.

"This is awful," Jenny whispered.

Ben nodded and raked his hand through his long disheveled hair. "I never would have dreamed I'd have to take money from your mother to keep my family off the street."

"Mom didn't mind. She was happy to do it."

"Yeah, I'll bet." Catching himself, he muttered, "It really was nice of her. She didn't have to do it."

Jenny sighed and looked helplessly around the room. Little Emily was so tired that she could hardly eat, so Jenny went over and pulled the cotton-topped five-year-old into her lap. "Come on, Emily. Let me help you with this."

She began to feed the child one french fry at a time.

"She needs a nap," Anne said. "She didn't sleep very well last night. Bobby kept coughing, and the car wasn't all that comfortable."

"Anne, if Bobby gets worse, you'll take him to the emergency room, won't you?" Jenny asked.

Anne shot Ben a look that said they couldn't do even that without money. "Yeah. Somehow, we'd convince them to treat him. There's always the health department. They treat indigents."

Ben stiffened, knowing that her remark had been intended to sting. "We are not indigent."

"Right," Anne said sarcastically. "We're

just homeless, penniless, and jobless. At least we're not sleeping under a bridge somewhere. I guess I should brace myself. That could be coming."

Ben went into the bathroom, the only place to which he could escape, and slammed the door behind him.

The sound woke Bobby, and he began to cry, making Ben feel even worse. He sat on the lid of the commode, rubbing his stubbled face, fighting feelings of terror and despair.

So he had come to this.

As always in times of stress, old tapes of Sharon's voice played in his mind.

You're irresponsible, Ben. When are you going to grow up and start acting like an adult?

You're selfish! You don't care about anyone but yourself. You think you've got it all figured out, with your artsy friends and your own set of rules. But this charade of a marriage is going to show everyone just how much of a loser you are.

She had been in pain when she'd said those words, reacting to his own cruelties. But knowing that didn't take away the sting of her accusations — and now he wondered whether he hadn't just proven that they were all true.

He only wished he hadn't spent every penny he made, always counting on the gallery to keep handing over monthly paychecks for his restoration work and the rights to show his work exclusively. He should have been smarter with finances, like his ex-wife was. In five short years, she'd gone from being a struggling real-estate agent to a six-figure wage earner. When she'd bought that house last year, he had convinced himself that it was intended as a slap in the face to him — a way of showing him what he could have had if he hadn't left her for greener pastures. But then he'd felt ashamed of those thoughts when he'd heard how she'd taken in a couple of unmarried pregnant women who'd needed a place to stay while they carried their babies, and then a family whose house had burned down. Her success, he'd finally realized, didn't have anything to do with him at all, one way or the other. She'd simply worked hard for herself and her daughters. His feelings that she was rubbing his nose in her wealth was his problem, not hers. He was the one who made comparisons. She had just gone on with her own life.

And he had his life with Anne. Although it had grown increasingly difficult as the infatuation had worn off and reality had set in, he had tried to make it work. He wasn't going to hurt two more children through a needless divorce. It's not as if he was a victim here. He had the power to turn this around.

But right now, he hated the feeling of Anne's disgust with him, so much like Sharon's. In fact, he realized, she had started reciting Sharon's tapes. Without using the same words, her very tone suggested that he was stupid, selfish, irresponsible, a loser . . .

But he'd prove to them that he wasn't a loser. He had to pull himself together, had to be rational. There was much to be done in the next few days.

Jenny was walking Bobby around the room, trying to make him stop crying so that Anne could eat, when a hard knock sounded on the door.

Anne, who was sitting with food balanced on her lap, sent a pleading look to Jenny. "Would you get that?"

"Sure." Still carrying the crying baby, Jenny stepped over Christy, who was sitting in front of the television, and opened the door.

Two men stood outside, one, a brunette dressed in jeans and a windbreaker and the other, a tall blonde, in khakis and a sport coat.

Bobby still cried, so the man in the sport coat had to raise his voice to be heard. "We're with the St. Clair Police Department," he said, flashing a badge. "I'm Detective Tony Danks, and this is my partner Larry Millsaps. We're looking for Ben Robinson. Is he here?"

"Sure . . . uh . . . just a minute." Anne began to put her food down, and Jenny stepped back over Christy and went to the bathroom, bouncing the crying baby on her hip. She knocked on the door. "Daddy, someone's here to see you."

Ben came out, looking more drawn and weary than she'd ever seen him.

"Someone's here," she repeated, then gave a worried glance back at the cops. "Policemen," she whispered.

Bobby's crying grew louder, and the baby reached for his mother. Anne took him, then followed Ben to the door.

"Officers," Ben said with a nod as he reached the door. "What can I do for you?"

"Ben Robinson?" one of the men confirmed.

"Yes," he said.

The one with the windbreaker pulled a pair of handcuffs out of his pocket. "I have a warrant for your arrest for the murder of Louis Dubose. You have the right to remain silent —"

"No!" Anne screamed, and Jenny rushed forward.

"Daddy!"

"Murder?" Ben asked as they got the cuffs on his hands. "What do you mean, murder?"

"He was found dead an hour ago," Tony Danks said. "You have the right to an attorney. If you can't afford an attorney —"

"There must be some mistake!" Anne cried. "My husband didn't kill anybody."

The baby was screaming louder, and now Emily and Christy abandoned their food and stood holding hands, fearfully watching the scene.

Jenny grabbed her father's arm as they tried to pull him toward their car. "Daddy, tell them you didn't do it! Tell them!"

"It's okay," Ben said hoarsely. "We'll straighten it all out."

But his family, stunned and terrified, watched as he was guided into the backseat of the squad car — and he looked anything but confident, trembling, his eyes wide. They watched wordlessly as the car pulled out of sight.

CHAPTER FIVE

The phone was ringing when Sharon walked into her house. She had just closed the deal on the house on Lewis Street, then had shown three houses to Mrs. Milford, a client who she suspected would never settle on anything. Dropping her purse and briefcase, she picked up the phone.

"Hello?"

"Oh, Mom, thank goodness you're finally home. I've been trying to reach you, but you never answered your car phone."

"I was showing houses. I must have been inside when you called. What's wrong?"

Jenny was crying, and her pain came right through the phone. "Oh, Mom!" She sobbed, caught her breath, and tried to go on. "Daddy's been arrested! They think he killed somebody!"

"What?"

"Mr. Dubose, the gallery manager, was murdered, and they think Daddy did it. Mom, he couldn't have! He was with us! But they won't listen — they don't believe us, and they say he was killed yesterday. Daddy was the last one to see him alive, so they're blaming him. Mom, I don't know what to do! My father is not a murderer!"

"I know he's not," Sharon said. "Jenny, where are you?"

"At the police station. We're all here. Anne's a basket case, and the kids are all upset . . . Christy and Emily don't understand, but they're smart enough to know that their daddy's going to jail! Mom, we've got to get him out!"

Sharon held the phone between her ear and shoulder and grabbed her purse. "Jenny, I'm coming down to the station. I'll be there in ten minutes. Does your father have a lawyer?"

"No. They can't afford one."

"I'll call Lynda," Sharon said. "She's one of the best lawyers in St. Clair."

"Yeah, I forgot she was a lawyer. Mom, ask her to hurry," Jenny said. "They're in there with him right now. Oh, and Mom? Could you stop by the store and get some cough syrup for Bobby? He's coughing his head off."

Sharon didn't like the thought of detouring on her way, but she muttered, "Sure. I'll bring it."

She hung up the phone and quickly dialed Lynda Barrett's number. They were good friends from church, and she knew the number by rote.

"Hello?"

41

"Oh, Lynda, I'm so glad you're home. I didn't have time to look up your office number."

"Sharon, what's wrong?"

"Ben . . . my ex-husband . . . he needs a lawyer. He's been arrested for murder."

"Murder?" Lynda repeated.

"Lynda, the man's one of my least favorite people, and he's capable of a lot. But he's not a killer. You've got to help him. I'll pay you, if he can't. He's at the police station, and they're interviewing him as we speak."

"I'll be there in five minutes," Lynda said.

Sharon hung up and breathed a sigh of relief. Then she rushed out, more concerned about the state of mind of her children than that her ex-husband was being accused of something he couldn't possibly have done.

CHAPTER SIX

Ben hadn't had a shower since yesterday, and as he sat in the over-heated interrogation room — no doubt kept that way by design — sweating and trying to answer all of their questions, he wished he'd at least had time to take a quick bath before the police had come. With his oily ponytail, a two-day growth of stubble, and clothes he'd had on for two days now, he must look like a biker who wouldn't think twice about killing his boss. Now he wished he'd never let his hair grow this long. But he liked the bohemian look that said he didn't have time to worry about his appearance because he was too busy cultivating his imagination. Part of the look was for effect, he admitted, but part of it was reality. Often he got so lost in his work that he *didn't* remember to shower, shave, or eat. That was why he still didn't have the mid-life paunch that most of his contemporaries had after crossing the forty-year mark. He had crossed it last October, and still prided himself on looking ten years younger.

"Look, I told you," he said, keeping his voice even so he wouldn't appear to be losing his temper. "The last time I saw Louis he was locking himself in his office."

"But you were angry at him, weren't you?"

"Yeah, of course I was angry. You'd be angry, too, if your boss threw you and your family out into the street, and wouldn't even give you your last paycheck!"

Lynda Barrett, who had burst in just moments before and announced that the family had retained her to be his lawyer, touched his arm to shut him up.

Ben had almost told her no-thank-you when he'd realized that the aggressive brunette was Sharon's friend. But when he'd seen that she knew the two cops well, he decided to accept her services. Maybe she'd have some pull with them.

"Larry, Tony, my client has already told you everything he knows."

"He hasn't told us why we found the murder weapon in a dumpster behind the gallery — a pistol that was registered to him. And his fingerprints were all over the glass," Tony said.

"No way," Ben argued again. "I've never owned a gun in my life. I don't even know how to use one."

"Were his fingerprints on the gun?" Lynda asked, taking notes.

"No. The killer obviously wore gloves."

Lynda looked up, smiling wryly. "Larry,

you said his fingerprints were all over the glass. If he was wearing gloves, how could that be? Make up your mind."

"I *did* put those fingerprints on the glass," Ben said. "We live in back of the gallery, and the day before I was fired, my little girl, Emily, was playing peek-a-boo with me outside the glass. We both got our fingerprints all over it. I meant to clean it off."

Tony pretended to be making a note. "Fingerprints due to peek-a-boo."

"I'm serious!" Ben said.

"There was obviously a struggle," Larry went on. "There was some overturned furniture."

"That doesn't mean I was there," Ben said.

"There was also a money clip next to the body. It obviously fell out of the killer's pocket. It had the initials BLR, and your fingerprints."

Ben sat straighter. "My money clip? I don't even know where that was. I haven't carried that in a couple of years."

"And there were strands of hair in Dubose's hands, like he'd gotten in a struggle and pulled it out of the killer's head. Blonde hair about your length. At first we thought it was a woman's, but now that we see you . . ."

"So I'm a killer because my hair is long?" Ben asked.

Lynda was still taking notes. She flipped her shoulder-length hair behind an ear. "Where was the entry wound, guys?"

"His back," Tony said, shooting Ben a look. "That ought to make you proud. Courage that matches the hair."

"I would never shoot someone in the back! I would never shoot anyone period!"

Lynda shot Ben a stern look, telling him to shut up. "So if he was shot in the back, then you must have figured out the range by now. How far away was the gun when it went off?"

"We're guessing a few feet."

"All right, then, how did he get a handful of Ben's hair if his back was to him and he was a few feet away?"

"They obviously fought before he turned his back."

"That's ridiculous!" Ben shouted. "I've never fought with him in my life! I don't fight with anybody! That's not my style!"

"Ben, let's go back," Larry said, playing the good guy in the good guy/bad guy routine. "Think about what you two talked about in your last few conversations. Was there anybody else there? Anyone you talked about?"

"No. He was kind of preoccupied."

"With what?" Larry asked.

"I wish I knew. Probably with his plans to throw me out. Then yesterday, out of the blue, he told me I was terminated and that my family and I had to be out of the apartment within the hour. I was stunned. I couldn't believe it."

"Angry, too, huh?" Tony asked.

"Of course I was angry. I was furious."

Lynda nudged his arm again. "That's enough, Ben."

"Not angry enough to kill him! But it was crazy. I tried to go up to my studio and get my paintings, but he said the gallery owned them — that they had paid me to paint them — and that I couldn't take them. I lost my temper when he refused to give me my last paycheck —"

"Ben, as your lawyer, I'm telling you that you've given them enough," Lynda insisted.

"But I have nothing to hide!" Ben said. "All we did was argue, and then he went up to that office of his and locked himself in. He said if I didn't leave within the hour, with my children and my wife and everything we owned, he'd have the sheriff escort me out. So I went to the apartment and started packing. We were gone an hour later. I tried calling him several times from pay phones to reason with him, but the line was busy."

"We can get the records from the phone company," Lynda told Larry and Tony.

"That'll only prove that a call was made to the gallery. It doesn't prove that Dubose was alive when he left him."

"Right," Ben snarled, slapping his hands on the table. "I got into a knock-down, drag-out fight with Dubose and shot him, then left my gun exactly where I knew you'd look for it, then called him afterward just to see if he was really dead."

The detectives both stared at him without amusement, and Lynda closed her eyes and began to massage her temples.

"I'm being sarcastic!" Ben shouted. "Why did I call the guy if I thought he was dead? And about that gun, you need to check out that registration, because I'm telling you, I have never owned one! Ask anybody. You won't find a registration with my name on it."

"We already have, pal."

Ben looked flustered. "You can't. It's impossible. I don't believe in owning guns. I have small children."

"Tell it to the judge," Larry said, jotting another note on his pad.

"People have been known to use other people's names and credentials to get guns," Lynda pointed out. "He has an alibi, Larry."

"Yeah, his wife. Big surprise."

"My children, too," Ben said. "One of them is sixteen years old. She's old enough to remember where I was when."

"Daughters are usually loyal to their fathers," Tony said.

"Then ask my ex-wife! She hates my guts and would probably love to see me rot in jail, but she'll tell you that Jenny was with me part of yesterday and this afternoon."

"We will," Larry said, getting to his feet. "But even if she corroborates what you've said, we've got enough to book you."

Ben covered his face with his hands, unable to believe what was happening. When both detectives had left the room, he turned to Lynda. "I'm gonna have to stay in jail?"

"Until morning, at least," Lynda said. "It'll be okay. You won't spend the most comfortable night of your life, but tomorrow morning I can probably convince the judge to let you out on bond. You have no prior arrests?"

"Not even a traffic ticket," Ben said wearily.

"That should play in your favor. Show up in court with your whole family in tow — all four kids — and maybe he'll show mercy and let you out pending the Grand Jury investigation."

Ben closed his eyes. "My children are all

49

going to know I'm in jail. What kind of image is that for a father?"

"They'll also know you're innocent," she said.

"How do *you* know I'm innocent?" Ben asked angrily. "You don't even know me. If all you know of me is what my ex-wife has told you, then you probably think I'm the scum of the earth."

"Wrong. Sharon's an intelligent woman, and she was married to you for a long time. She wouldn't have married a maniac."

Ben breathed a laugh. "You haven't talked to her lately, have you?"

Actually, she had. "She says you're a good father, Ben. That tells me a lot. She just thinks you were a lousy husband."

Ben shook his head. "That's why I hate this town. You make one mistake, and everybody in town knows about it."

Lynda wore a half-smile as she got up. "Look, I believe your story, and I think I can get you out tomorrow. Then we can start working hard on your case."

"There's a killer out there," Ben said. "Nobody's even looking for him. He got away with it."

"Well, maybe we can put our heads together and figure out who it is." She stuck her notebook into her briefcase and shut it.

"Ben, they're going to put you into a holding cell for the night. Just be patient. You'll probably be in a cell alone, so you'll be safe. I'll see if I can pull some strings to get them to put you in the new wing. The old one is kind of creepy. Oh, and the hearing is early tomorrow." She reached for the doorknob.

"Hey," he said before she could leave. "Tell my wife it's going to be all right. Try to make her feel better about this. She's a good person, regardless of what Sharon may have told you."

"Sharon hasn't said anything to me about her," Lynda said honestly.

"Right. Then you heard it from the famous St. Clair grapevine. All those church ladies who spend all their time exchanging gossip disguised as prayer requests."

Lynda couldn't help chuckling. "Don't worry. I'll forget whatever I've heard. See you tomorrow at the arraignment."

CHAPTER SEVEN

The small St. Clair Police Department was teeming with cops, people filing complaints, criminals waiting to be booked, and friends and family members waiting to bail them out. Sharon, who was able to fit in almost anywhere from soup kitchens to inaugural balls, felt as though she stood out ridiculously in her business suit and heels. She stood uncomfortably at the door and looked around for her children. She spotted Christy sitting with Emily in the middle of a crowd of seething gang members. Jenny sat a little farther down, between two women who could have been hookers. Anne was pacing and bouncing Bobby as he screamed at the top of his lungs.

Sharon rushed across the room and grabbed Christy's hand to pull her out of the midst of the street gang. Five-year-old Emily followed as they found vacant seats at the other end of the waiting area. Jenny got up and followed as they passed her.

"Mom, thank goodness you're here," she whispered. "Anne doesn't handle a crisis very well. She's really losing it."

Sharon shot Anne a look. The woman saw

her and quickly turned her head.

Sharon dug into her purse and pulled out the bag with the cough syrup. "Here, Jenny. Give her this. I also got one of those little measuring spoons I used when Christy was younger, so she can give it to him now."

"Thanks, Mom," Jenny said, then dashed to her stepmother.

Anne took the medicine reluctantly, looking more chagrined than grateful. Without acknowledging that Sharon had brought it, she headed for the bathroom to give it to the baby.

Sharon was glad she was gone. "Where's your father?"

"In that room over there. He's been there since I called you. Anne and I both signed statements saying that he couldn't have killed Mr. Dubose, because he's been with one or both of us since yesterday. But they're saying he did it when Mr. Dubose fired him. He's the only one they can prove was there yesterday, even though Anne saw him alive through the window when they were leaving their apartment."

Sharon looked toward the room. "How does your father get himself into these things?"

"*Mom!*" Jenny's tears had a hair trigger, and they filled her eyes now. "Daddy didn't have anything to do with this. You know that!"

She was instantly ashamed. "You're right; I'm sorry. Your father picks bugs up in his hand and takes them outside to keep from killing them."

"That's right!" Jenny said victoriously, as if that would be just the evidence she needed to clear her father. "Mom, tell them. They'll listen to you."

"I will, when I get the chance."

The door to the interrogation room opened, and Lynda Barrett came out. "Wait here with the girls," Sharon told Jenny, and hurried across the floor to meet Lynda, her heels clicking a staccato beat on the dirty tiles.

"Lynda, what's going on?" Sharon asked.

"Well, it doesn't look good," Lynda admitted. "He's going to have to spend the night in jail. His arraignment is tomorrow morning, and maybe then we can get him out on bond."

"Bond? They're not really charging him with murder, are they?"

"I'm afraid so."

Flustered, Sharon leaned toward her friend, intent on making her understand. "Lynda, I was married to the man for twelve years! He's not capable of murder! He's never even been able to bring himself to spank the kids. He's a lot of things, but he is *not* a killer."

"Sharon, the murder weapon was registered to him."

"Well, what did he say about that?"

"He said that it couldn't have been, that he's never owned a gun in his life."

"That's probably true. He wouldn't even know how to use one."

"Everybody knows how to pull a trigger. That's all the court cares about. He probably will be arraigned, Sharon, but if things go well, we can at least get him out pending an indictment."

"Excuse me!" The voice behind Sharon was Anne's, and Sharon swung around and saw the seething woman, still holding her crying baby. "This is none of her business," Anne said to Lynda. "If you're my husband's lawyer, you should be discussing my husband with me, not her! She doesn't even have the right to be here."

Sharon's teeth came together. "I'm here because I didn't want my children unattended in a police station, Anne."

"They're not unattended. They're with me."

"Forgive me if I thought you might be a little preoccupied, seeing how your husband has just been arrested for murder and all." People were starting to watch them. Sharon lowered her voice. "Look, I'll just go talk to my daughter, and you two can have a private conversation."

Her face was burning by the time she reached Jenny.

"What did she say?" Jenny asked anxiously.

"That this was none of my business. She's got so much nerve. It never fails to amaze me."

"She said that? Really? But I thought —"

"After I gave her that money, and brought the cough medicine, and hired a lawyer . . ."

Jenny's face changed. "Mom, I was talking about Lynda! What did *she* say about Daddy?"

"Oh." Sharon felt stupid and mentally kicked herself. Why was it that her dignity began slipping away bit by bit whenever she was near Anne and Ben? She tried to shift her thoughts. "Lynda said that he would have to spend the night here."

"No!" Jenny cried. "Mom, he can't! There are criminals in jail! He didn't *do* anything."

"Tomorrow is the arraignment, honey."

"What's that?"

"That's when they ask his plea and decide whether to set bond."

"Well, then he'll get out, won't he? There's not any evidence. He can tell them he wasn't there and prove it!"

"Honey, the arraignment is not really for presenting evidence. But Lynda feels sure he can get out tomorrow."

Jenny wiped her eyes. "This is like a nightmare."

"It sure is," Sharon whispered.

Anne turned away from Lynda, mascara-muddled tears staining her face, and she called Emily. Both Christy and Emily came to her, holding hands. "Come on, honey," she told the five-year-old. "We're going back to the motel."

"What about Daddy?"

"He's going to stay here tonight. We'll see him in the morning."

Sharon stood back as Jenny went to kiss Emily and Bobby good-bye. "Anne," Jenny said, "do you want me to come and help you take care of the kids?"

Anne glanced stoically at Sharon and lifted her chin, as if to hide any evidence of vulnerability. "No, thanks. We'll be fine."

"Okay," Jenny said weakly.

"You'll be here in the morning?" Anne asked.

"I sure will," she said. "Try to get some sleep, okay?"

Anne nodded and gave her a hug, then leaned down and kissed Christy on the cheek. Christy returned it easily, a gesture that bothered Sharon more than she ever would have admitted. Christy didn't follow as Anne led Emily out of the building. "Poor Anne," Jenny said, watching her go. "It's like her life is falling apart."

"I remember that feeling," Sharon muttered.

"Mom!"

Sharon took Christy's hand and started to the door. "Come on, girls. Let's get out of here."

Later that night, as Christy was changing into her pajamas, she found in her pocket the little army men that Emily had gotten in her Burger King bag. Emily had no pockets in her own pants, so she had asked Christy to hold them for her.

Christy set the little men up on her dresser and wondered if Emily had missed them. She had been so excited about them when she'd gotten them, even though Christy had found them a disappointment. Emily didn't have many toys, though, and the ones she did have were packed in a box in the back of their car. Carefully, she picked the little army men back up and held them securely in her fist. She would call Emily, she thought, and tell her she had them, so at least she'd know they weren't lost. And maybe she could offer her something else, just to make her feel better about Daddy.

Christy looked around her room for something Emily would like.

Her collection of porcelain dolls lay carefully arranged on the French provincial canopy bed, but she knew that Emily wouldn't really like those, because they broke so easily. On her shelves was a menagerie of stuffed animals. Though Emily had never been in her room before, Christy knew that she would like Simba, the little stuffed lion, better than any of the others. She climbed up on her chair and reached for it.

It was soft and good to sleep with, she thought. Maybe it would keep Emily company, and keep her mind off her troubles.

Clutching the stuffed animal in one hand and the army men in the other, Christy ran down the hall to Jenny's room. Jenny was on the phone, as usual.

"Jenny," she whispered, as if keeping her voice low would not disturb her. "Do you have the number of the motel?"

Jenny put her hand over the receiver. "Why do you need it?"

"I want to call Emily," she said. "She left

her army men. They're real important."

Jenny frowned. "Christy, those aren't important. It can wait."

"She'll cry if she thinks she lost them," Christy said. "She doesn't have anything to play with. I want to tell her that she can have my Simba, too."

Jenny stared at her for a moment, then smiled. "That's sweet of you. Okay, just a minute, and I'll look up the number."

Christy waited as Jenny continued her phone conversation while simultaneously searching the phone book. "Here it is," she said. "I'll circle it for you."

Christy looked hard at the circled phone number. Then, stuffing Simba under one arm, she took the book and headed down the stairs to the study, where her mother had a separate phone line. She climbed into her mother's big chair behind the desk, laid the book open on the desktop, and set the toys down. Picking up the phone, she punched in the number slowly, checking and rechecking each digit against the phone book.

"Holiday Inn," a woman's voice said.

"Can I speak to Emily, please?" she asked.

"There's no one named Emily who works here," the woman said. "Can someone else help you?"

Christy hesitated. "No, I need Emily."

"Emily who?" the woman asked, irritated.

"Emily Robinson. She's my sister."

The woman's voice softened. "Honey, you have the wrong number."

Tears of frustration filled Christy's eyes, and she hung up the phone. Had they gone back home? she wondered. Had they forgotten to tell her where they were?

She dialed their old number and waited through three rings. Finally, an operator's voice cut in. "I'm sorry. The number you've called has been disconnected . . ."

"I want to speak to Emily!" she cried over the voice. When she realized it was a recording, she slammed the phone down and looked helplessly at the phone book again. How could she get in touch with her?

She sat at her mother's big desk, looking at Simba staring expectantly at her, and those three army men poised to strike. What if they had put Emily in jail, too? she thought. What if they had put Bobby and Anne there?

Helpless about her father's plight and about all the other things she didn't understand, she began to cry into her small hands.

Her mother came to the door. "Oh, Christy . . ."

Sharon crossed the room and pulled Christy up into a tight hug, then sat back down with the small girl in her lap.

"I miss Daddy," she squeaked. "And Emily forgot her army guys."

"We'll take Emily her army guys tomorrow when we see her, okay?"

"But she'll cry when she thinks they're lost, and I wanted to call and tell her, but she's not there."

"Honey, it'll be okay. She's probably so tired after everything that's happened that she won't even think about them. Tomorrow will be soon enough. You're going to see her first thing in the morning. And your daddy, too."

"I am?" Christy asked hopefully.

"Yes. You and Jenny are going to court, and they'll both be there."

She wiped her eyes. "Will you be there?"

Sharon thought about that for a moment. "Yes. I think I will go. I'm worried about your daddy, too. But Daddy needs for you and Jenny to sit with Anne and Emily and Bobby, so the judge can see what a beautiful family your daddy has."

The words, though delivered softly, had a little bit of a bite to them, and Christy recognized it. Wiping her eyes, she sat up on her mother's lap. "I want to sit with you. Will you sit by us, too?"

"No, honey," she said. "Anne wouldn't

appreciate that. But I'll be there if you need me."

Christy suddenly felt very tired, and she began to cry again. Her mother hugged her tighter as she laid her head on Sharon's shoulder. "Mommy, can I call and talk to Daddy?"

"No, sweetheart. They don't let him have phone calls where he is."

"I know where he is," Christy said. "He's in jail. You don't have to act like I don't know."

"It's all just a mistake, honey. He'll be out soon."

"You promise?" Christy asked.

Sharon hesitated, and Christy knew that she wasn't going to promise. Sliding off her mother's lap, she grabbed up her Simba and the army men, and started for the door.

"Where are you going, honey?"

"To bed," Christy muttered.

"But it's still early, and you don't have to go to school tomorrow since we have to go to court."

"I'm tired," Christy pouted, rubbing the tears on her face. "I need my rest."

Ordinarily, Sharon would have smiled, but the words were spoken with such dejection that she didn't find them funny.

"All right. Come on, and I'll tuck you in.

And we'll pray for your daddy."

Christy slept with Simba and the army men that night, eager for morning to make sure her father was all right.

CHAPTER EIGHT

The cell was cold and dimly lit. Ben lay on his two-inch-thick mattress stretched across sagging steel springs and tried to sleep. A few cells down, a man sang out a painful dirge in a voice that could have made him millions. How had he wound up here?

Same way I did, he thought. He watched a roach crawl across the ceiling and closed his eyes as it got directly overhead. Jail. He couldn't believe it.

He rolled onto his side and pulled the threadbare blanket up to cover him. Two voices exchanged curses down the way, and a third screamed for them to shut up. Someone closer to his cell banged out a rap beat with a spoon on the edge of his bars, a sound so annoying that he too longed to scream "Shut up!"

Anne was probably scared to death. Anne, who had once made him feel like such an important man; Anne, who had believed in his work and his dream to become a renowned painter; Anne, who had vowed that she would follow him to the ends of the earth, regardless of the consequences, if he would just make her his wife. Over the past five years, after two children and a lot of ups and downs, that deep passion had faded into a more practical (and even cynical) kind of relationship, the kind that he had fled from with Sharon. Did Anne have even an ounce of love for him left? He doubted it. Instead, she was probably wondering what she'd ever seen in him in the first place. He was wondering that himself.

Anne deserved a husband who was strong, resourceful, able to provide. Up to now he'd been none of those things. It was long past time to change that. No matter how many paintings he'd sold, no matter how many important showings he'd had, no matter how many art critics were writing positive assessments of his work, it didn't amount to anything when he was broke, homeless, and lying in a jail cell.

The roach dropped onto his chest, and he jumped up and brushed it off. He kicked it under the bars, out into the corridor, then leaned against the cold iron and looked up the darkened hall.

Would they let him out tomorrow? They had to. He couldn't bear the thought of being in jail until his Grand Jury hearing, separated from his children and his wife.

Somehow, he had to get out tomorrow. And Lynda Barrett was the only one who could get him out. She was Sharon's friend, and one of those superstitious Christians. Still, he did trust her.

After all, he had little choice. There were ways to change his family's luck. But he had to be free to pursue them.

CHAPTER NINE

It was after midnight when the telephone rang in Anne's motel room. She hurried to answer it before it woke her children. "Hello?"

"Anne, is that you?"

The voice sounded distant, and the static over the line made it difficult to hear. "Yes. Who is this?"

"Nelson," the voice said. "Nelson Chamberlain. I'm in London, but I've just heard about Louis's murder."

Chamberlain, who lived in St. Clair even though he traveled most of the time, was one of Ben's biggest supporters. He'd bought at least four of his paintings and sold several more for him in just the past year. He had also been one of Louis Dubose's closest friends. "It was a shock to all of us," she said, shoving her hair back from her face. "Did they tell you who's been charged with the murder?"

"I heard they'd arrested Ben. Is that true? Anne, what's going on?"

"Nelson, it's a long story, but Louis fired Ben yesterday for some unknown reason and told us to move out. The police think that

Ben killed him for revenge or something. He's in jail right now." Her voice cracked, and she looked up at the ceiling, trying to fight the tears. "The arraignment is tomorrow. I don't know what we're going to do. I'm worried sick that they'll hold him until the Grand Jury investigation. Longer, if he's indicted. He's been framed, Nelson. All the evidence points to him, but I swear he didn't do it."

"This is incomprehensible," Nelson said. "I can't believe it's happening."

"Me either. And if they do set bond, I have no idea how to come up with it. A bail bondsman might not give it to us — we're not even employed."

"Don't worry about the bond, Anne," Nelson said. "I'll post it. I'm not at a number where I can be reached tomorrow, since I'm hoping to fly home to St. Clair for the funeral, but I'll phone the courthouse in the morning and have the money wired to them."

She caught her breath. "You'd do that?"

"Of course I would. I know Ben didn't kill anyone. We've got to get him out of jail."

"You're saving our lives," Anne cried. "I don't know how to thank you."

"Thanks aren't necessary. Just tell Ben to

keep his chin up. I'll call you when I get back."

When she had hung up, Anne sat back against the headboard of the bed and savored the relief that she would at least be able to post bond. Nelson hadn't set a cap on the amount he was willing to pay, and she knew that he'd get his money back when Ben was acquitted. It was the one bright spot in an otherwise horrible day.

She slid back under the covers and tried to sleep. But sleep didn't come. She lay on her back, staring at the ceiling, until morning intruded on the room.

CHAPTER TEN

The day was unusually cold for Florida, but that was no surprise. Everything else seemed out of kilter, too. Sharon walked into the courtroom and glanced around at the faces of other family members, lawyers, and accusers who had come to face the judge today. On one side of the courtroom sat the row of inmates awaiting arraignment. Ben was among them in his orange jumpsuit, looking as haggard and disheveled as she had ever seen him.

Jenny had brought Christy earlier; they were sitting with Anne. Jenny was holding little Bobby in her lap, bouncing him to keep him content, while Emily squirmed restlessly in her mother's lap — holding the army men that Christy had insisted on bringing her this morning. Christy sat beside Anne, dark circles under her eyes, dressed in her Sunday best with a big white bow in her long hair.

Lynda Barrett was the only one among them who looked confident and unafraid, as if she knew what she was doing here. Risking Anne's wrath, Sharon approached Lynda and quietly leaned over her shoulder.

"How's it looking?" she asked.

Lynda looked up at her hopefully. "Things are moving pretty fast this morning," she said. "The judge must have a golf game this afternoon."

The judge hammered his gavel, marking the decision in the previous case, and Sharon found a seat a couple of rows back.

"St. Clair versus Robinson," the bailiff called out.

Ben got to his feet, and Lynda went to stand beside him. After hearing the charge, the judge asked, "What is your plea?"

"Not guilty," Ben said loudly.

Lynda requested that Ben be released on his own recognizance pending the Grand Jury investigation, but the prosecutor pressed to keep him in jail, citing the violent nature of the crime Ben was accused of and suggesting that the streets of St. Clair weren't safe with Ben free. Lynda refuted his points one by one, making special note of Ben's alibi.

"Your honor, since my client has no criminal record, not even a traffic violation, it would be senseless to keep him in jail. He has a wife and four children who depend on him." She gestured toward them.

The judge regarded the family. Then, taking off his glasses, he read back over the forms on his table. "Miss Barrett," he said, looking up at Lynda and shoving his glasses back on. "I see here that Mr. Robinson was evicted from his home just two days ago."

"That's right, your honor."

The judge braced his elbows on the table and leaned forward, peering at her with impatient eyes. "Explain to me how I can release him if he doesn't have an address."

Lynda didn't hesitate. "Your honor, he's going to get an address very soon, but he has to be out of jail to do so. He was just evicted the day before yesterday. Yesterday he was arrested. He hasn't had time to find a place for his family to live."

The judge shook his head. "I'm sorry, but in light of the fact that this is a murder charge, and he is homeless, I can't in good conscience release him. It's hard enough to keep up with people until a trial when they do have an address. When they don't have one, it's just impossible."

"But your honor, it's not his fault he was evicted!"

"Your honor," the prosecutor interrupted. "The fact is, the murder followed the eviction. The murdered party was his landlord. It seems obvious to me that his homelessness and the murder that took place shortly thereafter are related, so I strongly advise you not to let this man back onto the streets."

The judge nodded as he looked back over the papers. "I'm sorry, Miss Barrett, but unless a man has an address, there's no way that I can release him. I'm afraid you're going to have to stay in jail pending the Grand Jury investigation, Mr. Robinson."

"No!" Anne cried, springing up. Jenny began to wail, covering her face and shaking her head.

Suddenly, Sharon rose. "Your honor."

The outburst surprised the judge, and he looked back into the crowd, trying to figure out who had had the audacity to interrupt his court proceedings.

"Your honor," she said again, drawing his attention to her. "I am Ben Robinson's ex-wife. My name is Sharon Robinson. And he does have an address."

The judge looked back at his papers. "Well, it says here —"

"Your information is out-of-date," she said, slipping out of the row she was sitting in and heading toward the bench. "Your honor, Ben and his family are going to stay with me until he's acquitted."

Jenny caught her breath.

Ben looked at her as if she had just turned into a chicken and begun to cluck.

Sharon couldn't believe what she had just done. She looked back at her older daughter, saw the gratitude in her eyes, and hoped that, alone, would be enough to see her through this.

"Your honor, I'm absolutely certain that my ex-husband did not commit this crime. And to prove that, I'm willing to have him and his family live in my home until the hearing. They will have an address, your honor."

The judge looked dumbfounded.

"Well, uh, Mrs. Robinson — it is Robinson, isn't it?"

"Yes," she said.

"This is highly unusual, and it's against my better judgment. The man doesn't have a criminal record, though, and looking out here at his family, I don't relish the thought of locking him up for an extended period of time. In my courtroom, I prefer to think that a man is innocent until proven guilty. Therefore, if I could have Miss Barrett's word that this is not some kind of farce, and that this man will not take this opportunity to skip the country, then I suppose I could grant you your request. I'll release him on $100,000 bond."

There was no relief in the breath Sharon took. In fact, it was full of dread.

Turning, she caught the full impact of Anne's reaction. Anne's eyes were narrowed, glaring with shock and anger, as if she had no intention of doing what Sharon had suggested.

"Thank you, your honor," Lynda said.

The gavel hammered again. The next case was called. And Ben was taken back out until his bond was posted.

Lynda hurried across the floor to Anne and Jenny to explain the procedure for posting bond. Sharon stood back, watching her teenager weep with a mixture of despair and relief.

Lynda ushered them from the courtroom, and Sharon followed them to the hall, keeping her distance as if she would be flogged if she were caught hanging too close. Christy spotted her and ran toward her, her bow bouncing as it slipped lower on her hair. "Mommy! Daddy got out of jail!"

"I know, honey," she said.

She looked toward them again, and saw Lynda starting back toward her. Her friend's eyes were sympathetic and grateful. Lynda hugged her. "That was a really great thing you did," she whispered.

Sharon's eyes were filling with tears already. "You can call for the men in the white coats now. I'm ready for them."

Lynda smiled. "It was the only way he could have gotten out," Lynda said.

"But how am I going to stand this?" she whispered. "I don't get along with his wife, and I barely get along with him."

"Then why did you do it?" Lynda asked.

Sharon glanced at Jenny, still weeping openly with joy. Christy wasn't sure what was going on, but she had gone back to Emily and was holding her hands and jumping up and down. "I did it for my children," she said. "It would kill them to think of their father in jail for any length of time. I'm not going to make them go through that."

"So instead you would put yourself through this?"

Sharon breathed a deep breath and wilted. "Don't overpraise it, Lynda. I wish I could say I'm doing this out of the goodness of my heart, but I'm afraid I'm going to spend the next few weeks seething. But I know that Ben is not a murderer. And the sooner we prove it, the sooner this nightmare will be over."

CHAPTER ELEVEN

An hour later, Sharon watched out the window as Ben's station wagon pulled into her driveway. She could just imagine what had taken place when Ben had encountered Anne. He'd probably been lambasted. By now, the whole idea of moving in with her husband's ex-wife had probably sunk in, and Anne must be livid.

Ben got out of the car with the baby on his hip and grabbed one of the suitcases he had stuffed in the back. Anne lingered behind as if to busy herself with something — anything — to delay her entrance into the home.

Ben came tentatively to the open door and peered inside. "Hi," he said.

"Hi," Sharon returned, all business. "Come on in. I'm putting you and Anne in the bedroom at the back, third door on the left down the hall. Emily can sleep with Christy upstairs in Christy's room, and I got our old crib out of the attic for Bobby. He'll be in the room next to you."

Ben whistled under his breath. "I guess I've never been farther in than the den. I didn't realize you have two extra bedrooms."

"It's a big house," Sharon admitted.

He stood there staring at her for a moment, holding that baby on his hip. If he'd been anyone else, she would have been reaching to hold the baby by now. She had always wanted another one of her own. But now she tried not to even look his way as he came in.

"This was really nice of you, Sharon," he said. "You didn't have to do it. It was the last thing I expected."

She turned away and began chopping carrots on the big island at the center of her kitchen. "I *did* have to do it," she said. "I saw the look on my daughters' faces. And last night, Christy was so upset — I'd do anything to spare the children from the pain of seeing their father stay in jail."

"Well, whatever the motive, I appreciate it."

A moment of loud silence passed between them as Sharon continued chopping the carrots.

"I didn't kill him, Sharon."

Sharon turned back to him and looked down at the floor, studying the big square parquet tiles. "I know you didn't, Ben."

"I'm gonna get out of this," he said. "I know it looks pretty hopeless, but I've got to fight it."

"I know."

She heard Emily and Christy giggling

and chattering as they walked up to the house.

Anne, on the other hand, was still bitterly angry. She marched into the house carrying a box and wearing a sour look on her otherwise pretty face. Sharon had trouble looking at her. She always had. "Hello, Anne."

Anne's face was red as she lifted her chin and faced Sharon. "I want you to know that I'm against this," she said. "I don't like it a bit."

Sharon nodded. "That's fair."

"I don't really know why you did it," she went on, tears filling her pale blue eyes. "But I don't trust you. I don't want any favors from you."

Sharon fought the urge to rail back at her that the last thing on earth she wanted was to do Anne Robinson any favors, but instead, she turned back to the carrots. "It doesn't look like you have a choice," she bit out.

"Maybe not for now," Anne told her. "But the minute I can get into my own place, we'll be out of here."

"Come on, Anne," Ben said cautiously. "We need to be thanking her instead of badgering her."

Anne turned on him then. "Don't you dare defend your ex-wife to me!"

"I'm not defending her," he said. "I'm just trying to point out that you're being a little irrational. We don't have a place to live, so she offered us her home."

Thick silence stretched out over agonizing seconds as Anne struggled with the emotions battling on her face . . . anger, humiliation, pride, distress. Finally, Ben handed the baby to her. "We're at the back room on the left. Why don't you take Bobby and go get settled in?"

"I've got a roast in the oven," Sharon said to Anne's back as she left the room. "It's for dinner tonight."

Anne shot her a scathing look, as if about to tell her that that dinner would go uneaten, but then she looked down at Emily and her face softened. The child would have to eat, as would the baby and her husband. Anne herself might fast for as long as she was here, but not her family.

Sharon almost felt sorry for Anne as she left the room, carrying her box of meager belongings in one arm and the baby in the other.

Jenny, who must have pulled into the driveway behind Anne and Ben, came to the door, her eyes lit up like a little girl in a doll shop at Christmas. Christy and Emily were on her heels. "Oh, Mom, you are so awesome! This is gonna be so great!" She threw her arms around her mother again, almost knocking her down.

Christy took Emily's hands and began dancing with her, her long blonde hair bouncing. "Emily gets to live with us! Emily gets to live with us! Mommy, it's gonna be so much fun! And Daddy'll be here right where we live, and we can see him all the time."

Bitterness welled back up in Sharon. If it hadn't been for Ben's recklessness with their marriage, Christy would never have had to know what it was like not to have her father living with them.

She turned back to the carrots, all her compassion for Ben slipping away. "Well, you guys have a lot of work to do," she said quickly. "Christy and Emily, why don't you go unpack? Give her some of your drawers, Christy. You two will be sharing a room."

The little girls squealed with delight, and ran up the stairs to Christy's bedroom. Ben followed them, knowing not to push Sharon any further.

When Jenny and Sharon were the only two in the kitchen, Jenny asked, "Mom, are you all right?"

"I'm fine. But Jenny, this isn't gonna be easy."

"I know," Jenny said softly. "But it'll work out. You'll see."

Sharon checked the stove, as if something might have changed in the last half hour since she'd put the roast in. If it hadn't been an electric oven, she might have considered sticking her head in it.

"Mom, I know you and Anne don't like each other."

Sharon breathed a laugh and closed the oven. "Now, there's an understatement."

"But don't you see?" Jenny asked. "That just makes it all so much greater. I mean, what you did. Letting her come live here, and Dad, and the kids. I mean, it's easy to do nice things for people you like, but when you do it for people you don't like . . ."

Sharon stiffened and turned around. "I did it, okay, Jenny? You don't have to keep on with this."

"But Mom, I mean it."

Sharon sighed and went to the medicine cabinet to look for aspirin. "I'm getting a headache."

"Maybe you and Anne will become friends," Jenny suggested. "She's really nice, most of the time. We've gotten to be kind of close, and —"

"I think the best we can hope is that we'll learn to tolerate each other," Sharon interrupted, hating the bitterness rising inside her. "And we've got a long way to go."

Jenny put her arms around Sharon's neck and forced her to look at her. She was as tall as her mother already, and it amazed Sharon that she had been as small as Christy not so long ago. Time was flying. Finding it hard to hold onto her bitterness with that sweet face smiling at her, she returned the hug.

"I love you, Mom. And you really are living your faith. I'm sorry about what I said yesterday."

"Oh, that's okay," Sharon said, letting her go. "I knew it was just manipulation."

"Hey, that's my job," Jenny said. She stepped back and gave her mother a serious look. "I'll help while they're here. It'll be good for me, too. I'll learn responsibility. I can help with Bobby and the kids. It'll be nice to have them around the house, won't it, Mom? To have the house full of kids?"

Sharon sighed. "Jenny, I know this is going to be fun for you. But I hope you'll be sensitive to the fact that some of us won't take very well to it. Not only that, but your father could still wind up in prison."

"He won't, Mom," Jenny said. "We're gonna find out who really killed Mr. Dubose. We're gonna prove he's innocent."

The determined tone in Jenny's voice alarmed her. An image flashed through Sharon's mind: Jenny out scavenging the streets in search of the real murderer. She took Jenny by the shoulders and looked straight into her eyes. "You are going to stay out of it. You are not going to pry around to find Mr. Dubose's murderer. Do you understand me? We're talking *murder* here. This is dangerous."

Jenny hesitated. "Mom, somebody's got to do something."

"I'll do everything I can," Sharon promised her. "I have as much at stake now as you do."

"What do you mean by that?"

"The sooner we clear your father, the sooner they can go back to their own lives."

Jenny's face fell so hard that Sharon thought she heard it crash. "Yeah, I guess it's not forever, is it?"

Sharon almost laughed, but she stopped herself. "No, honey, it's not forever. Now why don't you go help the girls get Emily's things put away?"

Jenny's mood changed quickly, and as she whirled to jog up the stairs, Sharon noticed the bounce in her step and the joy in her eyes that her family had finally been grafted back together again.

★ ★ ★

Anne had managed to get Bobby to sleep by the time Ben made it back to the bedroom. As he entered, she was sitting on the window seat, gazing out over the backyard. There were plenty of trees, and a swing set for Christy, and that tree house that Sharon had hired someone to build. It was clear from the way she gazed out the window that Anne envied Sharon's home.

He stood behind her and began to massage her shoulders. "You okay?"

When she looked up at him, he saw the tension on her face. "This is hard, Ben. Really hard."

"It doesn't have to be. The kids are thrilled."

"The kids don't have a clue." She jerked away from his massaging hands, got up, and went across the room to the suitcase. As she began to unpack, tears came to her eyes. "How did all this happen?"

"It'll be okay," he said. "Just trust me."

"I *have* trusted you," she snapped. "When I told you I was worried about our being so dependent on the gallery, you said to trust you. When I told you that we needed our own home for security, you said to trust you."

"Owning our own home wouldn't have

helped us today, Anne. I still would have been set up for murder charges."

"Yes, but we could have gone back to our own house, instead of living off of your ex-wife." She stopped and looked up at him, her eyes tormented. "It's humiliating, Ben. It's my worst nightmare."

"You're being melodramatic," he said.

"No, I'm not!"

"Look, if you're worried about something going on between Sharon and me, it won't. I'm married to you now."

"Being married didn't stop you before, did it?"

It was a low blow, and he took a step back. "If I recall, you played a part in that, too."

She didn't like being reminded of that, so she turned back to the suitcase and jerked out a stack of his shirts.

"Anne, look at the bright side. I get to be with my kids. Emily and Christy get to together."

"That's right," she said, swinging around again. "One big happy family, huh? Just like it was before I came into the picture. Daddy and Mommy back in the same house. The only thing wrong with this picture is me!"

He turned to the window. "Anne, it may not have occurred to you, but I'm the one who spent the night in jail. To have to come crawling to my ex-wife for help, to let my kids see me destitute and in trouble — you think I wanted it this way?"

"I don't *know* what you wanted," she said, flinging more clothes into the drawer. "I have no idea. All I know is that your name is being smeared all over the papers as a common murderer, and you've got me living in my archenemy's house. From where I stand, life with you isn't looking too good right now."

Ben looked back at her. "Anne, I need you to pull yourself together. You're my only alibi. If you start falling apart —"

"Alibi?" she almost shouted, then quickly lowered her voice. "That's another thing, Ben. I told them I was with you the whole time yesterday, but the truth is, I wasn't. When you went for that walk, you were gone over an hour."

"We needed some distance, Anne — because we were fighting, just like we are now," he said. "What do you think? That I jogged over to the gallery and killed Louis in that hour?"

"No!" she cried. "I don't think that. But *they* might if they knew!"

"Then don't tell them!"

She turned away and jerked another stack of clothes out of the suitcase. "This is a nightmare, Ben. I hate it."

"So do you want out? Is that it?"

"Out of what?"

"The marriage. The commitment to stand behind me no matter how tough things get."

"Where would I go, Ben?" she asked through compressed lips. "Whatever money I came into this marriage with is gone now. I can't even afford to take my child to the doctor. And I'm not really up to taking more money from your beloved ex!"

"Then get a job! If you're so dead set on getting away from me, then make some money and leave!"

"I'm not leaving without my kids, Ben."

"And I'm not letting you take them."

"Fine." Her face was reddening, and she crumpled over and dropped on the bed, breathing out a heavy sigh. "I'm stuck with you, then."

Ben had never been one to keep the tough-guy act going when a woman started to cry, so he sat down on the bed next to her and let out a ragged breath. Putting his arms around her, he pulled her against him. "Look, I've messed up once before, and my kids had to pay for it. I don't want another family to break up. Please, just relax and try to get through this. We can do it. We've had tough times before."

"Not like these," she cried.

"No, and neither have the kids. We have to be strong for them."

She tried to pull herself together. Wiping her face, she said, "I'm tired, Ben. I haven't slept since we left our apartment. How many days ago was that?"

"We've only been gone two nights. But I know how you feel. I haven't slept much, either. Can we just write this fight off to fatigue? Can we just forget the stuff about leaving each other for now?"

Again, she pulled away. "I don't know, Ben. I just don't know how much more of this I can take."

"You need rest," he said. "Why don't you take a nap while Bobby's asleep? It may not last long. If he wakes up, I'll take care of him."

"And what will you be doing?" she asked suspiciously. "Puttering around in the kitchen with your first wife?"

He sighed. "No, Anne. You don't have to fear Sharon. I'm the last man on earth she'd be interested in now."

"Oh, great," she said. "But if she were interested, it wouldn't be a problem for you, right?"

"Wrong. You're putting words in my mouth."

"No. I'm just interpreting them." She got up and started out of the room. "I don't think I can sleep right now. I'll go help Emily get unpacked."

Sharon decided to set the table alone, dreading the moment when everyone came to the table. When she'd finally gotten all the food into serving bowls and put them on the breakfast counter so that everyone could serve themselves, smorgasbord-style, she went to round everyone up.

Ben was on the telephone in her study talking to Lynda about the possibility of hiring a private investigator to try to find the real killer. Sharon knew that she would have to foot the bill for that, and the fact that he hadn't even asked her made her angry. On the other hand, it was worth whatever it cost to get Ben off the hook and out of her home. Jenny, who seemed not to know the purpose of chairs, sat on the floor in front of him, listening intently.

She told them both to come to the table. "Where's Anne?" she asked Jenny before she left the room.

"I think she's watching TV with the girls. I'll tell her."

"That's all right," Sharon said, determined not to let her feelings inhibit her.

"I'll tell her myself."

She walked up the hall and went into the den. Christy sat on the floor next to Emily, both of them engrossed in some sleazy tabloid show that she normally didn't allow Christy to watch. Since it was just going off and a preview of the news was flashing on, she let it go. Anne sat in a recliner staring at the screen, but Sharon suspected that she didn't see any of it. Her mind seemed a million miles away.

"It's time for dinner, everybody," Sharon said in a light, upbeat voice. "Wash your hands, girls."

"Okay, Mommy." Christy got up to reach for the remote control. But just before she could turn the television off, the news came on — and a picture of her father flashed across the screen as the headline story. "A local man is the primary suspect in . . ."

"Mommy, look! It's Daddy!" Christy shouted.

Sharon froze, and Anne slowly leaned forward. "Ben Robinson, local artist, was arraigned today on murder charges. The gallery owner where he worked was found dead —" As the anchor spoke, footage showed the body covered with a sheet being wheeled out on a gurney. "And evidence points to the disgruntled artist who lived in the studio and had been fired the day of the shooting. We'll have this and other stories when we return in a moment."

Sharon rushed forward to turn off the television as Christy and Emily gaped up at her, their eyes round with horror over the image of the dead man in their father's gallery. The man the newscaster said their father had killed.

"Go wash your hands, girls," Sharon snapped.

Christy couldn't move. "Mommy, is that the man they said Daddy —"

"Your father didn't kill anyone," Sharon said quickly. She turned to Anne angrily. "I would think you'd be a little more careful about what the children watched, especially today."

Anne bristled. "I had no idea that was about to come on. You were standing there, too."

"But I never would have allowed them to watch that stupid tabloid show. Whatever happened to Barney?"

Anne's tired face reddened. "This isn't about Barney or a tabloid show, Sharon. At least have the decency to say what you mean."

The girls left the room quickly, and Sharon watched them go, flustered. "You're right," she said through her teeth. "It isn't about the tabloid show. It's about them seeing their father called a murderer on television. We're going to have to be careful and monitor what they watch. Any fool would know that today of all days —"

"Oh, that does it!" Anne said, springing out of her chair and heading for the door. Sharon watched her, furious, and saw the girls still hovering together in the hall. "Girls, I said to go wash your hands!" she yelled.

Anne spun around. "Hey — you can order your kids around, but leave mine alone!"

"Fine," Sharon grated through her teeth. "Dinner's ready." She stormed out of the room, but Anne was right behind her.

"Hey, you know, this wasn't my idea. I don't like it. Like you said, I'm here because I have no choice."

"I know that," Sharon said. "But I did have a choice. I invited you to come here of my own free will."

"Why?" Anne shouted. "What's in it for you?"

Sharon stopped midstride and spun around to face Anne. "My children love their father, and it killed them to know he was in jail. I did it for them, not for either one of you!" she returned. "But that doesn't change the fact that I have rules in this house about television, and I don't want my children watching graphic images on the news about how their father murdered some guy —"

Ben walked in and Sharon stopped in midsentence.

"What are you guys talking about?" he asked.

"The news!" Sharon blurted.

"Yeah," Anne said, turning on him and beginning to cry again. "You're already all over it. Everybody we know is going to think you're a killer. You're a disgruntled employee, after all!"

"The news?" he asked.

Sharon knew she shouldn't add fuel to this fire, but she felt the need to enlist Ben's help. "Ben, your wife just let your children see Dubose's dead body being taken out of the gallery."

"Give me a break!" Anne shouted. "I had no more idea that was coming on than you did!"

"You should be more careful!" Sharon yelled.

Jenny walked into the room, carrying Bobby. "You woke him," she said quietly.

The censure in her voice stopped them

both, and Sharon felt like a child being reprimanded by a teacher. Gritting her teeth, she
went into the kitchen and began sticking
serving spoons into the bowls. "Someone's
gonna have to start eating," she said through
gritted teeth. "Come on, Jenny. Eat!"

Jenny put the baby into the high chair that
hooked onto the edge of the table and began
to fix herself a plate. Sharon heard Anne
whispering behind her to Ben, and she
wanted to scream. Instead she just decided
to leave the room.

"Where are you going, Mom?" Jenny
asked when she was almost out of the
kitchen.

"To find Christy and Emily," she said.
"They ran out of the room upset."

Jenny shot a glance to her father and Anne,
then silently took her plate to the table.

In her room, Sharon closed the door of her
bedroom and struggled with the emotions
coursing through her. She wanted to tell
Anne to get herself and her family out of her
house, and not to expect any more help from
her. But the truth, Sharon admitted, was
that she hadn't done what she'd done for
Anne's sake at all — she'd done it for Jenny,
and she'd done it for Christy. And she had
even done it for Ben, though he was the last

96

person she ever wanted to feel compassion for.

Her only choice now was to quickly get this murder resolved so that they could get out of her house.

She picked up the phone and dialed Lynda's number.

"Hello?"

"Lynda, it's me," Sharon said.

"How's it going?" Lynda asked knowingly.

Sharon couldn't even speak for a moment. "Lynda, you've got to help me."

"I'm doing everything I can."

"I know," Sharon said. "But I mean, *really* help me. I'll pay for the private detective you were talking to Ben about, no matter what it costs. We've got to find out who really killed Dubose and get Ben off the hook so we can get them out of my house."

Lynda was quiet for a moment. "What happened?"

"Let's just say that Anne and I rub each other the wrong way. There's so much friction that I'm afraid I'll catch fire."

Sharon could hear the smile in Lynda's voice. "Well, I had a feeling that might be a problem."

"He's being set up, Lynda. Someone's framing him. And it couldn't be that hard to figure out who."

"That's my thinking exactly," Lynda said. "Look, relax and try to get through this. I know this is hard for you, but as soon as I find out anything I'll be in touch. I know Ben's life hangs in the balance. Trust me, I'm not taking this lightly."

"I know you're not," Sharon said, falling back on her bed. "But you've been a little distracted lately with Jake and falling in love and all that kind of stuff —"

"You act like I'm a boy-crazy teenager."

"Call it jealousy," Sharon said, her tone serious. "I just can't remember what it's like."

Lynda chuckled. "Well, having Ben around might remind you a little bit."

Sharon quickly shook her head. "I'm wondering what I ever saw in the man in the first place."

"See how far you've come since the divorce? There was a time when you thought your life was over, and that you'd never get over Ben. Now you can't even remember feeling that way."

"I guess God has a way of anesthetizing us against those painful memories," she said. "And time heals. As far as I'm concerned, I wish Anne and him the utmost happiness — far, far away from here. Meanwhile, I just have to keep reminding myself that this is the right thing to do."

"It is," Lynda said. "There didn't seem to be an alternative — at least not one that would be fair to the kids. But you'll be all right. You're a sweet lady, and God can use you in this."

"You're a good friend, Lynda," Sharon said. "And a pathetic optimist."

"Let's hope I'm a good lawyer. Ben's gonna need one."

CHAPTER TWELVE

Eric Boudreaux sat in his opulent suite at the Tampa Biltmore, studying the stock quotes in the newspaper that had been delivered to his suite that morning. His appointment was in less than two hours, but he still hadn't heard from Louis Dubose.

The television news droned in the corner. Occasionally, he glanced up to see if anything interested him.

"... art gallery owner Louis Dubose ..."

Startled, Boudreaux looked up at the screen to see the face of the man he had never met before, except by phone. Leaning forward, he grabbed the remote and turned the volume up.

"... was found dead after being shot in the back. Police sources say the gun, which was found in a dumpster near the gallery, was registered to Benjamin L. Robinson, a local artist who was residing in the gallery. According to sources, Robinson was fired and evicted the day of the murder ..."

Eric listened, stunned, trying to follow the words, but all he was certain of was that Dubose was dead. How could that be?

He had flown from France for this very

appointment, anxious to get his hands on the prize that would make him even richer than he already was. If Dubose was dead —

The phone rang, and he snatched it up. "Boudreaux," he said in his heavy French accent.

"Yes, Mr. Boudreaux," a voice said cheerily. "So nice to hear your voice. I trust your flight was a good one?"

Boudreaux frowned. "Who is this?"

"My name is John Lieber, and I'm a close friend and colleague of Louis Dubose. I'm afraid I have bad news."

Boudreaux looked back at the screen, but a commercial was playing now. "Yes. The murder."

"The murder," the man said sadly. "You've heard the news, then. Our friend was murdered brutally. A terrible thing. So unexpected."

Boudreaux was quiet. Dubose had not mentioned another contact, although Boudreaux had suspected that he wasn't involved in this business alone. He would act cautiously, he thought. It was difficult to trust Americans, and he did not like doing business with them.

"I was Dubose's partner in our little enterprise," the man said. "And I see no reason that it can't go on as planned. I'd still like to meet with you and make the exchange."

"You have it?" Boudreaux asked hopefully, his thick eyebrows arching.

"It's in a safe place," Lieber said. "It may take me a short while to secure it."

"How long?" Boudreaux asked. "I must return to France."

"Just another day or two. I give you my word it will be worth your time. After all, you didn't come all this way just to return home empty-handed."

Boudreaux considered that for a moment. He couldn't take the chance of walking into a trap. He had an impeccable reputation, and no one had ever suspected him of being involved in anything that wasn't legal. What if somehow he had come under suspicion, and international art detectives were setting him up? Things weren't going smoothly enough. Yet he wanted what he had come here for . . .

"How . . ." He tried to put the words together correctly. "How may I trust you?"

"You *have* to trust me," Lieber said, "because I have the greatest find in the art world this century. If you don't trust me, you'll lose out."

Boudreaux nodded slightly, but didn't say a word.

"Please. Just stay where you are for another day or, at the most, two. I'll be back in touch as soon as we can make the exchange. Dubose would have wanted it this way. He wouldn't have wanted this sale to be jeopardized because of some unfortunate circumstances."

Boudreaux wasn't convinced. His instincts all screamed for him to get on the plane and head back out of the country. But Lieber was right. This was the find of the century.

"I will stay until I hear from you," he said grudgingly. "If I do not hear within two days, I will leave."

"Fair enough," the man said. "I'll be in touch. And Mr. Boudreaux? You won't regret this."

CHAPTER THIRTEEN

The children were missing.

While the others were looking inside, Ben went out back to see if they were in the yard. The little tree house nestled in the oak in the backyard was a new development since he'd last been here. Sharon had hired someone to build it for Christy because she loved to climb.

But building a tree house was the father's job. He should have been the one to design and execute it, and that bothered Ben as he peered up the ladder. It looked sound enough, though. The truth is, he probably couldn't have done a better job. But it was the principle of the thing. If Sharon had asked him, he'd have built the little house.

On the other hand, Anne would have probably had a fit about his being over here at all, and it would have gotten too complicated . . .

Sharon had probably done the right thing. Christy deserved a tree house. She shouldn't have to deal with the divorce fallout every time she wanted something. Besides, her mother could afford it. Despite the financial pit Ben had left her in, Sharon had thrived since the divorce. She had a way of always bouncing back. No matter how bad things looked, good things came out of it for her. She was lucky that way.

His luck hadn't been so good.

He heard crying in the tree house. Gripping the rungs, he slowly started up the ladder. He got to the hatch at the bottom and knocked lightly on the floor of the house. "Anybody home?"

The hatch opened and Christy's wet, red face greeted him. "Come in, Daddy. We're crying."

The announcement almost amused him, but when he pulled himself in, the sight broke his heart. Christy moved back to sit by Emily. They both sat Indian style, holding hands as they wept.

"What's wrong, girls?" he asked softly.

They looked at each other. "Nothing."

Ben climbed farther up into the tree house and tested the boards to see if it would hold him. It had been well built, he admitted. But these days Sharon did everything first-class. She had the money to.

He sat down on the floor next to Christy, and Emily climbed into his lap. He pulled Christy up onto his other leg and held both of his children tight. "Now, tell Daddy what's wrong."

"It was the news, Daddy," Christy said. "They said you killed Mr. Dubose."

"You know I didn't. You do know that, don't you?"

"But we're scared."

"You know Daddy didn't kill anybody, don't you?" he asked again.

Both of the girls nodded, and fresh tears rolled down their faces. Ben buried his face in Christy's hair.

"Girls, this is the worst time in Daddy's life. Sometimes things just don't go like you plan. But I didn't kill Mr. Dubose, and I'm gonna find out who did, and it's gonna be okay. Let's look at the good side," he said, trying to cheer his daughters up. "We're all here in the same house together."

"But Mommy hates Miss Sharon," Emily said, rubbing her eyes.

Ben shook his head, saddened by the complications adults, in their weakness, throw at the children who depend on them. He kissed his youngest daughter's cheek. "Honey, it's just real hard for them. They were both married to me, and it's kind of weird, all of us living here together."

"Are they gonna fight all the time?" Emily asked.

"Let's hope not."

Christy touched Ben's face, rubbing the

rough growth of stubble. He hadn't shaved since they'd been evicted. "I've been praying for you, Daddy."

"I know, sweetheart," Ben said. "You just keep right on doing that."

He looked around at the little building they sat in. "I haven't been up here before, Christy. Nice place you've got here."

"Thank you," she said, wiping her face.

"But it needs a little paint, doesn't it?"

She looked around as if she'd never noticed it before.

"I tell you what," he said. "Since I'm gonna be here with nothing to do for a little while, maybe we can start a project."

"What kind of project?" Emily asked, her face brightening. "You mean a painting project?"

Emily loved to paint, but his studio had always been off-limits to her. The idea of being involved in one of his projects now had enough appeal to distract her from her sorrow.

"Yeah," he said. "How about if we come up here tomorrow and start painting? We could paint the walls, and the floor, and the ceiling, and —"

"We could paint pictures on it," Christy piped in.

"Sure, we could paint a mural. It would be gorgeous."

"Nobody can paint a mural like you can," Emily said.

"All right, then, we have some plans to make. I want you two to go inside and eat supper, and then after supper, get some paper and draw pictures just like what you want on the walls of the house."

"Can we paint on the outside, too, Daddy?" Christy asked.

"Sure we can. We'll paint anything you want, as long as we clear it with your mom."

Christy and Emily forgot their grief as their minds reeled with possibilities. Ben wiped both their faces and kissed them on the cheeks.

"I love you guys."

"I love you, too, Daddy," they each said.

"Now, go in and eat supper. Your moms are worried about you. Then you can get started on the designs. I'm just gonna sit up here for a minute by myself."

He watched as they scurried down the ladder, and for a moment he hesitated, thinking about what had just taken place. Here he sat in the little tree house built by someone that his ex-wife had hired because Ben himself was no longer a factor in their family. And here were his two children, one from each marriage, best friends and loving each other as sisters. Now, arrested for murder, he was back in the home, but with his new wife and children . . .

Nothing about this was natural. It was as bizarre a set of circumstances as he could have imagined.

How in the world had he come to this? No job, no income, facing the possibility of going to prison . . .

The depression and anger that had been pulling him like quicksand since Dubose had fired him pulled him further under. Miserably, he slipped out of the hatch and climbed back down the ladder.

CHAPTER FOURTEEN

Sharon didn't have an appetite for the meal she'd cooked, so she stayed away until everyone had left the table. Then she ventured back into the kitchen to clean up. Anne was already loading the dishwasher, and when she looked up, Sharon saw that she was crying.

Sharon pretended not to notice.

"I'm cleaning up," Anne said.

"That's all right," Sharon told her. "I can do it. Why don't you go take care of the kids?"

As if Sharon's words had been an indictment, Anne dropped the pot on the counter and wiped her eyes. "Look, Sharon, the kids are being taken care of. They're playing upstairs, and Jenny's with them. Don't act like I'm neglecting them."

"I didn't say that," Sharon said. "Did I say that?"

"I know what you were thinking."

"All right," Sharon said, crossing her arms and squaring off with the woman. "What was I thinking, exactly?"

"You were thinking that you've waited six years to see us in this position," Anne said, tossing down the hand towel she was holding. "You were thinking that we deserve all this, and you're secretly delighted that we're in all this trouble."

"That's not true," Sharon said. "And I resent it."

"I can see right through all your generosity, Sharon!"

"That's enough, Anne." The words were Ben's, and both women swung around.

Anne's tears came harder now. "Don't you dare defend her!"

"I'm not defending her," Ben said. "She doesn't need defending. Now calm down." He crossed the room and cupped his wife's chin. "Anne, look at me," he said.

She looked up at him with her red, furious eyes.

"You're really stressed out, honey, and I understand that. So am I. But lashing out at Sharon is not going to help. It'll just make things worse, and we need to concentrate and keep our heads clear right now, okay? We don't have time for all this bickering."

She fell against him, and he held her for a moment, letting her cry. Sharon turned away, suddenly feeling like an intruder in her own home.

"Look, you go lie down," he whispered to Anne. "You need a break. Just go take a nap, and let Jenny look after the kids. She loves it."

"But Bobby's sick. It's almost time for his cough medicine."

"I'll give it to him," Ben said. "Go on now. I need you to be rested. There are going to be a lot of sleepless nights between now and the Grand Jury hearing."

Sharon watched her leave the room. Ben turned back to Sharon and shot her an apologetic look. "Sharon, I'm sorry. She's not herself. She's usually a sweet, warm person. Once you get to know her —"

"Spare me." Sharon turned away and started wiping the counters.

Ben's voice trailed off, as though he knew his mouth was leading him down the wrong path. "Okay, never mind. Listen, if you don't mind, I need to make some calls. Do you mind if I use your study?"

"Fine," Sharon said. "Oh, and if you need to paint, we could probably find some place around here for you to do it."

He shrugged. "Thanks a lot. I'm just not feeling real creative right now. I did promise the girls we'd do some painting in the tree house, though. You don't mind, do you?"

"No, I think it's a good idea. It's about time Christy's father got involved in her life." She turned back to the dishes and began scrubbing them with a vengeance.

Ben couldn't think of a response that wouldn't just make things worse, so he started out of the room. The phone rang, and he turned back. "I'll get it. It might be Lynda."

He picked it up. "Hello?"

He hesitated, then in an agitated voice, asked, "Who is this?"

Sharon turned around. "Who?" she whispered. He only shook his head, indicating that he didn't know.

"What are you talking about?" His face began to redden. "I have no idea what you're talking about!"

"What is it?" Sharon asked in an urgent whisper.

Ben put his hand over the phone. "Call the police," he mouthed. "Trace the call."

"It's him?" she asked in disbelief. "The killer?"

He nodded frantically and gestured for her to hurry.

As Sharon rushed to the car where she could call from her cellular phone, Ben continued the conversation. "You've got to tell me what you're looking for," she heard him say. "I can't read your mind."

She reached the garage and threw open her car door, and frantically dialed 911 on her cellular phone. After hearing what she had to say, the dispatcher transferred her. She waited, on hold, wishing someone would pick up.

After a moment, Ben burst through the door with Anne on his heels. "Do you have the police department?"

"Yes," she said. "But it takes an act of Congress to speak to the right person. I'm on hold —"

"He's looking for something," Ben cut in, raking his hand through his long hair. "I don't know what it is. He wants me to leave it at the airport at 10:30 tonight, but I have no idea what he's talking about. He threatened me. Said he'd go into the next phase of this nightmare if I didn't bring him what he wants."

"Well, what could it be?" Anne asked. "Didn't he give you a clue? Are you supposed to guess?"

"He thinks I already know," Ben said. "That's what's so bizarre."

Giving up, Sharon slammed the phone down. "Come on, Ben, we've got to go to the police station."

Anne looked stunned. "He doesn't need you to go with him."

Sharon felt reprimanded and quickly got out of the car. "You're right. Go! Somebody needs to tell somebody. Here. Take my car so you can call Lynda on the way. She probably needs to know about this."

Ben looked back toward the house. "What about the kids?"

"We'll take care of them," Sharon said. "Between Jenny and me they'll be okay."

Anne started running back into the house. "I'm not leaving Bobby. I'll take him with us."

Sharon looked as if she'd been slapped down, but she said nothing.

As they waited, Ben tried to work back through the conversation. "He said to get a black Travel-Lite garment bag from Walmart. That's what I'm supposed to deliver it in. He was very specific that it had to be that brand."

Sharon frowned, wondering why. "Well . . . all right. I'll leave Jenny with the girls and I'll run to Walmart and get one while you're gone. Who knows? Maybe it'll come to you. Maybe you'll figure out what he's looking for."

He nodded. "If the police believe me, this could clear me, Sharon. If they could catch him tonight . . . I could be off the hook."

New hope brightened her eyes. "That's right!"

Anne came back out, carrying Bobby with

one arm and the diaper bag and her purse on the other. "Okay, let's go. I'm ready."

"Good luck," Sharon told him. "And don't forget to call Lynda. She probably needs to meet you at the station."

CHAPTER FIFTEEN

Tony Danks scribbled on a legal pad as Ben related the phone conversation, every nuance of his body suggesting that he didn't believe a word of it. Larry Millsaps looked doubtful, too, though his eyes remained focused on Ben's as he spoke. Lynda sat beside Ben, occasionally prodding him with more questions that she thought might strengthen his story. Anne stood in the corner of the room, quietly swaying to keep Bobby from waking up.

"So . . . did you record this phone conversation?" Tony asked without looking up from his scribblings when Ben finished the story.

"No," Ben said. "Of course not. I didn't know he was going to call."

"He already told you that Sharon tried to get a trace started, Tony. She got put on hold," Lynda pointed out.

"Did anyone pick up on another line and hear any part of the conversation?" Tony asked.

"No, I don't think so," Ben said. "Why?"

"I just wondered if there were any witnesses."

"Sharon saw me talking to him."

"Oh, that should hold up in court," Tony said sarcastically. " 'Your honor, my wife saw me on the phone.' Case closed."

"She's not his wife," Anne clipped. "I am."

"Oh, that's right," Tony said. "He lives with both of you."

The statement only further inflamed Ben, and he stood up, knocking his chair back with a clatter. Leaning over the table, he asked, "What do I have to do to prove that he called?"

Tony glanced at Larry, who seemed to be deep in thought with his hands clasped in front of his face. "Well, we checked the phone records," Tony said. "There is a record of a call that came to that house at about that time, but it was from a pay phone. It really doesn't prove anything."

"Why not?" Ben asked. "The guy obviously didn't want the call traced."

"Because it could have been anyone," Tony said. "How do we know it wasn't a salesman or something? You could have played this out to throw us off your scent."

"Then come with me tonight," Ben said. "I'll deliver a black garment bag just like he said. Someone will pick it up, and you can get him. Then you'll see."

"What will you put in the garment bag?" Tony asked. "Your story is that you don't know what he wants, remember?"

Ben wanted to break something. "It's not a story, man! This is all so crazy, why would I make it up?"

"Why?" Tony laughed and glanced at his partner, who didn't join in his amusement. "Well, let's see. You've been accused of murder. All the evidence points to you. You're probably going to spend the rest of your life in prison — I don't know, Larry, can you think of any reason he'd want to make this up?"

"It's a pretty common ploy," Larry said matter-of-factly. "Cast suspicion on someone else. Try to get the magnifying glass off you."

Ben threw up his hands. "I don't *have* to make it up! I didn't do this! And I can't believe you morons are sitting on your duffs while some murderer is walking free out there. It hasn't even occurred to you that you could be wrong — that *if* I'm telling the truth, the trail of the real killer is getting cold while you just sit there. That's what's wrong with our criminal justice system. It depends on idiots like you!"

Lynda had stood up halfway through his outburst, and now touched Ben's arm to calm him down. "Come on, Ben. This won't get you anywhere." She looked back at the two cops, who looked more stubborn and determined than ever. "Gentlemen, if we have to tell a Grand Jury that we gave you the opportunity to catch the real criminal, and you declined, it isn't going to look good. And the fact that my client just called you idiots shouldn't change the way you investigate this crime at all. His temper may be on edge right now, but I'd say ours would be, too, if we'd been accused of a murder we didn't commit." She sat back down and leaned on the table to face Larry. "What do you say, Larry? Tony? Can't you at least escort him to the airport tonight? See what happens?"

Larry glanced at Tony and shook his head. "Lynda, if we jumped every time a suspect pointed us to someone else, we'd never get any sleep. I left before dawn this morning to investigate a shooting in a bar, and I'm tired. Besides, I have a wife at home who's expecting me for dinner."

"She understands what you do for a living," Lynda said. "If I know her as well as I think I do, she wouldn't want you to pin a murder on the wrong guy just so you could be on time for dinner. And we both know that you've gone without sleep to get the job done before this. What about you, Tony?"

Tony laughed under his breath. "So let me get this straight. After working fourteen hours today, I'm supposed to go with this guy to the Tampa Airport — which is roughly an hour from here — so that he can respond to a phone call he can't prove, by leaving an empty bag by a window so that an imaginary person can pick it up?"

"Forget it!" Ben said, shoving the chair again. "Just forget it. I'll go myself."

"No, you won't, pal," Larry said. "You're not allowed to leave town until you're cleared."

"What if he's telling the truth?" Lynda shouted, making them all look at her. "What if — just what *if* — he's telling you exactly like it happened? Whoever was on that phone *threatened* him if he didn't deliver that bag! Larry, put yourself in his shoes. What if it happened to you? What if you tried to tell the police everything that had happened, but they wouldn't listen?"

Something about those words softened Larry's face. He looked up at Ben, his eyes lingering pensively on him. Tony kept scribbling.

Anne stepped forward, her eyes full of tears. "I'll go."

Everyone looked up. "What?" Lynda asked.

She cleared her throat. "Somebody has to go. I'll do it. I'll take the bag and leave it where he said, if Ben can't leave town. Maybe that would be okay. And we can stick something in the bag. Even if it's not the right thing — what he's looking for — maybe it would be enough time for the security cameras to get a picture of him as he takes it. Or maybe I could take a camera and get his picture somehow . . ."

Ben slammed his fist against the wall. "No way! This guy's a murderer! I'm not letting my wife do this."

Larry shook his head.

"I can get permission from the judge to let Ben go," Lynda said. "But to do that, I'll have to explain how the police force refuses to cooperate."

Larry looked up, rubbing his fingers down his face, leaving it red. "Forget it, Lynda. I'll go with him."

"You will?" she asked.

"Yeah. And there'd better be something to see." He looked wearily at Tony, who rolled his eyes as if he couldn't believe his partner had caved in. "Are you in, Tony?"

Tony blew out a breath heavy enough to puff his cheeks. "I guess so."

"All right," Lynda said, getting down to business. "Now, I want you two to start thinking like cops. Think you're up to that?"

Neither of them appreciated the question, and neither answered.

"What should he put inside the bag? How does the man intend to get it without being seen? And why would he want such a specific brand of garment bag?"

"It's obvious," Tony said with a sigh. "It's the most common garment bag sold. This alleged criminal is probably going to bring one just like it and make a quick exchange. If he doesn't, we'll know that our friend here was pulling our strings all along."

Ben disregarded that. "What should I put in it? He didn't give me a clue about what he's looking for. It could be anything."

"It's obviously something that would look natural in a garment bag," Lynda said. "Maybe you should just pad it with pillows or something. You're just going to have to wing it."

Ben sighed. "All right. He said to set it beside the window next to Gate C–23 just after the last flight from Atlanta lands at 10:30."

"You'd better mark the bag, so that you can prove that he took yours. And guys —" She turned back to the two cops, who looked less than enthusiastic. "At the airport, shouldn't you be watching for anyone who has a bag like this? Maybe searching them?"

"Lynda," Tony said impatiently, "if there's a guy waiting to make an exchange, the last thing we'd want to do is alert him to the fact that we're there. Besides, if we catch him before the exchange, there won't be any clues that he's the guy. We'll call Tampa PD and Airport Security and let them know what's going on, and make sure a security camera is taping in that spot. If he makes the exchange, we'll be there, and we'll see him." But he didn't sound as if he expected to see anything.

"You'll have to get him immediately after the exchange," Ben said. "Otherwise, he'll see that he's been had, and he'll retaliate."

"Retaliate how?" Larry asked grudgingly.

"I don't know," Ben said. "But frankly, I'm not real anxious to find out. He's messed my life up enough as it is."

As Ben and Anne drove back to Sharon's house, Anne was quiet, brooding, and he knew what she was thinking. She was blaming him for all of this, and he supposed she had every right to.

Christy and Emily were sound asleep when they got in, and Jenny was upstairs working on something in her room. Sharon was closed into her bedroom as if she'd had enough of them all.

Quietly, they made their way through the house and put Bobby down into the crib.

They went to their bedroom, but the tension in the room was too stiff for either of them to relax. It was like the tension before he'd left Sharon, when she'd known he was having an affair: so thick you could slice it open.

"Why don't you go on to bed?" he asked. "I'll wake you when I get home."

She shook her head and sat down on the bed with her feet beneath her, looking like a little girl. "I won't be able to sleep until I know what happened."

He sat and put his arms around her. "It's gonna be okay. Tonight we'll catch the guy who's doing this to us, and by tomorrow they'll drop all charges against me."

"Then can we move out of this place?" she asked.

"Yes. I'll get Lynda to get a court order to get my paintings out of the gallery, and I'll find another gallery to display them. We'll be back on our feet in no time, and we won't depend on anyone else."

She seemed to relax.

The doorbell rang. Ben kissed her gently and got up. "Time to go," he said.

She looked so pale and tired that he hated

to leave her. "Good luck," she said. "And be careful. *Please* be careful."

"I promise." He hurried out into the hall and saw Sharon on her way to answer the door. She was wearing a long robe, and her feet were bare beneath it.

"It's for me," he said in a low voice. "Tony Danks and Larry Millsaps. We're going to make the delivery. Did you get the bag?"

"Yes," she said. "It's on the couch." She followed him to the living room and answered the door as Ben examined the garment bag.

"Hi," she said to the two men as she let them in.

Tony Danks smiled at her. "Did we get you up?"

"No," she said. "I was waiting to see what came of this. You guys have a long drive to Tampa. Are you gonna make it?"

"If we leave now," Larry said, checking his watch. "It's 9:00. We should be there by ten." They stepped into the living room and saw Ben stuffing the garment bag with some wadded paper grocery sacks.

"What are you doing?" Tony asked.

"Filling the bag up. It has to at least look like it's holding something."

The two cops just stood back, hands in

pockets, looking as if they couldn't care less whether the bag looked convincing or not.

"I'll drive in my car, in case he's watching for me," Ben said. "You guys can follow me."

"You try to get on a plane, Ben, my boy, and we'll drag you off before it's even off the ground," Tony said. "Got it?"

Ben's face hardened, and he shot Sharon a look. "They don't believe me," he said. "They think this is all a hoax."

Sharon caught her breath. "Then why are you going?" she asked the cops.

"Just doing our jobs," Larry said.

She moaned. "I can promise you that it's not a hoax. Please — don't drop the ball on this."

Tony smiled reassuringly. "We'll do the right thing, Ms. Robinson. You don't have to worry."

She looked at him uneasily. "All right. I guess you'll just have to see for yourself."

Ben lifted the bag. "I marked the bag with this yellow thread on the shoulder strap, so that if we don't see him take it, we can catch him with it afterward. It shouldn't be noticeable."

"Good thinking," Larry said, obviously humoring him.

Trying not to let their obstinacy distract

him, Ben headed out the door and got into his car.

The two cops started to follow, but Sharon grabbed Tony's arm and stopped him before they were out the door. He towered over her, but she looked up at him with determination in her eyes. "I'm his *ex*-wife. I haven't been a fan of his in six years. But I can promise you that he's not lying. Please take this seriously."

His blue eyes softened, and he smiled slightly as he patted her hand where it still held his arm. "Don't worry," he said.

She stood at the door and watched as both cars pulled away.

At the airport, they parked in the short-term parking area. After watching to see that Larry and Tony were behind him, Ben got out and took the garment bag from his backseat. Carrying it by the hook at the top and slung over his shoulder, he headed into the airport.

He paused at the flight schedule monitor and scanned it for the last flight coming in from Atlanta. It was ten minutes late, he saw, and coming in at Gate C–23.

Tony followed him up the stairs, then watched him stop at the security gate to lay his bag on the belt. As it made its way through the X-ray, he glanced around.

He grabbed the bag when it reached the end, headed to the C terminal, and counted off the gates.

Tony slowed his step as Ben reached the gate where a couple of dozen people milled around, waiting for the plane from Atlanta to arrive. Ben went to the window where the caller had told him to leave the bag, and keeping it hanging over his shoulder, looked out into the night for the plane.

Tony could see no sign of it yet. In the window, he saw the reflections of people behind Ben. No one looked suspicious. No one carried a bag like Ben's. Milling by, Tony went into the terminal, looking like anyone else about to catch a flight. His eyes scanned the faces there: those of women walking by with strollers, couples holding hands, tired, rumpled businessmen waiting to catch their flights home. Was one of them really a killer, or was this all some grand hoax?

He spotted lights to the north as a plane began to land. It touched down, slowed, and turned. As it taxied toward their terminal, he heard the announcement that Flight 438 from Atlanta had landed.

He could see Ben's hands trembling as he set the garment bag, doubled over, down beside the window. He looked around, then crossed the corridor and headed for the men's room. Neither Tony nor Larry followed. Tony ambled closer to the bag to peer out the window, waiting for something to happen. He knew Larry kept his eye on Ben as he came back out of the rest room.

The ramp door opened and passengers began filing off. A crowd quickly formed in the hall outside the gate, blocking Tony's view of the garment bag.

Concerned that the bag may have been switched while view was blocked, he pushed through the crowd and headed back toward the security gate, looking for anyone who carried a bag like Ben's with a yellow thread tied to the shoulder strap. He saw several similar bags, but none with the yellow thread.

He looked back up the corridor, wondering if Larry had seen anything. Slowly, the crowd by gate C–23 began to thin out, and he saw the bag still lying there, the yellow string still tied to it.

He saw Larry on the other side of the gate, still looking casual in his windbreaker and jeans. The perfect time to switch the bags would have been when the crowd was crushing in. The fact that it hadn't happened might mean that something was wrong.

Frustrated, Tony started toward the men's

room, caught Ben's eye, and nodded for him to follow. Tony didn't acknowledge him as he came in. He went into a stall, pulled a notepad out of his pocket, and wrote, *No one's made the switch yet. Go home and we'll keep watch. There's another cop parked beside you in the garage. He'll follow you home. Don't try anything stupid.*

He shoved the paper into his pocket.

Ben was washing his hands when Tony took the sink next to him. He reached into his pocket, pulled out the note, and set it on Ben's sink without looking at him. Then he dried his hands as Ben read it, watching as the artist closed his eyes in frustration.

Tony found a seat next to Larry at one of the nearby gates, in perfect view of the garment bag, which lay there by itself, waiting for anyone to pick it up. It would probably be taken, all right, Tony thought, but not by the killer.

He watched as Ben came out of the rest room and trudged back down the corridor toward the main terminal.

Sharon was asleep on the couch in the living room when Ben got home. The door woke her, and she sat up. "What happened?"

"Nothing," he said. "He didn't come. At

131

least, not while I was there. Have you heard from Larry and Tony?"

"They weren't with you?"

He shook his head and dropped into a chair. "I left them there. They had another cop follow me home. They could still be waiting, for all I know. If this guy doesn't show, they'll be convinced that I made it all up. They're pretty much convinced, already."

"Did they jeopardize anything?"

He rubbed his face. "No. Actually, they did a pretty good job. No one would have known they were cops or that they were with me." He dropped his hands and shook his head as he leaned it back on the chair. "I just can't figure out what happened."

The phone rang, and they both jumped. "I'll get it," Ben said, snatching up the extension on the table next to him.

"Hello?" His face reddened as he listened to the response, and Sharon got up and stepped toward him.

"I took the bag like you said," he insisted. "I put it exactly where you told me."

She held her breath, certain he was talking to the killer. Ben sighed heavily. "Okay, so I faked it. But you have to believe me. I have no idea what you're looking for, or I would have given it to you. There's nothing I know of that's worth a murder rap."

Sharon covered her face with her hands. The killer knew he'd been set up. Now what were they going to do?

Ben's breath was coming faster. "What do you mean, something worse?" He paused, and his face drained of color. "If you'd just tell me, straight out, what you want, I know I could get it. Why won't you just say it? Just tell me, and —" He looked up at her, his eyes dismal. "He hung up."

Sharon's eyes were as defeated as his as she watched him hang up. "What did he say?"

Ben closed his eyes. "He could tell when he saw the bag that it wasn't what he wanted. I folded it over when I laid it down, and that clued him. It must be bigger. Longer. I don't know. Maybe it's a painting. But which one? There's nothing of mine that's valuable enough for murder. Even the pieces I was restoring weren't that important. And there were some reproductions in the gallery, but who would kill over a reproduction?" In frustration, he threw a pillow across the room. "I just don't know what he wants!"

She tried to sort it all out, but she was too tired. "Well, there's no point in hashing this out right now. I'd go to bed if I were you.

There's nothing more you can do tonight."

"You go ahead," he said. "I'll call the police station and report this call. At least they can pull Larry and Tony out of there. No use having them stay there any longer for nothing." He blew out another frustrated breath. "If only I'd had time to hook up a recorder before that call. The cops still don't believe the first call ever came, and they're sure not willing to use their own resources to prove it."

Wearily, Sharon got up and padded to the doorway, then turned back. "Anne said to wake her up when you got home. She wanted to hear."

He nodded. "I'm glad she slept. It's been a while. I think I'll just let her keep sleeping."

"Whatever." She paused awkwardly for a moment, then finally whispered, "Good night."

"Good night," he said, then picked up the phone and started to dial.

CHAPTER SIXTEEN

The crying baby woke Sharon in the middle of the night, and she lay in her bed staring at the ceiling and waiting for someone to quiet him. The crying went on for fifteen minutes, and finally she got up and pulled on her robe. Someone was going to have to attend to him. His parents were so tired that they might not wake up.

Quietly, she padded up the hall toward the room where she had put his crib, stepped in — and jumped when she saw Anne rocking the screaming baby in a rocking chair.

"Oh! I didn't know you were up."

Anne shot her a contemptuous look. "You thought I was just letting my baby scream?"

Sharon sighed. She really wasn't in the mood for this. "I'll just go back to bed, then."

"I'm sorry he woke you up," Anne said. "He's sick. He's got a fever."

Sharon hesitated at the door, then turned back and bent over the baby. She touched his forehead; he was burning up. "Do you need a thermometer?"

"Yes," Anne said quietly. "If you have one."

Sharon went to the kitchen and found the thermometer, the pediatric Tylenol syrup, and an infant measuring spoon. She brought the thermometer to Anne and watched as she stuck the digital thermometer under the baby's arm. "Can you give him this?"

"What is it?"

"Tylenol," she said.

"It might help." Anne took it, and under her breath, added, "Thank you."

Sharon stood there a moment, waiting to see what the temperature was. The little thermometer beeped, and Anne took it out from under his arm. "A hundred one," she said.

"He's pretty congested," Sharon said, "so he may have an ear infection. Mine used to get them all the time."

"I've already thought of that," Anne said wearily. "I just don't know what I can do about it."

"Well, do you want to take him to the doctor?"

"I can't afford it," she said through clenched teeth, shifting the baby to hush him. "We have no money. Don't you understand?"

Sharon felt slapped down again. "Look, I'll be happy to pay the doctor bill."

"I don't want any more favors from you."

"Your child is sick!" Sharon blurted. "Besides that, no one in the house can get any sleep until he's well. Will you please take him to the doctor and let me pay the bill?"

Tears came to Anne's eyes as she stared off into the darkness. "All right," she said. "I guess I have no choice. I'll take him in the morning."

Sharon stormed back to her room and flopped onto the bed, her blood boiling. What had she done to deserve this woman's wrath? After all, it was Anne who had broken up their family, who had come between Sharon and her husband. How dare she come in here and act like Sharon was her enemy? And while Sharon was trying to help her, for pete's sake.

She tried to pray but the words wouldn't come, and as the baby continued to cry late into the night, she lay sleepless and exhausted, desperate to figure out a solution to this problem that seemed to have no end.

CHAPTER SEVENTEEN

The police station was less chaotic than last time, Sharon thought. She stood just inside the door scanning the desks for Larry or Tony. Dark circles ringed her eyes, and she felt as though she had been beaten during the night.

As she spotted Tony slumped over his computer, looking just as tired as she felt, she resolved to do something about that situation right now. She headed for his desk, but he didn't look up from his computer as she approached. He had the weary, distracted look, yet his face reminded her of a younger version of Robert Redford.

Since the first time she'd met him, she'd been wary of him, for his good looks were like a big red warning sign to be careful. Ben had been too handsome for his own good, too, before he'd grown his hair so long and cultivated that bohemian, too-creative-to-care image. Good-looking men needed constant affirmation and consistent hero worship — if they didn't get it, they strayed, and told themselves they were right to do so.

But Tony didn't look as if he'd spent a lot of time in front of the mirror this morning.

He had shaven, but his hair looked more rumpled than usual. His eyes were blood-shot, and she suspected he'd gotten about as much sleep as she had.

She cleared her throat to get his attention, but still, he didn't look up. She stepped closer and tried again.

"Excuse me," she said. He looked up unappreciatively, but when he saw her, his face changed instantly.

"Mrs. Robinson," he said, standing up and reaching to shake her hand.

"Sharon," she corrected. "I do still use Robinson, but I dropped the 'Mrs.' six years ago. I was hoping you'd be in this morning. I was a little doubtful, since it's Saturday and you worked so late last night."

He gestured for her to sit down and sat back in his own chair. "Yeah, nothing like wasted time."

She sat down and leaned forward, trying to keep her voice low enough that others wouldn't overhear, but loud enough that he could hear her over the din in the station. "That's why I wanted to talk to you. I was worried that what happened last night might have led you to believe that . . ." Her voice trailed off, and she struggled to find the right words.

"That Ben might have been leading us on

a wild-goose chase to get himself out from under the glass?"

She shrugged. "Something like that. I was afraid that you'd come back here and stop investigating — just write the murder off to an angry employee, and quit looking for the real murderer."

He leaned his elbows on his desk and took a deep breath. "Sharon, you're very loyal. That's admirable. But has it ever occurred to you that your ex-husband may really have done this?"

"No," she said with certainty. "Not for a second. It goes completely against everything I know about him. And I've known him for twenty years. Two before we were married, twelve years during, and six after."

He clasped his hands in front of his face and studied her as she spoke. When he didn't answer, she leaned back hard in her chair. "Why would I be so intent on proving him innocent if I didn't believe that?"

"Because you're the mother of his children," Tony said. "Most mothers don't want their children growing up with the stigma of having a father in prison."

"Oh, for heaven's sake," she said, leaning forward again. "It goes completely against his character, in every way. He's a make-love-not-war kind of guy. If you knew him like I did, you'd know how absurd this all is."

"I've seen his temper, Sharon. He's even admitted to losing it with Dubose." Tony's gaze didn't leave her face as he asked, "When he cheated on you, did you feel you knew him then?"

She sat slowly back and held Tony's gaze. "How do you know that's what happened?"

He nodded toward his computer screen, and she saw Ben's name in a block at the top. He had been looking into his background.

"When I count back from the birth of his next child, I don't have to be a genius to see that wife number two was pregnant already when the divorce papers were filed."

Sharon was getting angry. Was he making *her* out to be a liar now? "So you know what led to my divorce. I don't see your point."

"Point is, you don't always know people as well as you think you do."

"Okay. And?"

"And, if he lied and cheated once, maybe he could do it again. Maybe he *could* have had some motive strong enough to make him want to kill his boss. Maybe it was anger, or maybe it was something else."

"Why would he do it?" she asked him. "He'd lose his job, his home, his credit cards, his income — why would he do something so stupid?"

"He'd already lost those earlier that day." He turned back to his computer and scrolled down. "I've been looking over his history here, Sharon. He looks like a man who doesn't do a lot of planning. His financial state is a good indication that he flies by the seat of his pants. He doesn't always think things out."

"All right," she conceded. "He's definitely guilty of that. But that doesn't happen to be against the law."

"No, but it could be a clue that the man isn't always going to be predictable. That maybe sometimes he could act in a fit of passion. Artistic temperament can be very bizarre sometimes. Remember Van Gogh?"

"Van Gogh was insane," she said. "Ben is not. He's a little irresponsible, a little self-absorbed, a little scatterbrained, but he is not insane. And he's not a killer. How could I let him and his family move into my house if I thought for a second that he was?"

"Instead of proving the probability of his innocence, Sharon, that could just prove the probability of your state of denial."

"Denial?" She got to her feet and leaned over his desk, putting her face close to his. "You think I'd take in the man who cheated on me and the woman who wrecked my marriage and the children she rubs in my face — all because I was in denial? Trust me, Tony, there's no denial here. Neither Ben nor Anne are my favorite people, and frankly, my first instinct is to let them sink or swim. Last night was close to the worst night of my life. This woman hates my guts for existing, and instead of being grateful that I put a roof over her head, she's spitting nails and acting like I've locked her in there by force. If I were in denial, Tony, there might be a lot more harmony around my house right now. But my only thought is to get them out of there as soon as humanly possible. The only way I see to do that is to help Ben prove his innocence. And it looks like I'm going to have to depend a lot on you to do that."

Her eyes seared into his, and he sat motionless as she unloaded.

"Now you can take the easy way out and stamp this case solved, or you can consider some other probabilities. For starters, the probability that I am an intelligent woman who wouldn't be in the position I'm in unless I had complete faith in Ben Robinson's innocence. If for no other reason than that, you should at least keep looking. Consider the probability that someone really did call him last night. That I wasn't hearing things when the phone rang. That someone threatened him and told him to make a delivery at the airport. That he doesn't have a clue what they want. Could you do that, Detective? Could you just consider it? Just in case you really don't have all this figured out, and there's some killer still out there who's laughing his head off at the St. Clair police for falling so easily for this frame-up?"

Tony took a deep breath and rubbed his eyes, then leaned back and crossed his arms over his chest. "For your information, that's why I came in today, even though it's my day off and I didn't get much sleep last night. I've already started working on locating other people who may have had vendettas against Dubose. We've been in touch with some of his other colleagues, some of his friends, some of the art dealers who frequented the gallery. We're looking for other motives, Sharon. That hasn't stopped just because Ben has been charged. But that doesn't mean that I'm optimistic about finding anything. Ben is the most obvious suspect. Those phone calls — frankly, Sharon, they prove nothing. So he has an accomplice. I'd have guessed that anyway. Probably a woman, based on his history. Sharon, everything points to Ben."

"Yeah, like a neon sign. Like big red arrows. What kind of fool would leave that much evidence behind? It's so obvious that it was a setup. And now this maniac is calling my house, making threats, and I'm afraid of what might happen next!"

"But you're not frightened of Ben?"

"No!" she said too loudly, then realized others were looking her way. Trying to calm herself, she lowered back into her chair. "How many times do I have to tell you? He can't even spank his children. He barely raised his voice to me in twelve years of marriage."

"That is some feat, considering your temper," he said with a half-grin. "Did you ever get in his face like you did in mine just now?"

She lowered her face into her hands and gently massaged her tired eyes. "Look, I'm sorry. I'm a little on edge. This may be just another case to you, but it's altering my whole life. It's serious."

He softened then and looked down at his hands. "I realize that. I didn't mean to make it seem like I was taking it lightly. I'm really not. I'm working hard on this case because I don't want to make any mistakes. Whatever you may think about the St. Clair PD, we're very thorough. Ask Lynda. She knows firsthand."

"Well, you can ask Lynda about Ben, too. We've been friends a long time, and she's heard it all." She was getting very tired, and she felt that her body showed it. She studied him for a moment. "Have you ever been married, Tony?"

He shook his head and grinned slightly. "Can't say I've had the pressure."

She lifted her eyebrows at the play on words. "Then it's no wonder that you can't understand how sure I can be that Ben is innocent."

Tony stared at her quietly for a moment. "I guess you're right. I can't understand it. But I'll respect it. And I'll keep it in mind. Fair enough?"

She nodded and got to her feet again. "It's fair as long as you find the killer. Do you think whoever did this will come after Ben? Or that he's a threat to any of us in the house?"

Tony shook his head. "Sharon, *if* Ben was set up, then he's the last one the murderer would want to touch. He wouldn't want to give himself away. And he sure wouldn't want to do away with his scapegoat."

She considered that. "I guess you're right." She reached out to shake his hand again. "I appreciate your time, Detective."

"Anytime," he said, getting to his feet and

holding her hand a little longer than necessary. "In fact, if you ever feel like you need to escape the pressure for a while, just give me a call and we'll go get a cup of coffee or something."

She smiled. "I will."

"And if you think of anything else I need to know, don't hesitate to call."

"All right. Thanks."

She said good-bye and headed back across the precinct, feeling a little better than she had when she'd come in. She wasn't sure whether the visit had been merely therapeutic, or actually helpful. She got to the door and waited as several people came in, then looked quickly back over her shoulder.

Tony was still watching her.

Her heart jolted, and she told herself that she'd have to take him up on that cup of coffee soon. As she hurried out the door and back to her car, she had the gentle beginning of a smile on her face.

CHAPTER EIGHTEEN

Ben unlocked the door with Jenny's key, and opened it for the girls. They had gone to the art store to buy supplies for their mural on the tree house, which Ben was determined to paint in spite of the mess he was in. The children were chattering nonstop as they bounced into the house. Then suddenly they fell silent.

Over their heads, Ben saw the open pantry, the cans that had fallen on the floor, the cabinet doors. The two little girls gasped. "What happened?"

Jenny grabbed his arm. "Dad, somebody's been in here."

Ben motioned for her to stay back and went into the den. The cushions were on the floor, and books had been pulled off the shelves. He saw that the girls had not obeyed his silent order, and had followed close behind him. He hurried into the living room, and they stood gaping at the scattered cushions and the open closet, its contents spilled out onto the floor.

"Dad, who could have done this?"

"Get the girls and go next door," he said quickly. "Then call the police. Wait there until I come for you."

"Why?" Jenny asked. "Do you think who-ever did this is still here?"

"I don't know," he said. "Just do it."

She grabbed the girls' hands. "Come on, kids. We have to go."

"But who made this mess?" Christy asked. "Mommy's gonna die."

"I don't know. Just come on."

"What about Daddy?"

Jenny didn't answer as she pulled them out the door.

The police were there in ten minutes, and while Ben followed them around the house, making sure that no one was hidden there, Larry and Tony came in.

Ben looked at them with resignation as they came up the stairs.

"What's going on now?" Tony asked wearily.

"Somebody broke in," Ben said. "We were all gone, and this is what we came back to."

"Anything missing?" Larry asked, looking into the rooms he passed.

"Nothing that I can see. Sharon would know better, though. She's showing some houses this morning."

"I saw her earlier," Tony said. "She didn't mention where she was heading."

Ben raked a hand through his hair. "I think they may have been looking for something."

"Looking for what?" Tony asked skeptically.

"I don't know. Whatever I was supposed to have delivered last night, probably."

"Oh. Right." Tony blew out a heavy breath. "Ben, was there anyone with you when you discovered this?"

Ben looked insulted, but not surprised. "Yes. My kids."

"Where are they? I want to talk to them."

"They're next door. I sent them over there as soon as we saw all this. I was afraid whoever it was was still in the house."

"All right," Tony said. "Larry, I'm going over there to talk to them. You can handle it from here."

Larry nodded. "No sweat."

Tony trotted back down the stairs. Just as he reached the kitchen door, it flew open, and Sharon burst in. "I saw the police cars!" she said in a panic. "What's going on?"

"Everyone's fine," he said to calm her. "We got a burglary call. According to your ex-husband, someone broke into your house."

She looked around at the contents of the pantry on the floor, the cabinet doors —

through the arched doors, she saw the mess in the den. "I'd say he's right. Is anything missing?"

"Televisions, computers, stereos are all still here. You might check your jewelry, and anything else you had that was valuable."

"Where are the kids?" she asked quickly.

"Next door. Ben sent them over when they got home."

"Good," she said, turning and rushing back for the door. "I want to go make sure they're all right."

"I'll come with you," he said. "I need to ask them some questions."

Christy watched out the window of her elderly neighbor's living room, fascinated with the police cars in her driveway and in front of her house. She saw her mother's car, which had not been there before, and she jumped up and down and yelled to her sisters. "Mommy's home! Can I go tell her what happened?"

Jenny came into the room, accompanied by Mrs. Milton, the retired schoolteacher who had gotten the girls a plate of cookies to distract them. "No, Christy. You stay here until Mom or Dad tells us to come home."

"But why? We're missing all the excitement."

Jenny pulled back the curtain and looked out the window. "I know, but — I can't believe all this. Somebody's really out to get Daddy."

"Mommy's coming!" Christy said as she saw her mother hurrying across the lawn with the cop who'd arrested her father trailing behind her. She jumped up and ran to the front door to fling it open. "Mommy, somebody robbed our house!"

Sharon bent down and hugged her younger child. "I know, honey. But it's okay." She looked up at Jenny, then at Emily hunkering in the corner, looking a little frightened. "Are you all okay?"

"Sure, Mom. We're fine," Jenny said. "Is he still in there? Did he take my computer or my stereo?"

"I don't think so," Sharon said. She looked at the widow still holding the plate of cookies. "Thanks for taking them in, Grace. I appreciate it."

"No problem," the older woman said. "Come in and relax for a minute. You look so tired."

"It's been a tough couple of days," Sharon admitted. "Grace, girls, this is Detective Tony Danks from the St. Clair Police Department. He needs to ask you a few questions."

"Me, too, Mommy?" Christy asked hopefully.

"You, too," Tony said, sitting down so he'd be eye level with the child. "Tell me how you found out the house had been broken into."

Christy's eyebrows shot up with excitement. "We came back from the art store, and there was stuff all over the place. Mommy, it's a mess!"

"I know, honey. I saw it."

"How long were you gone?" Tony asked Jenny, and she sat down across from him, much more serious than Christy.

"About an hour, I guess," she answered. "Daddy is going to help the girls paint a mural on Christy's tree house, and we went to get some art supplies. Most of his paints are still at the studio."

"All right," Tony said, pulling out the pad he kept in his pocket and making a note. "Jenny, Christy, Emily, I want you guys to think real hard when I ask you this question. When you left, who was the first one in the car?"

"I was!" Christy shouted, shooting her hand in the air.

Emily raised her hand, too. "No, it was me. We tied!"

"If we tied, then how could you be there

first?" Christy asked. "I was first."

"No, I was."

"Okay, so you both got out there first," Tony said, chuckling. "Who was next?"

"I was," Jenny said, frowning. "Why?"

"So your dad was the last one out of the house?"

"Yes," Jenny said. "He locked up."

"How long was he in there before he got to the car?"

She looked disturbed at the question, and looked questioningly up at her mother. Sharon shrugged and nodded for her to answer. "Well, I don't know. A few minutes. He said he couldn't find his wallet."

"Did he find it?"

"Yes, and he came on out."

"I see." He made a note of that, then glanced up at Sharon. She was getting that look on her face that said he had a lot of nerve, but he pressed on. "Now, you went to the art store, and bought supplies, right? Did you stop anywhere else?"

"No," Christy volunteered. "We went right there and right back."

"All right. Who was the first one back in the house?"

"We all went at the same time," Jenny said. "The girls went in first, then Dad and I were right behind them."

"And which rooms did you see?"

Jenny looked confused. "Well, uh . . . I saw the kitchen, and the den, and then I went into the living room. That's when Dad sent us over here."

"So you didn't see the rest of the house?"

"No."

"Did any of you?"

"No," Jenny said. "Dad wanted us out in case he was still there."

Sharon was getting impatient. "What are you getting at, Detective?"

"I'm just asking questions," he said. "Now, your dad's wife. Emily's mom. Where is she?"

"She took Bobby to the doctor," Jenny said. "He's sick."

"And how long has she been gone?"

"Hours," Jenny said. "They had to work her in, because she didn't have an appointment."

He made another note, then looked up at Mrs. Milton. "Grace, did you see any cars over there earlier? Anybody who didn't belong there?"

"No, I'm afraid not," the woman said. "I didn't know anything was wrong until the girls came running over."

"Okay. We'll question some of the other neighbors to see if anyone saw anything."

"Good," Sharon said.

He got up and held out a hand for Christy, and she shook proudly. "Thanks for your help," he said.

"Sure. Can we go home now?"

"Stay here until the police get finished. Sharon, can I speak to you outside?"

"All right." She thanked Mrs. Milton again, then followed him out into the yard. "What is it?"

He saw Larry on his way across the yard to speak to him.

"Sharon, in light of our conversation this morning, I know you're not going to like what I have to say," Tony said as Larry approached.

"Oh, no. You're not going to blow this off like it didn't happen, are you? You're not going to ignore this! This is *my house!*"

"I'm not convinced anything happened," he said. "Ben was the last one to leave the house. He hung around in there long enough to have pulled the cushions off, opened some doors, upset some shelves. Jenny only saw the front rooms when she came back. Between the time they got home and the time the police showed up, he had plenty of time to go through the rest of the house, making it look like someone had been there. There was no sign of forced entry, no one has seen anyone who didn't belong here —"

"You haven't questioned everyone yet! You don't know!"

"And it doesn't look like anything was taken," Larry added. "It doesn't look like a robbery."

"You people are nuts. Why would Ben do this?"

"The same reason he staged that little drama last night. To throw us off. Make us think we've got the wrong guy. He's desperate, Sharon, and frankly, I'm beginning to wonder if it isn't dangerous having him in the house at all."

"So what are you saying?" she asked, keeping her voice low so her neighbors and kids wouldn't hear. "That I should send him back to jail? Just because you refuse to believe that someone actually could have broken into my house to look for whatever it is he thinks Ben has?"

"It just looks too suspicious, Sharon."

"And it may not have been Ben who did it," Larry conceded. "It could have been his wife, trying to help him out."

"No way," Sharon said. "There's a killer out there, and he's framed Ben, and he's called and threatened him, and now he's broken into my house, and you aren't going to do one thing about catching him, are you?"

"Sharon . . ."

"I had more respect for you when I left the station this morning, Tony. I thought you might really have a conscience, that you'd do a good job no matter what it cost you. That you were a good cop. But I was wrong."

He looked as if he'd been slapped across the face. "Sharon, I'm doing my job."

"No, you're not! You're passing the buck because you're too lazy to consider any other possibilities."

"We are considering them, Sharon," Larry said. "We just have to tell you what our gut instinct is. It's not unusual for someone accused of a crime to try to throw us off the track. We have to tell you if we think the man living in your house is putting your family in danger."

"We're in danger, all right," she bit out. "But I obviously can't turn to St. Clair's finest for help. The danger isn't coming from my ex-husband, detectives. It's coming from your apathy!"

She turned and fled into the house, leaving them both standing in the driveway. Tony stood there for a moment, watching her go. Finally, he turned and started walking away from the house.

"Where are you going?" Larry asked.

"To question the neighbors," he said irritably. "Might as well get started. We have a lot of ground to cover."

The police were finishing their report and clearing out as Sharon came back into the house. She found Ben sitting alone at the dining-room table, his hands covering his face.

"What was he looking for, Ben?" she asked, leaning in the doorway, suddenly feeling too weak to stand straight. "What does he want?"

"If I knew . . ." He rubbed his eyes and looked up at her. "Do you at least believe he was here? That I didn't do this?"

"Of course I do. I wish it *had* been you. I wouldn't be so scared."

"I ought to just let them take me back to jail."

"Right," Sharon said. "That should solve everything."

"Well, look at your house. He ransacked it."

She shook her head. "Actually, it doesn't look so bad. We can put it all back together. It just feels so creepy, knowing he was here."

He rubbed his temples, trying to think. "I was just going back over everything with the cops. In the second phone call, he said it was too long to fold the garment bag. That's how he knew it wasn't what he wanted. It's got to be a painting . . . something really valuable . . . maybe rolled up. I've been trying to think of all the things I was working on in the studio. There were a couple of things Dubose bought recently that I was restoring. They had some value, but not this much."

"Maybe if you could get back into the gallery and look around, you could find it."

"If that's where it is, why didn't he find it when he killed Dubose?" He looked up at her with helpless eyes. "Sharon, I know how this looks."

She heard a car pulling into the garage, and glanced out the window. "Anne's home."

"I don't know how much more she can take," he said.

Sharon knew the feeling, but she didn't voice it. "Guess I'll get busy putting Humpty Dumpty back together again."

He got up wearily. "I'll help. We'll all help."

Sharon left the room before she had to confront Anne again.

CHAPTER NINETEEN

The telephone in Eric Boudreaux's elegant hotel room rang, and he picked it up quickly.

"Yes?" he said in his French-accented voice.

"Mr. Boudreaux! How are you?"

Boudreaux was quiet for a long moment. "Impatient. As a matter of fact, I was just planning to ring the airport and book a flight back tomorrow. That is, unless you have something for me."

"I, uh . . . I need another day or two. Please. I'm trying to be very careful so as not to call too much attention to us. One can't be cavalier about an exchange of this sort."

"You do not have it, do you, Monsieur Lieber?"

A pause. "Of course I have it. And you want it. Dubose showed you the snapshot of it, didn't he?"

"He did. But I have yet to touch the picture."

"You'll touch it, my friend," the voice said with a chuckle. "Very, very soon. Don't return home just yet. I want you to have it, but if you return home, I'll have to offer it to another buyer."

"This was not in the agreement," Boudreaux said. "I was to stay for two days, then return with the picture."

"No one counted on Dubose's untimely death."

"No, you are right," the Frenchman said. "And I must tell you that I am growing quite suspicious, myself. I don't relish the idea of being a — how you say — accomplice to murder."

"I had nothing to do with his death. Nothing at all. It was an unfortunate coincidence that it happened the very week you were to meet with him."

"But if his death was motivated by greed because of this picture," Boudreaux said, "I would hesitate to do business with anyone involved. My reputation is flawless, and I intend to keep it that way. My crimes have always been harmless."

"And they will continue to be, sir. Trust me."

"Then when will you deliver?" Boudreaux asked.

"Soon."

"Tomorrow," he insisted. "If I do not hear from you tomorrow, I will leave."

There was a sigh. "You'll hear from me. Please, wait until you do. I anticipate having the painting by tonight. You will have it immediately after that."

"If I do not, you will have to bring it to me in LeMans," Boudreaux said. "Smuggling it through customs will be your problem, not mine."

"I'll be in touch tomorrow, Mr. Boudreaux. You won't be sorry you waited."

"I sincerely hope not," Boudreaux said, and hung up the phone.

CHAPTER TWENTY

Sharon took the easy way out and ordered pizzas that night, so that they wouldn't have to subject themselves to a sit-down dinner all together. She worked into the night putting things back where they belonged. When they were finished, everyone went to their bedrooms early, and Sharon went up to tuck in Christy and Emily.

"I'm glad Bobby's better," Christy said as her mother covered her with the Laura Ashley comforter. "He had a bad ear infection."

"And an earache, too," Emily added.

Sharon smiled. "Well, he should sleep better tonight."

"Mommy, are you scared?"

Sharon's smile faltered. "Why do you ask that?"

"Because that man was in our house. What if he comes back?"

"He won't," Sharon said. "Everything's locked up tight, and we're all home now. He won't come while we're home."

"Are you sure?"

"Positive," she lied. "Emily, are you comfortable? I could get you a softer pillow if you need it."

"I like this one," Emily said, snuggling up next to Christy. "I wish I could live here all the time."

Sharon smiled in spite of herself. She took a deep breath and asked, "How about if we say prayers together?"

"Okay," Christy said, "but you lie down between us."

Sharon crawled between them on the bed and got under the covers. She put her arm around Christy, and Emily snuggled up to her as well, expecting the same affection. Sharon grinned and slid her arm around her. The children didn't understand the politics of their family, she thought. And that was good.

She prayed aloud for their father, and for the man who was out there causing so much trouble, and for Bobby's ears and his cold, and for the safety of everyone in their home. When she finished, she lay there a moment, holding both girls.

"Tell us a story, Mommy," Christy said. "Please."

"I'll tell you part of one," Sharon said. "And then you tell me part."

Christy giggled. "Okay. You start."

Sharon sighed and thought for a moment. "Once upon a time, there was a little girl named . . ."

"Named Beth," Christy said. "Can that be

her name, Mommy?"

"Okay, Beth. And she lived in a beautiful little cottage with flowers all around."

"And it had this cool climbing tree in the front yard, didn't it, Mommy?"

"That's right."

"No, that's wrong!" Christy changed her mind and sat up in bed. "The cottage was *in* the tree!"

"Okay," Sharon said. "And Emily, what color do you think the flowers were?"

"Purple!" Emily cried.

"That's right," Sharon said. "How did you know?"

Emily shrugged and giggled.

"But one day, something terrible happened."

"What, Mommy?" Christy asked, her eyes growing big. "Did somebody break into her house and rob her?"

Sharon thought for a moment. "No. One day, she went ice-skating on the pond near her house, because she didn't live in Florida, she lived in . . ."

"Alaska!" Christy provided.

"That's right. And she went ice skating, and while she was gone, some mean man came and . . ."

"Picked all her flowers!" Christy said. "And he sold them at the flea market, because they had fleas!"

They all laughed and lay back down, and Sharon went on with the story.

Anne climbed the stairs and walked up the hall to say good night to Emily. As she neared the door, she could hear laughter. It was good to hear Emily giggle again, she thought, and she paused and listened. Then she heard Sharon's voice, embroidering a story that had them both enthralled.

She went to the door and looked in. Sharon lay between the two girls on the big canopy bed, an arm around each of them, giggling right along with them.

Anne stepped back, suddenly jealous again. Not only were they beholden to Sharon because of their dependence on her for shelter and money, but she feared that Emily was getting too attached to this home and this family. She was losing Ben, she was losing Emily, and she'd already lost control of her life . . .

Slowly, she went back down the stairs to Bobby's room. He was sleeping soundly now that he'd been given the medication he needed. She sat down in the rocking chair in the darkened room, trying to figure out where to turn with the anxious, dangerous emotions holding her in their vicious grip.

CHAPTER TWENTY-ONE

The phone rang once, and as usual, Jenny quickly answered it. After a moment, she yelled down the stairs, "Daddy! It's for you!"

Ben took the call in the study, hoping it was Lynda. "Hello?"

"Ben, it's good to hear your voice."

"Nelson?" he asked.

"Yes. I'm still in London. I had hoped to get home to attend Louis's funeral, but there was too much fog on the ground, so the planes weren't taking off."

"How did you know where I was?"

"When I had the money wired to the courthouse, the secretary there told me you had moved in with your ex. I have to admit it was a little surprising. If I'd known you really didn't have a place to live, I could have offered you the use of my house."

"Yeah, well, I appreciate it, but it's a done deal now. We have to stay until this whole thing is cleared up. Listen, thanks for the bond money. I promise you'll get it back. I'll be acquitted."

"Of course you will. Have they got any leads?"

"I seem to be the only one. Despite the

fact that this guy even broke in here today."

"Broke in? Are you serious?"

"The police don't seem to think so. They think I did it."

Nelson paused a moment, as if thinking. "Look, the moment I arrive, I'll go straight to the police and vouch for you, for what it's worth. This is ludicrous. Ben, do you think Louis was involved in something we don't know about?"

"Who knows?" Ben asked dejectedly. "When do you think you'll be here, anyway?"

"Probably in the next couple of days, if the weather clears. Have you thought about what you're going to do for money?"

"Yeah, a lot," Ben said. "I didn't get my last paycheck, and my paintings are all still locked in the gallery."

"Well, I've picked up a few things here that need some restoration work. Do you feel like doing them?"

"Of course," he said. "I need the work."

"Fine. Well, just cross your fingers that I'll arrive there soon. It's all going to work out, Ben. You'll see."

CHAPTER TWENTY-TWO

Home was a word that Tony only had a passing acquaintance with, especially these days when he spent so much time working. As he came in now, he shrugged wearily out of his sport coat and unfastened his shoulder holster. Dropping it on the counter, he carried the sport coat through the immaculate living room and into the bedroom. He hadn't slept much in the last few days, but the bed was made, anyway. Everything was in its place, perfectly in order. Normally, he found some degree of comfort in the small house he had built for himself, once he realized that he would probably never be married.

He walked across the white carpet and into the walk-in closet, where he hung his coat. Then, stepping out of his shoes, he padded back into the living room. Slumping down into his favorite chair, he pulled up his feet and stared at the vaulted ceiling.

It had been a horrendous, grueling afternoon, grilling neighbors who had seen nothing but wanted to waste his and Larry's time talking, trying to find out what was going on in the interesting and complex family that occupied the Robinson house. He'd learned more details than he'd ever intended to gather today — that Sharon Robinson rarely dated, that she was very successful on the real-estate scene, that her children were the best behaved on the street. He'd heard stories of how she'd helped elderly neighbors during the power outage last summer when the temperatures had soared to over 100 degrees. One single mother had shared how Sharon had kept her kids for an entire week while their mother was hospitalized for a ruptured appendix, then took care of her for a couple of weeks more until she had recovered.

She was too good for her own good, some of the neighbors agreed. And they all lamented the fact that she had been bamboozled into taking in her no-account ex this way, especially when everyone knew he'd killed that Dubose fellow. He suspected there would have been neighborhood complaints about his even being in the neighborhood, if it weren't for their great respect for Sharon herself.

But it wasn't those conversations that kept playing through his mind, but the one he'd last had with her. She'd said his apathy was dangerous. He worried that her generosity was.

He glanced at the phone and thought of

calling her, just to let her know that he had taken it all seriously, that he had interviewed neighbors and had spent much of the early evening running down a list of people found in Dubose's Rolodex, matching them with his desk diary, and trying to determine who they needed to talk to next. But none of that mattered, he thought. He had done all that work mostly to humor Sharon. In his mind, Ben was the murderer, and all the work he did would only prove that. He just couldn't understand why it was so hard for her to see.

Maybe it was because she'd been married to the guy, he thought. She couldn't admit that she had been blind all those years. That he was ruthless and cold-blooded. That she'd had children with a man who could kill.

No one liked facing up to facts like that.

But he worried about her, and about the undying loyalty and unwavering faith that could get her into trouble. He wondered if she'd cooled down, or if, in the dark quiet of her night, she was wondering if, just maybe, Tony could be right. If Ben might have done all this, after all.

His eyes strayed to the telephone, and he started to pick it up. Then he thought better of it. He didn't need to entertain these lingering thoughts about Sharon Robinson. She had too many problems. He needed to do his job and stay away from her. Wasn't that what he'd told Larry so many times? His cardinal rule — not getting personally involved in his cases — had always stuck, even when his partner disregarded it.

But he wasn't sure why he couldn't shake her from his mind. He could pick up the phone right now and call any number of women to have dinner with him and go have a drink at the Steppin' Out across town. Or he could just show up there, and meet new ones. It was his common MO for Saturday night.

Tonight, however, his heart just wasn't in it. And he wasn't interested in meeting any other women. Tonight, only Sharon Robinson occupied his thoughts.

He tried to rationalize. He told himself that this case wasn't about her. She was only involved by virtue of her former marriage to the defendant. If he called her, it wouldn't be a conflict of interest, would it?

He looked at the phone again, and finally picked it up. Quickly, he dialed information, asked for her number, then punched it out. He waited as it rang once, twice . . .

"Hello?"

It was her older daughter's voice, and he

cleared his throat and said, "May I speak to Sharon, please?"

"Yes, just a moment."

She was polite, he thought, just as the neighbors had said. He waited for a moment, then heard another extension being picked up, as the first one cut off.

"Hello?"

"Sharon? It's Tony."

"Yes?" she said coldly, obviously still perturbed at him.

He smiled. "I just wanted to see how you're doing."

"Fine, thank you."

He could see that this wasn't going to be easy, so he softened his voice and gave a stab at being contrite. "Look, I'm really sorry I made you mad today. But I spent the rest of the day interviewing neighbors. None of them saw anything, so now I'm working on friends and colleagues of Dubose who might have had a vendetta against him."

She let that sink in for a moment, then asked, "What about the fingerprints?"

"They all belonged to those of you living in the house. No one new."

She was quiet again. "Well, at least you're trying. I appreciate that."

His smile returned, then faded again. "Are you sure you're okay?"

He imagined her sinking into a chair, letting down her guard. "Yeah, I'm okay. Just tired. I don't know how well I'll sleep tonight. Tony?"

"Yeah?"

"I'm sorry about all the things I said to you today. I was under a lot of stress, but I had no right to lash out at you like that. You were just doing your job."

"You didn't think I was doing it well. You have the right to that opinion."

"Yeah, but I didn't have the right to beat you up with it. I'm sorry."

He couldn't believe he had called her to apologize, and had wound up getting one from her.

"You work really hard, don't you?" she asked. "Day and night, weekends . . ."

"It depends on what I'm working on. It's not usually so bad."

"But you and Larry are the only two detectives in the whole force, aren't you?"

"That's right," he said.

"Then you get all the junk. How do you ever have any time to yourself?"

He smiled. "I take time. I could say the same thing about you. From talking to your neighbors, I'd say that between being the best real-estate agent in town and the best neighbor on your block, not to mention the best mother and the best ex-wife, I can't imagine how you ever get time to yourself."

She laughed softly, a sound that lightened his heart.

"For instance, what were you doing when I called? I'll bet you were cleaning up the mess from the break-in."

"Wrong," she said. "I finished that earlier."

"What then?"

He could hear the smile in her voice. "If you must know, I was under the fig tree."

"Under the fig tree?" he asked. "Is that a fig tree in your backyard?"

She laughed louder now, and he couldn't help grinning. "No. That's an oak. 'Under the fig tree' is just an expression."

He let his feet down and sat up. "What does it mean?"

"Have you ever read the Bible, Tony?"

He frowned. "No. I can't say I have."

She didn't seem surprised. "Well, there's a passage in the first chapter of John, where Jesus is calling his first few disciples. He finds Philip and tells him, 'Follow me,' and then Philip goes and tells Nathaniel that he's found the Messiah. Nathaniel doesn't believe him, so Philip tells him to just come and see. Nathaniel goes with Philip to meet Jesus, and when Jesus sees him, he says,

'Here is a true Israelite, in whom there is nothing false.' And Nathaniel asks him how he knew him."

"Yeah?" Tony asked, a little surprised that a Bible story could hold his interest for this long.

"Jesus says, 'I saw you while you were still under the fig tree before Philip called you.' "

"So? He saw him under a tree. What's the big deal?"

"In those days, 'under the fig tree' meant 'seeking God.' When a man wanted to pray, often the coolest place was under a fig tree, so he'd go there to be alone and to pray. It became a common expression. Instead of saying you were praying and seeking God, you'd say you were 'under the fig tree.' "

"Oh," Tony said. "So you meant that you were praying?" The thought made him a little uncomfortable. As long as they were talking about some story in the Bible that had nothing to do with him, he was fine. But he hated it when these spiritual subjects cropped into his own comfort zone.

"Right," she said. "So you see? I do get some time to myself now and then. Sometimes I just have to take it."

"But I didn't mean praying time. I meant time that's good for you. Recreation. Something that's not an obligation, but a pleasure."

"I don't pray to fulfill an obligation, Tony. And it's pure pleasure. Even when I'm on my knees begging him for answers."

"Yeah, I know," he said, though he didn't have a clue. "But I just mean . . . well, you know, people like you . . . like us . . . they're prone to burnout. It's a big danger, you know. You have to take time out. Do things for yourself. Go to a movie. Out to dinner. Whatever."

He didn't know why he was getting so tongue-tied and nervous. He asked women out all the time, and he was smooth. Very smooth. Tonight he felt like an awkward kid asking the homecoming queen for a date.

"Well, yes," she agreed. "Those things are nice. If you have someone to do them with."

"Well, of course. I mean, not by yourself. Maybe with someone. Like me." He grinned then and winced, covering his face and kicking himself for sounding like a jerk. He leaned forward, holding the phone close to his ear. "Sharon, I'm trying to ask you for a date, but I'm doing an incredibly poor job of it."

There was a stunned silence for a moment. Finally, she said, "Well, yes. I mean, if it's okay. Not a conflict of interest or anything. I mean, you are working on Ben's case."

"It should be okay," he said.

She drew in a deep breath and let it out quickly. "Well, okay. When?"

"Well, we could wait until the case is over . . . but that could be a while. And frankly, I don't want to wait that long. How about tomorrow?"

"Tomorrow's Sunday," she said. "I go to church twice on Sundays. But you're welcome to join me."

He had walked into that one, he thought, but he could walk right back out. "Church and I don't really get along," he said. "How about after church tomorrow night? What time do you get home?"

"About seven-thirty," she said. "I guess dinner would be all right."

"Are you sure?"

"Yeah, why not?"

He smiled. "Okay. Great. I'll make reservations someplace nice. And I'll call you tomorrow afternoon and let you know what time."

"All right," she said. "I'll look forward to it."

Again, he felt like that awkward kid as he leaned back in his chair and mouthed "yes!" to the ceiling. Then trying to temper his voice, he said, "Well, I'll talk to you tomorrow then. Good night, Sharon."

"Good night."

He hung onto the phone as she hung up, then dropped it into its cradle and stared back at the ceiling again. What had he done?

He was going out with a woman who was tied up in a case he was working on, and she was a Christian, and she had kids, and she had her ex-husband who was quite possibly a killer living with her . . .

Great going, Tony, he thought. *You know how to pick 'em. The more complicated, the better. Like you don't have enough problems already.*

But it didn't matter to him as he sprang out of his chair, fully renewed, and headed for the kitchen to find something to eat.

Across town, Sharon smiled and stared at the telephone for a long moment. She had consented to going out with the cop who was trying to prove Ben's guilt. She had consented to going out with a guy who had never read word one of the Bible, a guy who was obviously uncomfortable talking about spiritual things, a guy who would never darken the doors of a church unless a crime had been committed there.

Was she crazy?

Probably, but it had been so long since she'd been attracted to any of the men who had asked her out. Maybe just one date wouldn't hurt. She could use the distraction — and the boost — after all the tension around here.

And there was no shortage of baby-sitters.

The truth was, she looked forward to it, but that anticipation only scared her. Tony was certain that Ben was a killer. Tony, who saw criminals every day, heard all their excuses, their alibis, their lies. Could it be that he saw something in Ben that she couldn't see?

She got up and pulled on her robe and padded up the dark hallway. What was Ben doing now? Where was he?

She saw a light on in her study, and went to the door. Standing back, she listened. Was he in there?

Slowly, she peered around the doorway.

Ben was there, reclining back in her leather chair, his feet propped on her desk. On his chest slept Bobby, his breathing much better now that he'd been medicated. Memories flooded through her of the same man lying on an orange bean bag with newborn Jenny on his chest. She had a snapshot of it somewhere. Could that same man have turned into a killer?

Confused by her disturbing thoughts, she turned and headed back to her room. She turned the light out and curled up on her bed. Wondering whether she'd done the right thing by agreeing to go out with the detective, she went back under the fig tree again.

CHAPTER TWENTY-THREE

It didn't feel like Sunday. To Jenny, the fact that her dad and Anne didn't care to go to church depressed her. It had felt weird, getting ready and trying not to wake them, and then there had been all the wailing when Emily had wanted to go with Christy, but her mother had awakened and tried to talk her out of it. Sharon had finally shamed Ben and Anne into letting the child go, and they had angrily gotten her dressed. The truth was, Jenny hadn't been so keen on going herself, since everyone there knew that her father had been arrested for murder. It was embarrassing, humiliating. But she needed their prayers, she thought, and she supposed that the gossip she would have to endure was worth it.

She had felt bad for her mother when she'd had to come home from church and cook a huge meal that would feed seven, since neither Ben nor Anne had shown enough initiative to start lunch before they'd gotten home. Then she had helped her mother clean up, since Anne stayed in the same room with Sharon as little as possible.

When Anne had asked Jenny to go to the

store to get some more formula and diapers for Bobby, Jenny had welcomed the opportunity to get out of the tense house. She had volunteered to take Emily and Christy with her, hoping to give her mother a little reprieve from all her responsibility. Since she was going anyway, Sharon had given her a list of other things they needed.

Now, as she pulled into the parking lot of the Kroger and saw how crowded it was, Jenny almost regretted agreeing to come. She cut off the car and looked into the backseat at the two blonde girls seat-belted in and holding hands. "Now, girls, I have a list," she said. "Don't beg me for candy and stuff. It'll drive me crazy."

Christy looked crestfallen. "Not even gum? Not even Popsicles?"

"Not even Reeses?" Emily asked.

"No! Nothing! Now, come on."

In the store entryway, Jenny spotted a video game. Perfect. She pulled out some quarters and handed them to the girls. "Here. Stay and play the game for a while. When you finish, come find me."

"Will you get Popsicles?" Christy asked.

"And String Things? And Reeses?" Emily added.

"No junk. Mom said."

"That's not junk. Popsicles are not junk!"

"Okay, but just Popsicles."

"But I need String Things," Emily whined. "Mommy always puts String Things in my lunches for school. I need String Things for tomorrow."

"All right," Jenny gave in. "I'll get some. Just go play. Please!"

The two girls headed for the game. Breathing a sigh of relief, Jenny went into the store, determined to fill her mother's list as quickly as she could.

Emily was not as good at video games as Christy was, and she quickly "died." Because they had both spent their fifty cents, they began to look around for something else to do.

Spotting the bubble gum machines outside, they headed through the electric doors. Christy checked each slot to see if anyone had forgotten their candy, while Emily wound each handle to see if it would miraculously release some.

They had almost given up when a man came by and, chuckling, reached into his pocket for a quarter for each of them. "Here you go, girls. It's on me."

Christy looked up at the man who wore a straw Panama hat and dark glasses. "No, thanks, Mister. I'm not allowed to take things from strangers."

"I'm no stranger," he said with a kindly smile. "Not to Emily." He pulled his glasses off briefly and winked at the child.

Her eyes rounded. "You're Daddy's friend."

"You know my daddy?" Christy asked.

"I certainly do." The man smiled and put his glasses back on, then inserted the money into a machine, turned the knob, and caught the candy as it came out. Giving a piece to each of them, he nodded toward his car. "As a matter of fact, I have something in the car that your father needs. Would you girls mind coming with me to get it? You could take it to him." He squeezed Emily's nose. "I also have some jelly beans in the car. If you like them —"

"We do!" Emily cried. "Come on, Christy!"

The two girls bounced out behind him as he led them to his car.

Jenny pushed her loaded cart to the long line at the cash register. Thankful that her sisters had not hounded her while she was shopping, she glanced over at the play area. She didn't see them.

Sighing, she got out of line and went to the candy aisle, expecting to find them there.

There were children admiring the colorful bags of treats for the Valentine season, but Christy and Emily weren't among them.

Frustrated, she decided to start at one end of the store and look down each aisle until she found them. She should have told them to stay where they were. And she should have known that they wouldn't.

She looked up every aisle in the huge store, to no avail. Again, she checked the play area, but they weren't there.

Then she remembered that Christy loved the candy machines, so she abandoned her cart and looked through the glass doors. No one was there.

She was beginning to get worried, but her anger at them overpowered it. She went to the manager's booth at the front of the store, and waited in line until it was her turn. "Could you please page my sisters over the intercom? They're somewhere in the store, but I can't find them."

They took down the little girls' names and sent out a page. When five minutes had passed with no answer, Jenny began to worry. Abandoning her cart, she went back to the first aisle; then her speed picked up as she turned a corner and ran into a stock boy, causing him to drop a box of cans. "I'm sorry!" she said, helping him pick them up.

"Have you seen two little girls with blonde hair?"

"No," he said, annoyed. "I haven't."

She looked back at the front desk. The children still hadn't answered the page. Quickly, she ran back to the front. "Look," she said, breathless, "they've got to be here."

"I'll try again," the manager said. "Just hold on."

The page went out again, but there was still no answer. She headed outside, thinking they may have broken the cardinal rule of leaving the store, and she searched up and down the sidewalk for them. Beginning to get frantic, she ran out to her car and looked inside. They weren't there.

Where could they be?

Perspiring and breathless, she ran back inside and headed to the back of the store where the swinging doors led into the warehouse. She burst through and found two workers. "Have you seen two little blonde-haired girls? Five and six years old? One was wearing . . . a little red outfit with hearts on it, and the other was . . . Oh, I don't know what Emily was wearing!"

"No, they haven't been back here," one of them said.

By now her breath was coming in gasps, and she pushed out of the doors and ran up each aisle and down the next, calling out for them at the top of her voice. Store patrons were staring, and a few started to join her in the hunt.

Realizing the problem was serious, the manager got on the intercom. "If anyone has seen two little blonde girls, ages five and six, who answer to the names Emily and Christy, would you please come to the front desk?"

Jenny was in tears by the time she had searched the whole store a second time. Frantic, she made her way to the desk. A customer was standing there talking to the manager.

"Miss?" the manager said, now visibly shaken. "This woman says she saw the children getting into a car with someone. We've called the police."

"A car?" Jenny asked, breathing in a sob. "They couldn't have. They were with me. They know better than that!"

"One of the little girls had on a red tunic with hearts and some red leggings, and the other one was wearing something purple, I think," the woman said.

Jenny felt dizzy, and her heart sank. "That was them. Who were they with?"

"A man," the woman said. "He had on a straw hat and sunglasses. I think his hair was brown, but I'm not sure. He was maybe 5'9" or 5'10", average weight. They looked like they knew him and got into the car willingly. They were smiling and laughing, so I didn't think anything of it."

"They *couldn't* have!" She began to tremble, then asked, "Can I use your phone? I have to call my parents."

Her hand trembled as she tried to dial the number. The phone rang, and she closed her eyes. After a moment, her father answered. "Hello?"

"Daddy?" she said, trying to control her voice. "You didn't come and pick up Christy and Emily, did you?"

"What do you mean, did I pick them up?"

"Did you or Mom pick them up?" she shouted.

"No. No one's gone anywhere."

She sobbed again, and dropped her head on the counter. "Daddy, someone's taken them! They're gone!"

CHAPTER TWENTY-FOUR

"Where are you taking us?" Christy asked tearfully as the man drove much too fast down Highway 19 leading out of St. Clair.

He didn't answer.

"He lied," Emily whispered. "He didn't have any jelly beans."

"We're gonna get in so much trouble," Christy whispered. "Jenny's gonna kill us. And Mommy will punish me for my whole life."

"Quiet back there," the man barked. "You're getting on my nerves."

They stopped talking, but continued to cry.

"Did you hear me? I told you to shut up!"

The girls put their arms around each other, trembling with fear and trying hard not to make noise.

He pulled off of the highway and turned onto a long dirt road.

"Maybe he's taking us home," Emily whispered.

"I don't think so."

"Then where is he taking us? What is he gonna do with us?"

"I don't know," Christy said. "Maybe he's

191

not really mean. Maybe he just likes little girls."

"He doesn't act like he likes us," Emily whispered. "Maybe he's gonna hurt us."

They clung to each other as he turned down a dirt road and took them far into a patch of woods. Finally, they came to a small structure that looked like a toolshed. The car stopped.

The back door opened, and the man reached for Christy's arm. "Come on. Get out."

She slid across the seat and got out, then with a burst of adrenaline, kicked the man with all her might. "Run, Emily!"

Emily took off running, but the man grabbed Christy around the waist and bolted after the other child. He caught her before she could get far, and grabbing a fistful of hair to guide her, he pointed them toward the shack.

"See that?" he asked through his teeth. "That's where we're going."

Christy's crying grew louder, and Emily screamed and struggled to make him let go of her hair. He dragged them, writhing and trying to break free, to the door of the shed, opened it, and threw them in. They each hit the dirt floor, and Christy bumped her head on the edge of a shelf. She screamed out, but the man only slammed the door behind them.

Christy curled into a ball, holding her cut head as warm blood seeped around her fingers.

They heard him locking the door, and then going back to his car. The car door slammed, the motor roared to life, and he drove off.

Emily was sobbing and groping around, trying to find Christy. "Christy, where are you?"

"Here," she cried.

Emily's hand reached out to touch her, and they clung to each other. "I want Daddy," Emily cried.

"Me too," Christy sobbed. Blood dripped into her eyes, burning them, and she wiped it on her sleeve. On her hands and knees, she groped until she found the wall, then the door. Emily followed close behind her, her little fist clutching the back of her shirt. Christy slid her hand up the door until she found the doorknob. She jiggled it, but it had been locked from the outside.

She tried to stand up, but Emily cried, "Don't leave me! I can't see!"

"I'm right here. I'm just standing up."

Emily stood with her, still clinging to her. She pushed on the door as hard as she could, then rammed her small shoulder against the wood, like she'd seen people do on TV. It was no use.

She kicked it with all her might, then began to bang on it. "Help, somebody! Let us out!" she screamed, pounding it with her fists. Emily joined her, pounding and screaming at the top of her lungs.

"Let us out! Help! Let us *out!*"

But they could hear the car driving away on the long gravel road.

As he drove away, Nelson Chamberlain smiled with satisfaction. Ben was probably squirming by now and preparing to make the exchange. Nelson had just provided Ben with an irresistible incentive.

He'd definitely gotten lucky. He had expected to have to take the teenager, too, which would have made the whole situation much more difficult to manage. But when she'd left the girls to fend for themselves, he'd had the perfect opportunity.

His smile faded, as he realized how deep he had gotten. Normally, he didn't like to get his hands dirty. It had been unpleasant enough working with the thug who'd had the fake IDs and credit cards made for him — one set under Ben Robinson's name so he could purchase the gun, and another set under the name of John Lieber. The murder had been even more distasteful. He had been lucky enough to find the money clip with Ben's initials; Ben had left it behind in the medicine cabinet of the gallery's apartment — along with a hairbrush, which had provided the strands of Ben's hair that Nelson had planted in Dubose's hands. Yes, all of this had been distasteful, but he'd had no choice.

He had come this far and didn't intend to stop now. Too much was invested. Too much was at stake. It wasn't easy maintaining the lifestyle he loved. A few bad investments had seriously depleted his funds. The financial injection he'd get from this transaction was essential. Things had to work out before his creditors and generous friends abroad realized he wasn't what they thought he was.

The hundred thousand dollars he'd donated for Ben's bond money had been well worth it. Ben couldn't deliver anything if he was behind bars. It would have been useful to frame Ben for Dubose's murder — that had been his original plan, and a good one. But now there was something he needed more than a fall guy, and only Ben knew where it was. This kidnapping, of course, would transfer suspicion away from Ben, even for the murder. But it couldn't be helped. Nelson was desperate to make the delivery to Boudreaux quickly. Besides, everyone thought he was still out of the country, so even if they did look earnestly for another culprit, they would never suspect him.

If things went the way he expected, he should have what he wanted and truly be out of the country, and out from under any chance of suspicion, before the sun came up tomorrow.

CHAPTER TWENTY-FIVE

The sound of Sharon's wailing when she heard the news cut through the walls of her house and could be heard all over the neighborhood. She ran out to her car and screeched out of the driveway. Ben, Anne, and Bobby were right behind her in the station wagon.

They were at the grocery store parking lot in record time, and saw the fleet of police cars with their blue lights flashing. Sharon pulled her car up to where she saw Larry and Tony with Jenny, slammed it into park, and jumped out. Ben's car screeched to a halt behind her.

"Jenny, where are they?" she shouted. "Weren't you watching them?"

Jenny was sobbing, and Tony set his arm around the teen to steady her as she looked up at her mother. "I'm so sorry, Mom. I lost them. I let them play at the video game, and the next thing I knew they were gone!"

"What are you doing to find them?" she asked Tony. "They're so little. They must be scared to death. You've got to find them!" Her voice was rising in pitch with each word, and Larry tried to calm her. Ben was standing behind her now, and Larry faced them both.

"We have an eyewitness who saw a brown-haired man with a straw hat and sunglasses, average weight, 5'9" or 5'10". Does that sound familiar to you?"

Sharon looked helpless. "It sounds like a hundred people I know."

"We also have a description of the car. It was a blue Taurus, a rental car, but our witness didn't notice the agency. We also have an all points bulletin out on it. We've got cars at checkpoints all over St. Clair, and we've notified the state police to watch for him if he leaves town with them. But right now we need your help. I know you're upset, but we need to keep our heads clear so that we can move as fast as we can."

"What do you need?" Ben asked.

"We need pictures so we can distribute them all over the area. And we need to set up some phone lines in your house so that we can trace any ransom call you might get."

"He said he would take something of mine," Ben said. "He threatened me, the night he realized I didn't deliver what he wanted."

Furiously, Sharon stood up to face Ben. "It's him, isn't it? He took our children!" She shoved Ben back against another police car. "Give him what he wants, Ben!" she shouted. "Give him what he wants so I can get my baby back!"

"I . . . don't . . . know . . . what he wants," Ben said through his teeth. "If I knew, I'd take it in two seconds flat. I have *two* kidnapped children, Sharon. Don't you think I would do whatever I could to —"

"Stop it!" Anne commanded as she stepped between them. "We don't have time for this. We have to find them!"

Sharon swung around to Tony and grabbed the lapels of his sport coat. "If you'd listened when Ben told you! If you'd looked for the killer instead of pinning it on him — this maniac wouldn't have my child!"

She saw that television crews were beginning to gather, and one camera was aimed at her. Shaking her head, she pushed through the crowd and back to her car. "I'm going after them. I'll find them!"

Tony stopped her. "Sharon, you can't! We have people looking for them, but we need your help here."

"All right!" she screamed, shaking his hands off of her. "Tell me what to do! But don't make me just sit here while he gets farther away with the girls!"

Hours later, as it began to grow dark,

there was still no word. Two cops stayed at their house, waiting for the ransom call, while Larry and Tony beat the streets trying to find any leads on who could have the children. This case took precedence over every other. There hadn't been a kidnapping in St. Clair in almost twenty years, and that one had been a parental abduction. Now the whole town of St. Clair was searching for the children. Posters were hung on every pole, every wall, every window. Church friends came to the house in a steady stream, bringing food — the only thing they knew to do — and leaving with stacks of posters with the faces of the two children.

Jenny had been sedated, and slept in her room. Bobby also slept peacefully now that he'd been medicated and was on his way to recovery. But Anne, Sharon, and Ben paced the living room waiting frantically for the phone to ring.

It was nearing dark when Tony and Larry returned to the house. Their expressions were grave, and Sharon began to feel nauseous at the thought of what they might say.

"Sharon, Anne, Ben — would you all please sit down?"

"You found them," Anne said, her face turning white with fear.

"No, no," Tony said quickly. "We haven't

found any trace of them. Not yet. But we need to ask you a few questions."

"Sure," Sharon said. "Anything. What?"

Larry looked uncomfortably at Tony. "We need to know every place any of you went today, starting with the time you got up until right after the abductions."

"Oh, here it comes," Ben said. "I should have anticipated it."

Puzzled, Sharon and Anne looked at him.

"Don't you see?" he asked. "It's the parallel investigation. While they're looking for the guy who took our kids, they start to consider that we might have done it ourselves."

"What?" Anne asked, astounded.

Sharon got to her feet. "Why would we do that?"

"We're not saying you did, Sharon," Tony said. "It's a matter of protocol. Really. Just routine. For our reports."

"Now I remember," Sharon said. "A couple of years ago, that kidnapping in Virginia or somewhere. They discovered that the mother had killed them. But you don't think . . ."

"Sharon, we're not accusing anyone," Tony said. "We just have to ask a few questions."

"It's me, Sharon," Ben said. "Since I'm an alleged murderer and a pathological liar, I had to have done this, right? Another ploy to throw them off my scent!" He swung an arm and knocked a vase off the table, sending it crashing to the floor. He turned and stormed out of the room.

"Where are you going?" Larry asked loudly.

"To call my lawyer," Ben said. "I'm not saying another word until she's here."

Sharon and Anne gaped at the two detectives as Ben rushed out. "He didn't do this!" Sharon shouted. "He's their father! He was here with us the whole time! You had a witness who saw them get into the car with a man! You need to expend your energy trying to find that man, instead of wasting your time on this!"

Tony sat down, looking weary.

"Sharon, we have to ask the questions," Larry said. "You need to help us by answering them. We haven't stopped the investigation. It's still going on. But it's department policy that we cover every possibility. And with the extenuating circumstances —"

"I don't care about extenuating circumstances," Sharon cried. "This whole nightmare has been extenuating from the beginning!" She wiped her face and paced across the floor. "What about me? Am I suspect?"

"No one is suspect," Tony said.

"Why not? Maybe I had some stupid ulterior motive. Maybe I had some deep hatred against Emily, so I hired someone to kidnap both of them."

"I guess being the stepmother," Anne said, "I'm a prime suspect, too, huh?"

"We told you! We're not accusing anyone."

"You're accusing Ben!" Sharon shouted. "Admit it. You think he did it, and that would be just as absurd as either of us. They're both his kids!"

"They're just questions, Sharon! Just questions!" Tony shouted.

Ben came back into the room. "Lynda's on her way over. She said that none of us should say another word until she gets here."

"Fine," Larry said, sitting back in his chair and crossing his arms. "We'll wait."

Tony nodded. "Fair enough."

Seconds ticked by, as everyone found some spot in the room to focus on. Finally, Anne cried, "Why doesn't that phone ring?"

"He wants us to sweat," Ben said quietly.

"But what about the children? It's getting dark, and they'll be so afraid. Emily doesn't have her blankie or her little doll that she sleeps with. What if he doesn't feed them? What if they're hurt?"

"They can't be," Sharon whispered. "We just have to pray that they'll be all right. We just have to have faith."

But her faith seemed as flimsy as Anne's and Ben's as they waited for Lynda to arrive.

They waited, Tony and Larry sitting on the couch, Sharon leaning stiffly against the piano with her arms crossed, Ben pacing, and Anne in a chair watching out the window, as if the kidnapper would suddenly drive up and let the children out.

The doorbell rang. It was Lynda and Jake.

"What's going on, Tony?" Lynda asked. "Why are you badgering these people?"

"We're not badgering them, Lynda. We just want to ask some questions."

"All right," she said. "Everybody sit down."

They all took places around the room, except for Jake, who hung back in the doorway. "I'm gonna go hang some posters, guys," he said. "Lynda, are you sure you can get a ride home?"

"No problem," she said. "I think I'll be here for a while."

He touched Sharon's shoulder and squeezed hard. "Sharon, I'm praying for them. We're gonna find them. We've got hundreds of people out looking. You know that, don't you?"

Sharon touched his hand and squeezed back. "Yeah. I have more faith in you guys than I do in these so-called detectives."

Tony looked up at her, stung.

"At least somebody's doing something," she added.

Jake nodded soberly. "I'll see you later then," he said, heading out the door.

After the sound of his car died away, Lynda spoke up. "All right," she said to Larry and Tony, "ask anything you want. I know that my clients want to give you any answers that can help you find the children. But I'm not going to let you bully or badger them, and you're not going to get away with hanging this on them."

"So now they're *all* your clients?" Larry asked.

"That's right," she said defiantly.

Ben leaned forward, looking ragged and haunted. "Look, before you ask anything, can I just ask you something?"

Larry shrugged. "Go ahead."

"Think of the logic here, guys. If I really killed Dubose, why would I leave all the evidence — the gun registered to me, the money clip, the fingerprints. And it's even more illogical that I would add to that by doing something with my own children —" His voice broke off. "But think about it. If

I'm being set up, and Dubose was killed because of whatever it is this maniac is looking for, then wouldn't it make sense that he'd kidnap my children to have leverage over me? He thinks I have whatever it is, so he wants to force me into handing it over."

"Sure, that would be logical," Larry said. "Logical enough for you to count on."

"What's that supposed to mean?" Lynda asked.

"It's the conspiracy theory," Sharon snapped. "Oswald didn't kill Kennedy — it was the Republicans. And this kidnapper didn't take our kids — Ben did, only he staged it so carefully that it would look like someone else did it. He was actually in two places at once, and he didn't look anything like himself, and it wasn't his car, but he was behind it, because the other way seems too blasted logical!"

Lynda touched Sharon's hand and gestured for her to be quiet.

"Just find my baby!" Sharon shouted, standing up and knocking over her chair. "Stop sitting here and find them before it's too late!"

CHAPTER TWENTY-SIX

Their eyes had adjusted to the dark. Above them, too far to reach, hung shelves cluttered with gardening tools. A bag of feed leaned against the corner, and a lawn mower was parked near the back. The whole space was no larger than Christy's walk-in closet at home, and the floor was made of dirt and getting colder the later it got.

"I'm hungry," Emily said, her voice hoarse from screaming.

Christy's head still throbbed, and the cut stung. Her bangs were bloody and matted to her forehead. "Me, too. But Daddy will come get us real soon. I know he will."

"What if he can't find us?"

"He will. He's real smart."

"But I want to go home *now*," Emily whimpered.

"Me, too," Christy said.

They listened hard to the wind whistling around the corner of the building, and the raindrops pattering on the roof. Thunder cracked, and both girls screamed.

"It's just thunder," Christy said, trying to sound brave.

"I hate thunder," Emily cried.

"But it can't hurt us," Christy said, remembering what her mother had told her so many times. "We're safe in here."

Emily began to wail as thunder cracked again.

"We could pray," Christy tried.

"I don't know how."

Christy put her arm around Emily. "Just close your eyes," she whispered, "and I'll do it."

"What if God can't hear us through the thunder?"

"He will," Christy assured her. "Thunder is no big deal to God. He always hears children's prayers. Mommy told me so. Now bow your head."

"I don't want to."

"Just do it!" Christy shouted. "Bow your head now or I'll quit trying to make you feel better!"

"You're *not* making me feel better!" Emily cried. "You're making me feel worse."

"I'm the one with the hurt head!" Christy snapped. "And I'm not acting like some whiny little baby!" She started to cry even as the words came out of her mouth, and finally Emily reached over and hugged her.

"I'm sorry."

Christy sucked in a sob and wiped her

eyes. "It's okay. Will you bow your stupid head now?"

Emily stuck her thumb in her mouth and bowed her head. They clung together as Christy started to pray.

"Dear God, we're really scared . . ."

The thunder and rain raged around them as Christy prayed, but before she even got to "Amen," Emily had drifted off to sleep.

Christy held her for a long time before she too finally surrendered to sleep.

CHAPTER TWENTY-SEVEN

The storm was getting more violent, as if the universe were conspiring against them. Sharon paced outside in her screened porch, while they continued questioning Ben inside. Desperately, she clutched Christy's Simba doll against her and railed mentally at God, bargaining with him, pleading with him to bring her child back. She was angry, she was frightened, she was confused.

When Tony stepped through the back door, she squelched the urge to throw something at him. "What do you want? I thought you were finished interrogating me."

"We are, for now," he said. "Sharon, are you all right?"

She breathed a despairing laugh. "Funny how things work out, isn't it? We were supposed to have had dinner tonight. Who knew that instead I'd be out of my mind with terror?"

"We'll find them. I know we will."

"Dead or alive?" she screamed at him. "Before or after it's too late?"

He looked down at his feet, and she clutched the Simba doll tighter. "I just want Christy back. I can't stand the thought of her being out there somewhere." She pressed her hands against the brick wall, staring out at the night. Lightning struck, brightening the night sky, then blackening it again. A sharp clap of thunder followed.

"That's it," she said, shoving past Tony into the house. He followed behind her as she grabbed her purse and started digging for her keys. "I'm going out there," she said through clenched teeth. "St. Clair isn't that big. I'll find them. I'll drive down the streets with my windows rolled down, and listen for their voices. I won't come back until I've gotten them."

She bolted through the kitchen and out the side door, Tony at her heels.

"You can't do this, Sharon," he argued.

"Yes, I can!" she screamed. "You can't stop me. I'm not under arrest! I can go anywhere I want to."

"You're not in any condition to drive, Sharon. And the weather's bad. If I have to, I *will* arrest you just to keep you from doing something stupid."

"But somebody has to look for the children!" she screamed. "We can't leave them out there. Do you know what it's like for a little girl in a storm? Even at home, she's terrified. She sleeps with a night-light on every night. And the hall light. And if it's damp and cold, she catches cold real easily. I've got to get to her . . ."

Feeling helpless, Tony reached for her. "You've got to leave it to the professionals, Sharon. Trust them."

"I *can't* trust them," she cried, shaking free of him. "I can't. Christy trusts me. I'm the only one. She knows I'm always there for her. I've never let her down. Never. When she's scared or tired or hungry or sick, I've always been there." Her voice broke. She was getting hoarse from crying, but she kept on. "I'll find them. I know I can. I know St. Clair better than anyone. I've sold property in every section of the town. I'll think of hiding places."

Tony glanced back toward the door. "All right, listen. I'll go with you. You're too upset to drive, so I'll drive and you can tell me where to go. Fair enough?"

She nodded and breathed another sob. "Yes, all right."

"Okay. Just let me tell Larry."

He went back to the door and saw Larry standing with Ben and Anne in the doorway. "Larry, I'm gonna take her for a ride just to make her feel better. She has a car phone, so give us a buzz if anything comes up."

Larry looked concerned. To keep Ben and Anne from overhearing, he stepped outside.

"Are you sure this is a good idea? You're a cop, not a social worker. It's not your job to make her feel better."

"Larry, it's either ride with her or arrest her," Tony said in a low voice. "She's losing it, just sitting here like this. I can't blame her."

"I want to go, too," Anne said from behind Larry. "Take me with you."

Sharon heard, and swung around. "No! You and Ben have to stay here in case they call!"

"You can't go," Larry added. "I still have some questions. We aren't finished."

"But we've told you everything!" Anne cried.

"Look," Tony said, "if we find one child, we'll find both. Your husband needs you. So does your baby."

Larry coaxed Anne back into the house before she could protest further.

Feeling as if he'd been caught on the front lines of a major war, Tony hurried out to her car before Sharon could leave without him.

Sharon insisted on Tony's driving twenty miles per hour with both windows down. His left side was getting drenched as they went, and her car's interior was beginning to soak up the rain like a sponge. They had been all through the rural parts of St. Clair, up one street and down another, searching for places where a deranged kidnapper might have hidden two little girls. One time, she had been positive that an old, condemned house was where the children were, and he had been forced to follow her through the muddy yard and the pouring rain, up the broken steps of the porch, and into the rat-infested house. The children hadn't been there, though there was evidence that someone had been using it for a crack house, and he made a mental note to follow up on that later.

Now, after driving for two hours, he wondered how to broach the subject of going back to her house.

"We'll never find them, will we?" she asked.

"Not like this," he said.

She shivered as the cold rain soaked through her. "I should have dressed Christy warmer today. I should have made her wear a jacket."

"It was in the seventies earlier, Sharon. You couldn't have known."

"Yes, I could have," she said. "We knew there was a killer out there already turning our family upside-down. I should have realized the kids were in danger."

He didn't know what to say. It seemed that everything he attempted only made things worse.

"You try to teach them things, you know?" she railed. "Like, never talk to strangers. Look both ways before crossing the street. Eat your vegetables. Brush your teeth. But you never really think about teaching them how to survive in an emergency . . . how to get help . . . how to get home . . ."

Tony reached for her hand and squeezed it. It was as cold as ice. "Don't underestimate their instincts. Even children have good ones."

"But I've sheltered her so. I didn't want her to know that evil like this existed."

"You were supposed to shelter her. That's your job. Don't beat yourself up because you didn't prepare her to be kidnapped."

Quiet settled over them for a moment. Rainwater soaked her hair and trickled down her face as she gazed at him. "I almost lost it with Anne before we left. I just couldn't take any more."

"That's normal," Tony said. "And you have a lot of anger in you. For good reason. It's natural that you'd want to lash out at them."

"I thought I was different," she whispered.

He looked at her. "Different how?"

"Better," she said. "I thought I had all the biblical principles down, that I knew how to behave in any circumstance, that I could stand up to any tragedy, that trials would only make me stronger."

"And?"

"And I think I've just been fooling myself."

Tony frowned and moved his eyes back to the wet road. "You think those principles don't work, after all?"

She shook her head. "No, that's not it. I know they work. I think I've been fooling myself about what I was capable of. Christianity isn't about becoming a better actress. Hiding your feelings. *Doing* all the right things. It's about changing your heart. And I think mine has a long way to go."

Tony let those words sink in. They were foreign to him, for he couldn't fathom anyone being more self-sacrificing than this woman who had taken in her ex-husband and the woman he left her for. "You have a pretty good heart, from where I sit."

"I have a *petty* heart," she said. "Petty and angry and vindictive."

"Vindictive? How do you figure that?"

She began to cry again and shook her head with disgust. "Vindictive because I wish Emily had been taken alone. That it was just their child who'd been kidnapped. That mine was at home, safe and sound . . . because some part of me feels that they deserve that." She looked at Tony, her eyes glistening. "Isn't that terrible?"

He came to a red light and sat still for a moment, looking at her, wishing he could touch her and offer some comfort. But he knew better. He was a professional and had to maintain some detachment. Still, her tears reached straight into his heart, and he found himself doubting the logic of his own strict rules. "Sharon, there's not a mother out there who has a child kidnapped, who doesn't wish it was someone else's child. You're not horrible. And you're not vindictive. You're just distraught because something has happened to your child that you can't control. I don't have any kids, but if I did, and this happened, I'd probably have snapped and killed twenty people by now. I think you're a very special lady for analyzing your own heart at a time like this."

She dropped her forehead into her palm and wept quietly for a long moment. No other traffic was on the road as the storm raged around them, so he ignored the green light and watched her cry.

He reached across the seat and took her

hand, almost tentatively. She accepted his touch, so he squeezed gently. "I want to find Christy for you," he whispered. "I'd kind of like the chance to get to know her. She's a pretty cool kid, from what I've seen. Any little girl with such a special mom is someone I'd like to make friends with."

She looked up then, and he saw the torment on her face and wished from the deepest places in his heart that he could take it from her and carry the burden for her.

"I'm gonna find her for you, Sharon."

She sucked in a sob and nodded as if she believed him. When he moved the car forward through the intersection, she leaned her head back on the wet seat. "Let's go home," she said. "Jenny might be awake by now. She's going to need me."

"Okay," he whispered. But he kept holding her hand as he drove her back to her house, where those who loved the two little girls still kept vigil through the night.

Back at Sharon's house, Ben, Anne, and Lynda still sat at the kitchen table with Larry, who had asked them a zillion questions a dozen times each. Ben had answered as patiently as he could, knowing how it looked to the police who had seen more bizarre cases than his, if not on their own turf, then in other precincts across the country. People did murder their bosses. Parents did sometimes do harm to their kids. He just didn't know how to convince them that he wasn't among them.

"All right, now, for a minute, let's assume that you're telling the truth, and that someone else killed Dubose, and wants something you have, and kidnapped your kids to force you into giving it to them. So let's go back over it all. Try to think of everyone who came into the studio to see Dubose the week leading to his death."

"I have," Ben said. "I've given you the names of everyone I could think of. None of them seemed angry at him or agitated in any way."

"Then can you think of a time in the days leading to his death when *he* was agitated or angry? Maybe after a phone call?"

Ben stared at the table, retracing the last few days. Dubose had been moody, quiet, and Ben had the feeling he was aggravated with him.

"There was something about his mood," he said, finally. "He was distant. Preoccupied. Like I had made him mad or something."

"Had you?"

"No. We usually got along real well. He

was happy with my work . . . and was real generous to us. I thought he might have some personal problems."

"Then you hadn't had any blow-ups with him?"

"None."

"Wait," Anne said, her eyes widening. "There was a blow-up, Ben. Remember a few days before we were thrown out, when you found that hidden painting? You said he bit your head off about that."

Ben frowned. "Yeah, but it was so silly. I thought he was just in a bad mood."

Larry leaned forward and gazed intently at him. "Why didn't you mention this before?"

Ben threw up his hands. "I didn't think it was related. It happened days before the murder. And it was such a little thing. I had gone up to the attic looking for an old-fashioned frame for one of my paintings. I thought I might find something up there, since he stored a lot of stuff there. But I bumped my head on something, and a rolled-up canvas fell out. I unrolled it, and it looked just like the famous painting *The Multitude*, by the sixteenth-century Italian painter Marazzio. I got excited — I'd heard that that painting had been stolen several years ago. So I took it downstairs and stretched it out on a table. It looked so authentic, I could have sworn —"

"Was it the real thing?" Larry prompted.

"Well, no. Louis walked in and saw what I had, and he blew a fuse. Started yelling at me that the attic was off-limits. Which was pretty strange, because that just didn't seem like him. I apologized and told him to calm down, and I asked him if he knew that *The Multitude* had been hidden up there in a specially built compartment. Someone else owned the gallery before Louis, and I figured *they* might have hidden it there — although, when you think about it, they wouldn't have left it there. Anyway, he finally did calm down, and he looked at the painting, and quickly discovered some mistakes. They were tough to see, because the picture has a crowd of hundreds of people, supposedly at the Sermon on the Mount. But Louis said he was very familiar with all of Marazzio's work, and this wasn't real. He knew his stuff better than anyone I know, and he had a keen eye because he saw a lot of fakes that people tried to pass off as originals. Of course, he admitted his main clue that it was a fake was that the original had been recovered a couple of years ago."

"What did he do with it?"

"I don't know. I told him we should frame the picture, reproduction or not, and display it in the gallery, but he refused. He took the painting and rolled it back up, and I never saw it again."

Larry stared down at his notes now, thinking. "Why would anyone have hidden a reproduction?"

"I have no idea. It really didn't make sense, but I figure someone might have mistakenly thought it was the real thing. Who knows?"

Larry's eyes were riveted on Ben's when he asked, "Do you think there's any possibility that this Marazzio reproduction could be the painting our kidnapper wants?"

Ben frowned and considered that for a moment. "No. Why would anyone kill over a reproduction? It's practically worthless."

"What if Dubose lied, or was just wrong about that stolen painting being recovered?" Lynda asked. "What if it was the real thing? Do you think a real Marazzio could cause all this trouble?"

"A genuine Marazzio, particularly *The Multitude*, would be worth millions. Yeah, somebody might kill over it."

"But wouldn't they realize that when they sold it, they'd be sitting ducks with a murder and kidnapping attached to it?"

Ben shrugged. "It depends. The statute of limitations in Italy for stolen art is ten years.

Paintings like that one disappear for a decade or more, then suddenly turn up at an auction one day, supposedly found by accident." He shook his head. "It doesn't matter, though. It was a reproduction. The real one was found a couple of years ago."

"Are you absolutely sure?" Lynda asked him.

"Yes. Louis knew his stuff. He traveled a lot, buying and selling important pieces of art, and he knew. For someone to go to all this trouble over a reproduction, they'd have to be fooled into thinking it was real. But I don't see that happening here. Anyone willing to pay what a real Marazzio is worth would check it out and find out that the real thing has been found."

"Then explain why Dubose fired you just a few days later, when you say it was completely out of his character. There must have been something else going on."

He turned his palms up and shook his head. "I don't know. I have no idea. Maybe the painting had nothing to do with it. Anyway, even if it did, I don't know where the reproduction is. I went back up there the next day to see it again, just out of curiosity, but it was gone. I don't know what he did with it."

Larry sighed. "We've got to find it. It

might be what he wants."

"If I had it, and knew that was what he wanted, I'd have given it to him by now, and have my girls back in their own bed tonight."

Lynda touched Ben's hand, as if to offer some small bit of comfort, and looked beseechingly at Larry. "Larry, the man's been through enough. Leave him alone. Go look for the children."

Larry stared at them both over steepled fingers, then nodded reluctantly. "All right, Ben," he said. "That's all for now. But I may have more questions later."

CHAPTER TWENTY-EIGHT

A light rain pattered against the window as Lynda Barrett sat at the desk in the corner of her den, hunched over the books she had picked up from the library on her way home from Sharon's. There had to be something here. Something that might give her an idea about what to do next. She felt helpless. It had been bad enough trying to defend a man for murder when all the clues pointed to him, but the kidnapping gave it a terrible urgency. She felt sure that Ben wouldn't be a suspect much longer, since they had confirmed that he was home with Lynda and Anne when the kidnapping occurred.

Desperate to get to the bottom of this complex case, she flipped through pages and pages of art books, trying to learn more about Marazzio and the painting that Ben had discovered. If it wasn't the original, then it probably had nothing to do with the case at all. But if there was even a chance that it was, it might be the key both to clearing Ben of the murder charges and to finding the kidnapper.

Coming to a chapter on famous lost paintings, she scanned the pages for Marazzio.

She found him listed halfway through and quickly began to read.

She heard a knock at the kitchen door, and before she could call "come in," the door opened. Jake, who had lived in her garage apartment since the plane crash that had changed his life, came in and peered around the doorway to the den. "Hi," he said. "I couldn't sleep and I saw your light on. Are you all right?"

She smiled up at him. He looked good, standing so tall without his cane, though he still had a slight limp. He was handsome — even more now than he'd been before the crash, because now she knew his true character. In her mind, his looks weren't marred by the scar that slashed one side of his face. That scar had special attraction for her, because it had special meaning. It was because of that scar that they had both bonded as human beings rather than adversaries. She cherished it now.

"I'm fine," she said, sitting back in her chair and holding out a hand to him. He came over to her and bent to kiss her. She reached up and touched that scar that felt so familiar beneath her fingertips.

"You sure? You were so shaken about the kidnapping."

"So were you."

"Yeah, well. That Christy's a character. I just hate the thought that . . ." His voice trailed off, and he slumped into a chair and looked at the floor.

"Yeah, me, too," she whispered. "I went to the library a while ago and got everything I could find on Marazzio — you know, the painter? I thought maybe that reproduction Ben found had something to do with all this. The police searched the gallery tonight and didn't find it. I can't help wondering — if it was just a worthless fake, where is it? Who took it?"

"Find anything?"

"No," she said, rubbing her eyes. "Well, a couple of things, but I don't know if they're important. I feel like I'm barking up the wrong tree with those kids out there somewhere. . . ." She dropped her forehead into her hand. "But then I tell myself that I have to leave the kidnapping to the police. My job is to help Ben. I have to somehow help him figure out who could be setting him up. *That* will tell us who the kidnapper is, and who the killer is."

"Not a very comforting thought, is it?" Jake asked. "That the kidnapper is the killer."

"No," she said. "It isn't."

"Well, I've been trying to think what I

could do," he said. "And it came to me. As soon as it's daylight, I'm gonna head out to the airport, and Mike and I are gonna take one of the planes up and scan the landscape. See if we can spot the Taurus they were taken in. Who knows? Maybe it's parked somewhere and we can see it. It's a long shot, but it's something."

She smiled slightly. Flying was Jake's passion, but he'd lost his license after the crash due to his temporary paralysis and his blindness in one eye. He was waiting for the opportunity to get his medical release and try to get his license back, but until now, he hadn't been ready. "You gonna do the flying?" she asked.

"I might," he said. "Mike's a certified instructor. As long as he's with me, it's not a problem."

"It's been a long time. Are you sure you're ready?"

"I've never been more ready," he said. "Maybe I'll see something. You never know."

She thought about that as her smile sobered. "Even if you don't see the car, make a note of any hiding places on the outskirts of town. We could try them."

"There's not much to go on, is there?"

"No, there's not." She closed the book she

was reading and stood up. "I just hope Larry and Tony will let up on the parents now that it's so obvious that they weren't involved."

"Sharon obviously couldn't have done anything like that. She's got a heart as soft as marshmallows. But what about Ben or Anne? Do you think they could have —"

"No," she said without question. "I think Ben was telling it straight from the beginning. He was framed. Somebody killed Dubose and left a trail that pointed to Ben."

"But why the kidnapping?"

"I don't know. There are still too many questions. It seems strange. If the killer wanted us to think Ben did it . . . then why would he kidnap Ben's kids? It would obviously indicate that someone else is the culprit, after all. The minute the police realize someone else is involved, Ben is out of the hot seat."

"Maybe the killer's desperate. Or maybe he's just sure he won't get caught. Maybe he's trying to manipulate Ben in some way. Needed the kids so he could work a deal."

"Yeah, but why? What does he want?"

"I'm with you. That reproduction keeps coming to mind."

Lynda looked back at the book she'd been flipping through. "But a reproduction isn't worth much. Certainly not all this."

They heard a car in the driveway, and Jake went to the kitchen and glanced out into the night. His mother sat there in the red Porsche that was once his — the toy he had cherished more than any other possession. It looked more ridiculous each time he saw her driving it. But he had given it to her free and clear. He had expected her to sell it and buy a condo or something. But she was having the time of her life driving it all over town.

"It's Mama," he said to Lynda over his shoulder. "She probably came to get some of the posters of the girls. She's working the late shift at the diner tonight and said she'd put some up and hand them out to her customers."

"Great."

Jake went to the door as his mother got out of the car, dressed in tight knit black pants, an over-frilly pink blouse, and four-inch heels. She had gotten her hair done, Lynda noted as Doris bopped in. Her roots weren't quite as black as they'd been the last time she'd seen her. Though the woman had been hard to swallow when she'd first come to St. Clair, Lynda was growing fond of her now. She was a lost soul, desperately trying to find herself. That it had taken the woman fifty-something years to do it was not her fault.

"Hey there, boys and girls!" Doris said, clicking into the kitchen and reaching up to pat her son's cheek. She took one look at Lynda and gasped. "Heavens to Betsy, girl, you look like something the cat dragged in."

Lynda's smile crashed. "I do?"

"You look like you haven't slept in a month of Sundays."

"Well, this kidnapping's got me really worried . . ."

"Of course it has!" Doris said in her Texas twang. "Those poor little sweet boys . . ."

"Girls, Mama," Jake said. "They're girls."

"Well, just imagine them out there with some awful person. It just makes my skin crawl. But honey, when this is all over, let me give you a make-over, won't you? If you're gonna keep my boy happy, you're gonna have to take better care of yourself. He's the type has to fight the ladies off with a stick, ain't you, Jake?"

Jake grinned and winked at Lynda. "No, Mama. Not really. And I think Lynda's beautiful. We're both tired, that's all."

"Well, we've got to get out there and find these kids," Doris said. "Now where are those posters you were gonna give me?"

He handed her a stack, and her face twisted as she looked at the sweet faces. "Bless their hearts. They're so little. Oh, maybe some of the truckers who come through the diner will know something. I'll give these out to everybody who comes in tonight."

"Good," Lynda said. "I've set up a television interview this morning for the parents. Maybe a personal plea from them will get people's attention."

"Television?" Doris asked, her hand immediately straying to the blonde mop piled on her head. "Why, you know, if you needed some help with that, I'll be off work at seven. I've had a little experience with this sort of thing. When my friend Spud McKinley ran for mayor of Slapout, I fixed his wife's makeup before they did their campaign ad. You remember Spud, don't you, Jake? The kid who used to shoplift cigarettes from the corner store? Lived in the trailer park across from us? Anyway, he didn't win, but his wife had the prettiest makeup job you've ever seen. If that mother looks anything like you do right now, she's gonna need a makeup job."

"That's okay, Doris," Lynda said with a smile. "We're not really concerned with makeup. Besides, there are two mothers. The children have the same father, but they're half-sisters."

"Is that so?" Doris asked, leaning back against the counter as if settling in for some juicy gossip. "Well, that's interesting. Are they all gonna go on TV together?"

"Probably."

"Hmmm. They'll probably sell that story to Hollywood and make one of them miniseries out of it."

Lynda didn't quite know how to respond to that. "Thanks for passing out the posters, Doris." She gave the woman a hug, and Jake followed his mother out the door. "You be careful now, Lynda. Messing around with murder ain't no picnic."

She smiled. "Jake's the one you should worry about. He's going to fly tomorrow for the first time since the crash."

"You're what?" Doris asked, spinning around to face Jake. "Son, are you out of your mind? After what happened to you, you would want to fly again? Lynda, you're not gonna let him do this, are you?"

Lynda laughed. "Since when have I had control over anything Jake did?"

"Honey, you've got more control than you know. You just don't use it right."

"Come on, Mama," Jake said, rolling his eyes. "I'll walk you to your car."

Lynda could hear Doris chastising Jake all the way out to her car.

CHAPTER TWENTY-NINE

It was raining outside when the doorbell rang and Larry let Lynda in. Since most of the police force was looking for the girls, Larry and Tony had decided to stay at the home all night in hopes that a ransom call would come. Jenny still slept, sedated, upstairs, and Sharon paced the house, clutching Christy's Simba doll and praying. Anne stayed busy with Bobby, who was still fussy because of his cold, though the tormented, distracted expression she wore and the swelling of her eyes testified to the fact that Emily was never off her mind.

"I couldn't sleep, so I thought I might as well come on over," Lynda said as she followed Larry into the dining room of the house, where all of their tracing equipment was set up in anticipation of the phone call. "I've been doing a little homework, trying to find a motive. I got some books on Marazzio's work. I thought maybe the reproduction was a clue, somehow, and that if we could just get to the bottom of the motive, we might have some lead on who the killer and kidnapper are."

"Good. I was thinking about doing the same thing."

"Then you'll finally admit that Ben was set up?"

"I'm not admitting anything," he said wearily. "It's too soon. But while we're sitting here waiting with no leads, we can at least get a little culture."

Tony came into the room and said hello to Lynda, then picked up a Marazzio book and began flipping through. "This about that artist guy?"

"He's not just any artist," Lynda said. "According to what I've read, Marazzio's paintings have a high price tag."

"How high?"

"Millions. Three of his paintings have been stolen over the past fifteen years. Two have been recovered, and sold for millions. But this book must be outdated. At the time of its printing — three years ago — *The Multitude* still hadn't been found. The book said it was worth a whopping twenty million."

"Get outta here," Tony said. "You can't be serious."

"It's true."

Tony looked more seriously at the book in his hand, and flipped through, looking at the shots of his paintings. "Do you think the painting Ben found could have been the real thing?"

"It's possible," Lynda said. "Though I

doubt it. Dubose was probably right. It probably has been recovered since this book was printed. Shouldn't be too hard to find out."

"This is ridiculous, anyway," Tony said. "People don't kill and kidnap over a picture slapped on canvas, do they? This has got to be about something else." He lowered his voice and said, "There's more here than Ben Robinson is telling. Mark my word."

"Maybe, maybe not," Larry said.

Sharon came to the doorway and looked in. It was clear that she had been crying, and she wore a fragile, haunted look. "Oh, Lynda, it's you. I thought maybe it was someone with news."

Lynda went around the table and hugged her friend. "We're working on it, Sharon."

Sharon looked down at the books on the table. "Marazzio?" She looked frustrated that they were wasting time on that. "You don't honestly think my child was kidnapped over that picture, do you?"

"No, I don't," Larry admitted. "But it's the only unusual thing that happened before Ben was fired and Dubose was killed. I don't know if there's a connection, but if there is, it might help us with the kidnapping, too."

"Instead of reading books and waiting for the phone to ring, you should be out combing the county for the girls. It's storming outside, and the whole night has passed without a phone call!" Her voice broke off, and she covered her face. "What if this maniac has hurt them?"

Tony got up and urged her to sit. Pulling his chair up close beside her, he said, "We've got people out there looking, Sharon. No one's going to get past our checkpoints with two little girls in the car. We're searching every boat and every plane that leaves St. Clair, and every man driving alone is going to have his trunk searched. We're also compiling a list of every rental car in the county with the description the witness gave. We'll find out who rented them, and that might give us some ideas."

Sharon whispered, "You think he put them in the trunk? That's horrible. Christy will be terrified. And it's thundering. She always sleeps with me when there's thunder."

"Maybe we'll find them soon. It'll be morning in a couple of hours, and we'll have the advantage of daylight."

Lynda bent over her and stroked her hair. "Sharon, as soon as the sun comes out, Jake and Mike are going up in a plane to see if they can spot the car anywhere, or get some idea where they may be. So that means all the bases are being covered. They'll be searching on the ground, in the water, and in the air."

"It's not enough!" she cried. "It won't be enough until they find them!"

The telephone rang, and they all jumped.

Ben bolted for the telephone in the kitchen, but waited and looked through the dining-room door to Tony — as he'd been instructed. Tony, who held his hand over his own phone, nodded that he was ready to begin tracing, and Ben picked it up.

"Hello?"

"Are you ready to give me what I want now?" the muffled, disguised voice asked.

"Where are my children?" Ben asked, the blood draining from his face. "Where are they?"

"I asked you a question."

Sharon rushed toward Ben. Anne already stood next to him, hanging on every word. "I don't even know what you're looking for!" he shouted.

"The painting, you con artist. You know I'm looking for the painting!"

"*What* painting?" Ben asked. "Is it . . . is it one of *my* paintings? Because Dubose didn't let me leave with any of them. But if you'll tell me which one, maybe I can get back into the gallery and get it. Please!"

"What do you want, Ben?" the voice

asked. "For me to spell it out for those cops sitting there with their tape equipment, waiting for me to state it for the record?"

Ben was silent.

"I'm getting tired of these games," the voice said. "Your girls are getting tired of them, too."

"Where are they, you scumbag? Where are my children?"

"They're in a damp, dark place. Picture it, Robinson. Those two beautiful little girls screaming for their daddy. And you're the only one who can help them. All you have to do is give me what I want."

"I don't *have* what you want!" Ben said, breaking into tears and leaning his forehead against the wall. "I don't *know* what you want!"

The phone went dead in his ear.

Sharon swung back to Tony and Larry, who were each on another telephone, and were now barking orders.

"Did you trace it?" she asked, her eyes wide with hope.

"Yeah," Tony said, putting his hand over the receiver. "He was at a pay phone on the east side of town. A unit should be there by now."

"He's gone," Larry said, shaking his head and dropping his own phone. "The booth was empty when our guy got there."

"Oh, no!" Sharon cried. "I don't believe this!"

"They're combing the area. It's not too late. They could still catch him."

They all waited as moments ticked by with agonizing slowness. Finally, the officers searching for the kidnapper called to say that they hadn't found him.

Tony dropped the phone back in its cradle and looked up at Sharon, Ben, Anne, and Lynda, who were all clustered in the arched doorway of the living room.

"They lost him?" Sharon cried. "Are they looking around the area? Did they block off the neighborhood around the phone booth? Maybe he has the girls with him!"

"They're still searching the area," Larry said. "But with this storm, it's unlikely that there were any witnesses."

"But you've got to *do* something!"

Tony rewound the tape of the phone call and looked up at Ben through the door. Ben was still leaning with his forehead against the wall, weeping. Anne was staring at them with a look of shock on her face.

They played the tape again, hoping Ben would recognize the voice, but he couldn't place it. Sharon was near the breaking point. Gritting her teeth, she turned to Ben and shoved him.

"Tell him where it is!" she shouted through her teeth. "Give him what he wants!"

"I don't know what he wants!" Ben cried. "How many times do I have to say it?"

"No more times," she shouted. "Just give it to him!"

"Please, Ben!" Anne threw in, and began to sob into her hands.

He turned to her, then back to Sharon. "Do you really think that I'd put my family through this for some stupid secret?"

"Why not?" Sharon shouted. "You've done it before. Once you even *destroyed* your family over a stupid secret!"

"I have never intentionally hurt my family," he said, quieter now, though his voice trembled. "I've always tried to do the best I could."

"It was the best you could do when you left your wife and children for another woman?" she screamed. "You had no regard for them then, and I don't believe you have any regard for them now."

"Shut up!" Anne cried. "You don't know how he felt! You don't have a clue what was going on —"

Ben broke in, raising his voice over his wife's. "So what do you think is going on here now, Sharon? Do you think I have something that could ransom our children, but I'd rather sacrifice them than turn it over? Is that really what you think of me?"

"Stop it!" Lynda shouted. "All of you."

All three of them turned to look at Lynda, sobs racking them as they glared at her.

"I think I know what he wants," Lynda said. "The Marazzio, Ben. I think it's time to seriously consider that what you found may not have been a reproduction."

CHAPTER THIRTY

Christy woke with a start and shivered from the cold. The night-light must have gone out, she thought, and Mommy must have forgotten to leave on the hall light. But as those thoughts came to her, she realized she was not at home, but lying on a dirt floor in the tool shed where the man had left them.

Emily still slept, her head resting on Christy's shoulder. For a moment, Christy didn't move, for fear of waking her. But as she sat staring into the darkness, feeling the cold creeping around them, despair fell over her. She began to cry quietly.

The feeling that she would never be found, that she and Emily would never get out, panicked her, and she suddenly felt the urgency to try to get out. She gently slid out from under Emily's weight, then helped her to lie down on the cold dirt floor. Emily curled up in the fetal position, trying to get warm, her thumb stuck in her mouth.

Christy tried to reach the shelves to look for something to cover her with, but they were at least four feet higher than she could reach.

Her stomach ached with hunger, and she

felt shaky and weak, but she went to the door and tested it again, as if hoping it had miraculously come unlocked during the night. They were still bolted in.

She sank down and listened to the sounds of the rain still pounding against the roof. Was Mommy out looking for her? Was Daddy? Had they called the police?

She wiped the tears from her face and set her hand down on the dirt by the wall. It was wet there. The rain was seeping under the walls, making the dirt floor soft. An idea came to her.

She felt around for a tool of some kind, anything she might dig with, but there was nothing. She tried using the heel of her loafer to start a hole in the dirt. It came loose, so she dug more, until she reached the softer, wetter earth underneath. Getting on her knees, she began to dig with her hands, raking away small handfuls.

"Mommy!" Emily woke, looked around, and began to scream. "Mommy!"

Christy grabbed her. "Emily, it's me. Christy. We're here, remember? In this place?"

Emily's wailing just got worse. "I want my mommy! Moooommmy!"

"She can't hear you," Christy said sullenly. "But I think I've found a way out. You have to help me. Now stop crying and look."

Emily hiccuped her sobs, but grew quieter.

"Look," Christy said, going back to the hole she'd been digging. "Help me dig under the wall, and we can get out."

"Dig with what?" Emily asked.

"Our hands," Christy told her.

Emily looked down at her hands. "I don't want to."

"Do you want to be here when that man comes back?" Christy asked her. "Or do you want to get out so we can go get help and call home?"

"Get out," Emily whimpered.

"Then help me."

Slowly, Emily moved over to the hole and began to help halfheartedly.

"If we dig deep enough, and get under the wall, we can run real fast into the woods."

"I'm scared of the woods," Emily said. "It has wolves and bobcats and alligators."

Christy hadn't thought of that. "Well . . . maybe we'll find a house. Maybe some nice grandma lives there, and she can give us some food. Maybe she has a phone."

Emily liked that idea better. "Okay, but I hope she has a heater. It's cold in here."

Together, they began to dig with their fingers, desperately trying to make a way to escape.

CHAPTER THIRTY-ONE

Sharon didn't know what to do with herself, so she set about to do something, anything, for Christy. First, she washed all her clothes. Then she pulled out a ready-made roll of dough and began to make cookies. The smell that filled the house made her feel that her child would be home by the time they were done.

But when she took them out of the oven, the children were still just as lost as they'd been before.

The house was deathly quiet, though she knew the two police officers sat in her dining room waiting for the phone to ring again. Larry and Tony had taken Ben to the gallery to look, once again, for the mystery painting, and two officers she'd never met were taking their place here while they were gone. The fact that they played a hand of cards in the dining room riled her, for she couldn't stand the thought that they were wasting time when they could be looking for the girls. It didn't matter that other cops — dozens of them — were combing the town for them.

She turned off the oven. Looking around at the clean kitchen, she realized there was nothing more to do. This busyness was crazy, anyway. It wasn't helping to give her any more peace.

She wandered upstairs to Jenny's room and checked on her. Heavily sedated, Jenny was sleeping soundly. Sharon touched her back and felt her rhythmic breathing. At least one of her children was safe. But what if something happened to Christy? Jenny would always blame herself. Her guilt over the kidnapping was overwhelming her already.

Feeling the weight of a couple of tons on her shoulders, Sharon adjusted Jenny's covers and left her bedroom. Slowly, she walked up the hall to Christy's room, trying to recover the feeling that her child was in there, tucked into bed, sleeping soundly. But as she neared the doorway, she was hit with the reality that her child was out in the cold, wet morning someplace, terrified and confused.

She burst into tears as she reached the doorway.

Anne sat there in the rocking chair in Christy's room, her knees hugged to her chest. For a moment the only sound was that of the rain pelting against the windows.

"Oh," Sharon said. "I didn't know you were in here." Anne started to get up, but Sharon stopped her. "It's okay. Stay."

Anne hugged her knees again, and Sharon could see that the misery on the woman's face reflected her own. "Where are they?" Anne asked on a whisper.

Sharon went into the room and sat down on the bed. She picked up one of the dolls propped against the pillow, and smoothed out its hair. "At least they're together."

"Yeah," Anne said. "I was just thinking that. Christy's not that much older than Emily, but she takes care of her. If either of them was alone . . ." Her voice trailed off, and she looked out the window again.

"He just wants the painting," Sharon said, trying to reassure herself more than Anne. "He has to keep them alive so he'll have something to bargain with. He can't hurt them. He just can't."

"He already has," Anne whispered. "Just by taking them, he hurt them. The trauma that they're going through . . ." She covered her face, and her voice came out in a squeak. "I know God's punishing me."

Sharon stared at her for a long moment, at a loss for what to say. There had been many times since her divorce when she had wished God would punish Anne, but in the last couple of years, those wishes had come less frequently. Why would such punishment come now, and include her own child?

Sharon grew quiet and followed Anne's gaze to the raindrops running down the window. She didn't know what to say.

"Do you remember during yours and Ben's divorce, when you told him that the pain for you was bad enough, but that he had traumatized his children and robbed them of their family? That they'd never be the same because of it?"

"I said a lot of things," Sharon whispered.

"That haunted Ben," Anne went on. "And I never let it haunt me. I thought kids were resilient. That they'd recover. That it wouldn't be a big deal."

Sharon had known that was Anne's attitude. She stiffened a little, wondering where the woman was going with this.

"But sometimes, I think God punishes people by giving them more of the pain they gave somebody else." She swallowed and hiccuped a sob, then kept going. "We traumatized your children, so now he's letting us see how it feels. Only this is even worse."

Sharon stared down at the doll for a moment, running her fingertip across the porcelain face and over the pink lips. "There's one problem with your logic on this, Anne. If it's the way you say it is, why would God make me go through it?"

Anne considered that for a moment, then

looked at Sharon. "I don't know. Maybe he's punishing you for something, too."

She dropped the doll and got up. "Maybe you're just wrong about all of it," she said. "Maybe God had nothing to do with any of this. Maybe he's just watching over them. Bringing them back to us."

"They're both so little," Anne said in a tormented whisper.

For a moment Sharon felt a bond with Anne that she had never felt before. The bond of one mother to another.

But she didn't want to feel that bond, and as the contagious agony caught up with her and brought her close to breaking, Sharon left the room, to suffer alone.

CHAPTER THIRTY-TWO

The gallery was almost as it had been the last time Ben left it. The same paintings still graced the walls, the same sculptures stood on their pedestals.

But everything was different.

Ben let his eyes stray to the chalk mark on the floor, and realized for the first time that a man he had respected and depended on, a man he had seen every day for the last five years, was dead. Some murderer had come in here and killed him, and if Dubose had not fired and evicted him, Ben and his family might have been killed, as well. He wondered if that was why Dubose had been in such a hurry to get them out. Did he know he was in danger? Was he trying to spare Ben and his family?

Somehow, that thought made the reality seem more difficult to bear. His eyes teared up, and he turned away.

Tony looked uncomfortable with the show of emotion. "So where was this painting you told us about? How about taking us there and showing us where it was hidden?"

Ben tried to pull himself together and started up the stairs, with Larry and Tony following behind him. He cut through the studio where he'd been the most creative, and looked longingly at the work that leaned against the walls or sat on easels. Without uttering a word, he crossed the room to the office where Dubose had worked.

The little door to the attic was at the back of Dubose's office. Ben turned on the light, and the wooden stairwell lit up.

Slowly, he led them up into the attic. A few bare bulbs hung from the ceiling, casting a weak glare over wrapped and stacked canvases, over empty frames hung haphazardly on the walls.

"It was right over here," he said, and the two cops followed him. "I was up here looking for a frame." He gestured toward all of the old frames, some broken, some just dusty. "I wanted a frame that was obviously old. I was going for the antique look for one of my paintings. I'll show it to you when we go back down. Anyway, I bent down like this to look at that frame over there, and when I stood back up, my head bumped on this compartment, and the painting fell out. It had been rolled up for some time, because when I started to unroll it, the paint cracked a little."

Tony stepped forward and examined the narrow box built into the rafter at the ceiling.

The door was hanging open, and he could see how the slanted compartment could have dropped its contents if it hadn't been closed properly. "Any idea where the painting is now?"

"I gave it to Dubose," Ben said. "I never saw it again."

"What might he have done with it?"

"Got me," Ben said. "He may have hidden it someplace else, though I don't really know why he'd go to all that trouble. I mean, it obviously wasn't the original."

Larry took a deep breath. "Well, maybe we'd better look around up here. It could be in a new hiding place."

"But didn't you say that the place had been rifled through? If it was here, the killer would have found it."

"We have to anyway," Tony said. So they set about examining every inch of the dusty, dark attic, moving frames and old cracked canvases, oil paintings that looked as if they'd be better suited to the dumpster outside than the attic, and broken sculptures that Dubose hadn't had the heart to throw away. There were no more hidden compartments, and very little of value there.

As they walked back through the studio, Ben showed them some of the things he'd been working on. "Pretty cushy job you had," Tony said, looking around. "Free rent, nice place to work, steady income whether you sell anything or not."

Ben's face reddened. "I sold plenty. People came from all over the country to buy my work."

"Do you think this is about one of your own paintings?" Larry asked.

Ben shook his head. "Why wouldn't he just call it by name? Describe it? Why the secrecy? Why does he think I know what he's talking about?"

They went through each of his paintings, then headed downstairs, studying each painting for something that gave it more value than the others. Nothing stood out as a work worthy of murder and kidnapping.

"All right, who can we call to find out for sure if that Multitude painting was recovered?" Tony asked.

Ben thought for a moment. "Come to think of it, Louis kept a set of books in his office that have information like that." He started back up the stairs, feeling excited. "I don't know why I didn't think of that before!"

They followed him back up, and he hurried into Dubose's office. "See?" he asked, pointing to the eight volumes on the credenza behind the desk. "*The Dictionary of*

Painters and Sculptors. I had almost forgotten. It has information about lost and stolen art, what it's worth now, and all that kind of stuff. Louis used it extensively."

He pulled out one volume and flipped through the pages until he came to Marazzio. "There it is," he said, setting the book down and pointing to the passage so that Tony and Larry could see. "Says *The Multitude* was stolen from a museum in Palermo over ten years ago." He frowned. "I don't get it. It doesn't say it was recovered. These other two that were stolen at other times, they were recovered three years ago, but nothing about *The Multitude*."

"How current are these books?"

"Very current. Louis kept them up-to-date. He just got this set about a month ago."

"Maybe he got *The Multitude* mixed up with one of the ones that really was recovered."

"Or he lied," Larry said.

"If the painting I found was really the original, stolen painting, then it probably is what the kidnapper wants."

"So where is it?"

"I have no idea," Ben said. "Maybe you should search his house . . . his car . . ."

"We searched it after the murder," Larry

said, "but we weren't looking for a painting then."

As they drove back to Sharon's house, Tony said, "That painting is the key to whatever is going on here. This painter. Mar—"

"Marazzio," Ben said.

"Yeah, Marazzio. He was pretty famous, huh?"

Ben chuckled, almost condescendingly. "I'd say so. He's considered one of the greats. Who knows? If it was a fake, maybe Dubose was going to doctor the reproduction and try to pass it off as the original, especially if he really did know the painting was still missing. See how many millions he could get for it."

"I'm in the wrong business," Tony muttered, and Larry laughed. "No, really. I'm artistic. I used to draw a mean Bugs Bunny."

"Used to? What happened?"

"I had to trade my crayon in for a gun."

"Tough life, buddy."

"Yeah. But if I'd known the money was in those crayons . . ."

They looked in the backseat. Ben wasn't laughing. But their bantering made him realize one good thing: they no longer considered him the killer.

"So where did Dubose buy most of the original art pieces he found?" Larry asked.

Ben shrugged. "He traveled a lot, went to a lot of auctions. And there were a few dealers he did business with. Some of them spent a lot of time at the gallery."

"Who were they?"

"Well, there were several. He had dealings with people all over the world. But some of the most frequent ones, I guess, were Leon Spatika, Nelson Chamberlain, T. Z. Quarternet. All three of them have bought paintings of mine."

Tony shot Larry a look. "Would their names be in Dubose's Rolodex?"

"Sure. Why?"

"We took it as evidence. Maybe we'll give them a call."

Larry looked over his shoulder. "If Dubose was such a big-time art dealer with all these connections, what was he doing in a little town like St. Clair?"

"He had about ten galleries across the U.S.," Ben said. "They're all as small as this one. It's a good outlet for some of the lower priced paintings he sells. Plus he liked to cultivate up-and-comers. That's what he considered me."

"Then there are other galleries with artists-in-residence?"

"Sure. But I doubt there are any others where the owner has been murdered and the artist's kids have been abducted."

They pulled into Sharon's driveway, but Larry made no move to get out. "Go on in, Ben, and tell John and Nick in there that they'll have to stay a little longer. Tony and I are going to search Dubose's apartment and his car again. Maybe we can find the painting."

"All right," Ben said. "But what if the kidnapper calls back?"

"John and Nick know what to do, and they'll get in touch with us."

"All right." He got out of the car, and headed inside to face the quiet left behind by his two little girls.

CHAPTER THIRTY-THREE

The hole the girls had dug was deep, and though their fingers had developed blisters, they both dug with a zeal that they hadn't felt since they'd come there. At the end of the tunnel they were digging with their hands was freedom. And food. And warmth.

They heard a car pulling up to the shack, its wheels popping on the gravel road.

"Daddy's come!" Emily exclaimed, jumping to her feet. "Daddy! Daddy!"

But Christy clapped a dirty hand over Emily's mouth. "It might be him!" she hissed. "The mean man. Be quiet and help me hide the hole!"

Emily's joy crashed instantly, and she looked around for something to move over the hole. There was nothing.

"I'll sit here over it," Christy said, sitting on the edge of the hole. "You lie down with your head in my lap, and he won't see it."

"What about the pile of dirt we dug out?"

"Lie down in front of it," Christy said. "Maybe he won't see it."

Emily got into place, and Christy could feel her trembling as she laid her head in her lap. "Do I pretend I'm sleeping?" she whispered.

"If you want."

Christy's hand was trembling as she laid it over Emily's arm. "Our hands," Emily said. "When he sees them, he'll know we've been digging."

Christy considered that for a moment. "I'll put mine under you. Put yours between your legs."

Both children hid their hands as the car door slammed. Footsteps came closer to the shed, and keys jingled.

"It's not Daddy, is it?" Emily asked on a whisper.

"No. I think it's *him*."

The door opened, and both girls stiffened. Emily closed her eyes and tried to pretend to be asleep.

The big man stepped inside holding two bags. "I brought you something to eat," he said, and thrust the bags at Christy. She took the bags, forgetting the dirt on her hands. The man didn't seem to notice.

"Thanks, Mister. Are we gonna get to go home today?"

"That depends on how much your daddy wants to keep you alive. It's up to him, kiddo."

Christy's eyes widened as she tried to understand. "It's cold in here. And dark. Real dark, and Emily's afraid of the dark." She started to cry, knowing that it wasn't the right thing to do, but she couldn't stop it. Then Emily's act crumbled, and she began to squint her eyes and cry, too.

"Please let us go home, Mister. We'll tell everybody you were nice to us. We won't tell them about this place."

The man laughed sullenly under his breath. "I told you, it's up to your father. When he gives me what I want, you can go home."

Both girls looked up at him, quiet.

"Eat your food. I don't know when I'll bring you any more."

With that, he closed the door and locked the bolt again.

"McDonald's!" Emily cried, and dug into the bag. "Drinks, too. Look, Christy!"

But Christy wasn't thinking about the food. Her mind was still hung on the fact that her father had the power to get them back, but hadn't done anything about it. More tears ran down the dirt on her face, and she wiped them away with a filthy, blistered hand, smearing mud across her face.

"Aren't you hungry, Christy?" Emily asked.

"Yeah," Christy said and took her drink

out of the bag. "Emily, do you think he's ever gonna let us go home?"

Emily bit into her burger, and chewed thoughtfully as she looked at her sister. "If he doesn't, Daddy'll come get us. He'll find us. He always finds me when we play hide-and-seek."

"This isn't hide-and-seek," Christy said miserably. "He doesn't know where to look for us. And the man said it was up to him. What if we have to stay here another night?"

"We'll dig out before then," Emily said solemnly. "We'll run away and find that grandma with the telephone."

Christy wiped her eyes again and moved away from the hole. The man hadn't discovered it. Maybe Emily was right. Maybe they could escape soon.

The baby's cry woke Sharon from where she half-dozed with her head in her arms at the kitchen table, and she jumped up. It was morning. That was Christy calling her! She rushed toward the stairs.

But the crying wasn't coming from upstairs, and as the fog from her brain cleared, reality jolted her. It was Bobby, not Christy. Christy was still out there with some maniac who'd already killed at least once.

She grabbed Christy's Simba doll and

wished she could at least get it to her somehow, so there would be some measure of comfort for her child.

She walked into the living room, and saw that Tony and Larry had come back and had fallen asleep on the two couches set at right angles to each other in the big living room. Tony stirred slightly, so she backed out and walked toward the sound of the crying baby.

As she grew closer, the crying stopped. She slowed her step and got to the doorway. Anne was there, holding the baby, humming to him and gently rocking him as he whimpered.

Maternal anguish washed over her, overwhelming her with pain. But it wasn't resentment this time, or jealousy. The sight just reminded her that there would be no outlet, none at all, for her emotions until Christy came back.

Then came the miserable, cruel, startling thought. *What if he's killed them? What if they're already dead somewhere? What if they cried and he got impatient? What if I never see Christy again?*

She covered her mouth to muffle her sobs. Rushing back up the hall, her head bent, she slammed right into someone coming toward her.

She caught her breath and yelped once,

before she realized it was Tony.

"Are you okay?" he asked, looking down at her.

She covered her face and shook her head viciously. "What if they're dead?"

He pulled her into his arms and held her as she sobbed violently against his rumpled shirt. "They're not dead," he whispered. "You can't think like that. We're going to find them. Come on. Sit down. You're exhausted."

She let him lead her to the couch, and she sat down and allowed him to pull her against him. She laid her head on his shoulder and hiccuped sobs that wouldn't stop as he whispered soothing assurances against her ear. "Go ahead . . . it's okay to cry . . ."

The human contact helped. Slowly, her sobs subsided, and she was left under a blanket of grief. He still didn't let her go.

He stroked her hair back from her face and wiped her cheek with the back of his fingers.

"I dozed off in the kitchen," she whispered. "And the baby cried, and for a minute, I thought it was Christy. Just a split second, where I believed it had been an awful dream, and I was waking up."

"You need to get some real sleep, Sharon. You're not a superwoman."

"I can't," she said. "Some part of me thinks that if I let myself relax even for a minute, that they'll just fade away, and I'll never see my baby again."

There was nothing he could say.

After a while, she pulled out of his arms and sat upright. "I guess I should make everybody some breakfast."

"That's not necessary," Tony said. "You have enough to cope with."

"No," she said. "It's something I can do. You and Larry have been here all night. I want to feel useful somehow. I'm going to do it."

Tony stood up with her. "Are you sure you're up to it?"

"Yeah," she said. "Thanks for the shoulder. You have no idea how much I needed it."

"Any time." Tony watched her disappear back into the kitchen, then went back into the living room where he and Larry had been sleeping.

Larry was sitting up now. "You're getting a little too close to this case, don't you think, Tony?"

Tony shot him a disbelieving look. "You're kidding, right?"

"No, man. You're here to help find her child, not fall in love with her."

"Fall in love?" He almost laughed. "She was upset, and I tried to comfort her."

"Be careful. That can become a habit."

"Yeah, well, you ought to know." He raked a hand through his rumpled hair and wished for a shower.

"I'm serious, Tony. The woman's really vulnerable right now. She's going through a lot. You need to keep your distance."

Tony turned back around and glared at his partner. "That's just hilarious coming from you, Larry. In fact, I can't believe what I'm hearing."

Larry grinned. It was no secret that he had married a woman whose case he'd worked on. It was also no secret that he'd never been happier in his life. "Look, I know what you're thinking."

"I'm thinking that I was telling you the same thing just a few months ago. 'You're getting too involved. You're not being objective.' "

"I was the exception," Larry said with a grin. "But this is different."

"No, it's not different," Tony said. "But don't worry. I'm not gonna get hurt."

"Get hurt?" Larry asked. "Mr. Confirmed Bachelor? I'm not worried about *you* getting hurt!"

Tony gaped at him. "Her? You think I'll

hurt her? What kind of lowlife do you think I am?"

"A noncommittal lowlife," Larry said matter-of-factly, though a twinkle of humor shone in his eye.

"Thanks a lot, pal."

Larry pulled on his shoes and got up, stretching. "Speaking of commitment, I think I'll go call my bride."

"Yeah, you do that." Tony sat down and watched his friend go out of the room. And some part of him resented that Larry had been so lucky. Tony hadn't realized he was lonely until he'd seen how happy Larry's marriage had made him. More and more lately, he had wondered if the bachelor life really had all that much to recommend it.

On the other hand, seeing the tangled web of *this* family reminded him that marriage wasn't all it was cracked up to be, either.

CHAPTER THIRTY-FOUR

The storm raged on, tormenting those who waited. It had been two hours since the short appearance they'd all made on the news, in which they had pled for the return of their children. In her despair, Sharon had offered a $25,000 reward for information leading to their return. But still, they hadn't heard a word.

Now Sharon wandered in and out of rooms like a phantom, racking her brain for some idea that would get her child back. In her mind, her prayer for Christy and Emily's safety played like a chant, repeating itself in the same cadence over and over. She wondered whether God was even hearing it.

She stepped out onto the porch and looked up through the screen to the cloudy, angry sky. Under this same sky the children were hidden. God knew where they were, and he was the only one she could trust to keep them safe. Tears came to her eyes as she looked up to plead with him, but a voice behind her startled her.

"I thought we'd have them back by now."

She swung around and saw Ben sitting on a bench leaned back against the wall of the house. His voice was hoarse, and she could see that he'd been crying. For a moment, she thought of going back into the house, but the brief connection seemed more important. Besides Anne, Ben was the only person in the world who knew exactly how she felt.

Quietly, she turned back around and looked up at the sky.

"I never thought we'd come to this," he said. "In my worst nightmares, I wouldn't have believed . . ."

Sharon didn't look at him. A million thoughts fled through her mind, thoughts of how he'd brought it on them somehow, how he was being punished for all the cruelty he'd inflicted on her and their children, and that the kidnapped children were just caught in God's crossfire. But some part of her knew that wasn't true.

"Despite what you might think, Sharon," he went on, his voice raspy and heavy with emotion, "and despite how cruel I was, I never meant to hurt any of you."

If he'd said that two days ago, she would have laughed sarcastically, then reminded him of all the little instances in which his hurting had seemed deliberate. But the fight had left her now, and all that remained was a dull numbness.

"I thought I'd forgiven you," she whispered. "At church, I even bragged about it. Lectured to other divorced women about letting go and praying for their exes. I told them that God loved their ex-husbands as much as he loved them. Even when I invited you to move in, part of me was patting myself on the back, thinking how everyone would see how I lived out my faith. What it looked like to truly forgive. I had it all worked out. I thought I'd even gotten some peace about it. But I didn't know what a farce it all was."

A long note of silence stretched between them as the cool wind whipped around the house, whispering through the leaves.

"I can't undo what I've done, Sharon," he said from his dark corner of the porch. "This whole week, it's been like my life has passed before my eyes. But it's done."

"That's right," Sharon said. "And none of it really even matters right now. I just want my baby back."

She turned and looked at him now, and saw that his eyes were closed as he struggled to control his emotions. "I guess it would make this a little easier if I thought you and I weren't enemies," he said.

"How could we be enemies, Ben? You're in my house. You're the father of my children."

"Neither of those things qualifies for friendship."

"Oh, is that it?" she asked, her sarcasm returning. "You want to be friends?"

"It'd be nice," he said. "We have a lot in common, you know. We both love our children. And we used to love each other."

She turned away again. "Love dies, Ben. You ought to know that more than anyone."

Before he could answer, Sharon went back into the house and left him alone.

CHAPTER THIRTY-FIVE

"Look, Emily. Light!" Christy clawed at the dirt, ignoring the bloody blisters on her fingers. "We reached the other side!"

"Can we get out now?" Emily asked.

"No. We have to dig the hole bigger! Help me!"

The two girls dug faster, the skin on their fingers raw and bloody and caked with the dirt through which they would escape. More light filled the small shed, giving them hope as the hole got bigger and the pile of dirt next to it piled higher.

"I think it's big enough," Emily said. "I can slide out."

"No, you'll get stuck. It has to be bigger!"

On their knees, they both pulled and clawed at the dirt, getting closer, closer, to the point at which they could slide under the wall and embrace their freedom.

Then they heard the car.

"He's coming!" Christy cried. "He'll see the hole!"

"I'm going now!" Emily fell down on her stomach and started to crawl into the hole.

"He'll see you!"

"But I'll get away," she said. "Come on. Hurry!"

They heard his car door close, and Christy hoped he had parked on the other side of the building. His footsteps in the gravel were growing closer. He was coming around the side to the door, and probably wouldn't see Emily escaping. "Go! Hurry!" she whispered.

Emily burrowed through the hole, then up on the other side, and turned back to help Christy.

Christy went head first into the hole, slithering under the wall, but as she tried to come up on the other side, she heard the door open.

"You brats!" the man thundered. Suddenly she felt a hand grab her feet, and she was jerked backward.

"Run, Emily!" Christy screamed. "Run!" She watched as the terrified five-year-old took off into the woods, screaming in fear.

Christy fought with all her might not to be pulled back into the shed, but he yanked her up, bruising and scraping her back on the bottom of the wall as he got her back inside.

She tried to fight him as he lifted her, but he was too strong. Cursing, he held her sideways with an arm around her middle and bolted out of the building. The car parked outside was different from the one he'd taken them in, and he opened his trunk and threw her in, then slammed it shut, encompassing her in darkness once again.

Terrified, she hunkered in a little ball and covered her mouth with her hand, trying to muffle her sobs for fear he would hurt her if she made too much noise.

And then she began to pray, as hard and as fast and as deeply as she'd ever prayed in her life.

Emily had to get away. It was their only hope.

CHAPTER THIRTY-SIX

It took only a few phone calls to confirm that the original Marazzio had never been recovered. Dubose had lied.

Larry sat over Dubose's telephone records, which he had finally managed to get from the phone company, and compared them to the names on Dubose's desk calendar. "This one guy keeps coming up," he mumbled, thinking out loud, "Eric Boudreaux. The page torn off of the desk calendar was for the day after Dubose died. From the impression on the next page, I can read the words 'Eric Boudreaux, 2:00.' The phone records show a call from Boudreaux in France the day before the murder." He looked up at Tony, who was studying some documents they'd brought from the gallery. "Have you got anything on him yet?"

"Yeah," Tony said, looking up and resting his chin wearily on the heel of his hand. He shuffled some papers around and checked his notes. "He's a museum curator in France. Nothing unusual came up. No prior arrests."

"Do you think Dubose was planning a telephone meeting, or was he going to meet him in person?"

Tony picked up the phone. "I'll call and ask."

He got the long-distance operator, placed the call, and waited. After several rings, a woman answered in French.

"Eric Boudreaux, please," Tony said.

She returned something in French that he couldn't understand, and he closed his eyes. "Excuse me. Do you speak English?"

"A little," she said in a heavy accent. "Uh . . . Monsieur Boudreaux is . . . not here . . . in town . . ."

"He's out of town? Where?"

"*Les Estats Unis.* Florida."

Tony's eyebrows shot up, and he looked up at Larry. "Do you happen to know what town?"

"Non, Monsieur. I could have him . . . phone back? Yes?"

"No, that's okay. Thank you very much." He hung up the phone and looked up at Larry. "Ten to one our boy is in St. Clair as we speak."

"Then you think the appointment was face-to-face?"

"Maybe he moved it up a little," Tony suggested.

Larry thought that over for a moment. "I'd say we need to talk to him."

"Without delay," Tony agreed, getting up. "Call for someone to relieve us while we pay him a visit, and I'll start calling the hotels until I locate him." He picked up the phone and started dialing. "Oh, and ask Ben if he knows anything about this guy. He might know something we don't know. And hurry."

Larry rushed into the kitchen, where Sharon and Ben sat stone-faced and silent over coffee that was turning cold.

"Eric Boudreaux," Larry said, leaning both hands on the table and leaning over it. "What do you know about him?"

Ben shrugged. "He's a well-known art dealer."

"Well-known how?"

"He makes some pretty amazing buys." He sat up straighter as something occurred to him. "A few years ago he found one of the lost Monets."

Larry tried to sort out what that might mean. "Where did he find it?"

"He claimed he bought it at an estate auction. That some deceased person had it, and no one knew how he'd gotten it. No one had realized it was an authentic Monet, one of the missing ones. He knew it immediately and seized the moment."

Larry went to the phone and dialed the

number of the precinct. While he waited, he asked, "Did anyone ever check out that story? Confirm where he'd found it?"

"What do you mean?" Ben asked.

"I mean, to make sure he hadn't stolen it himself, or bought stolen goods, or that sort of thing?"

Ben breathed a laugh. "Actually, there was so much hoopla about finding the painting that I don't think too many people were concerned about how he'd found it. Art theft is big business, and it's rarely prosecuted, even when the people are caught. The discovery of a stolen Monet is a very big deal."

Larry turned away long enough to ask for relief officers, then hung up and turned back. He began to pace, trying to figure this out. "Okay, let's just pretend. Let's say that Dubose had some important original. And let's say that he had made contact with this Boudreaux guy to sell it. How much did the book say the original lost Marazzio would sell for?"

"Probably around twenty million."

Larry whistled.

Sharon got up, interested now. "You think this Boudreaux person is the killer? The one who has Christy and Emily?"

"No, now wait. It's a hunch. A possibility."

"But why would he kill Dubose for the painting? Why not just buy it from him?"

"Maybe the profit margin was higher if he did away with the middle man."

Ben thought that over for a long time, silently trying to work it all out in his mind. "So you think Eric Boudreaux is the one?"

"I hope so, man." He saw the squad car pull into the driveway, and Tony came into the kitchen.

"He's at the Biltmore. Let's go."

"I'm coming with you!" Sharon said, heading out the door.

Tony lassoed her with an arm and pulled her back in. "Oh, no, you don't. Let us do our work, Sharon."

"But the children could be there with him!"

"We'll call you immediately if anything breaks," he said gently. "Just trust us."

Reluctantly, she went back in. "Please. Call us if you find out anything!"

"I promise," Tony said, and they headed for their car.

CHAPTER THIRTY-SEVEN

Emily heard his footsteps coming closer. Breathless, she kept running. She wove through trees and bushes, leapt over logs, tore through briars and thorns.

She cried as she ran, and kept looking back over her shoulder. She couldn't see him yet, which meant that he couldn't see her. Soon she would be to that grandma's house she and Christy had talked about, and she could go in and call the police, and they would come and get them so they could go home.

But the house never came into sight, only deeper, thicker woods, a forest prison that frightened Emily the farther she ran. But what came behind her frightened her more. She could hear his heavy breathing, his feet hitting the ground with weight and speed . . .

She looked back and still couldn't see him, but she could hear him getting closer. She kept running, slipping under branches and tangled vines.

Then she stopped.

She stood at the edge of a gully, looking down into the stream bubbling by. Would the stream be too deep for her if she slid

down into it? No, she couldn't do that —
there was no place to hide down in the gully.
He would see her, slide after her, and catch
her.

Panicked, she turned around and searched
for a hiding place. There was a tree with low
branches beside the ravine. Without thinking, she began to climb it. She climbed from
one big branch to the next, knocking away
smaller branches and vines entangling it,
climbing higher and higher, where the man
would never think to look.

Certain she was hidden by the leaves beneath her and the vines webbing through the
tree, she found a sturdy branch and sat still,
holding her breath.

Within seconds, the man was beneath her,
searching. She saw him reach the edge of the
gully and almost fall down, but he caught
himself. He stood still for a minute, looking
up and down the gully, but then turned back
around.

She shrank into a tighter ball as he looked
up into the trees. His eyes passed over where
she sat, and she breathed a sigh of relief that
he had not seen her.

Slowly, he walked back through the trees
and brush the way he had come, and she
watched until he was out of sight.

She thought she was safe — until she

looked down at the branches she had climbed to get there, and didn't know if she'd ever have the nerve to go back down. Would she have to stay here, in this scary tree, even when it got dark? What if no one found her?

And where was Christy? She started to cry again. She had heard Christy scream for her to run, and she had, but then she hadn't heard anything more from her sister. What if the man had caught her? What if he had hurt her?

She put her filthy, bloody thumb into her mouth, then quickly spat it out. Wiping a smear of dirt and blood on her shirt, she tried again. The dirty thumb gave her some comfort, but only enough to make her cry harder.

Daddy would find her somehow, she told herself. This was harder than hide-and-seek, but it was more important. He had to rescue them both. He had to.

Hurry, Daddy. Hurry.

CHAPTER THIRTY-EIGHT

There was no answer at the door to the room at the Biltmore where Eric Boudreaux was staying. Larry and Tony knocked again, then looked at the manager who had accompanied them up. "We have a warrant to search his room," Larry said, flashing the paper they had gotten from a judge on the way to the hotel. "Could you let us in, please?"

"Sure. But he isn't here. He checked out." The manager used his key to open the door. Gesturing for them to go in, he asked, "Is this guy in some kind of trouble?"

"We don't know yet," Tony said. "Thanks for your help." Tony looked around at the room. It hadn't been cleaned yet since he'd checked out, but the man had left little behind. He went to the trash can and stooped down next to it, while Larry went into the bathroom.

"At least we have some fingerprints here," Larry said.

Tony nodded as he sorted through the sundry papers that had been dropped into the can. A Delta boarding pass stub, a couple of receipts with credit card numbers, a rolled up newspaper, a small sheet of paper with a phone number on it.

"Hey, Larry," Tony said. "There's a phone number on here. You'll never guess what it is."

"The number of the gallery?" Larry asked.

"You got it."

"Well, that doesn't mean anything. We knew he had an appointment."

"This piece of paper here has the name John Lieber written on it."

"Keep it and we'll check him out." He looked around. "No evidence of any children having been here."

"Nope. If he's got them, he's got them someplace else."

Tony reached for the newspaper and shook it out. It was the edition put out on the day of the murder, and it was folded so that Dubose's picture was on top. "Well, he knows about the murder. No doubt about that."

"Where is he now?" Larry asked.

"Who knows? We'd better check out all the flights leaving in the next few hours. He could be at the airport as we speak."

"What about the children?"

Tony shook his head. "Who knows?"

CHAPTER THIRTY-NINE

Emily had waited what seemed a very long time, but the longer she sat, the more afraid she got. She had seen a TV show once about snakes, and how they loved to hide in trees. Still sucking her thumb, she clung to the trunk and looked around her.

The thought that some unseen creature might be sharing this hiding place with her made her want to get down, but she was still afraid of the man, too. She hadn't heard him since he had walked away into the forest, and she hoped he had given up the search and gone back to the car.

She reached for the next branch with her foot and stepped down onto it. Trembling and perspiring, she made her way to another branch, and then another. She looked around for any sign of snakes and saw a shadow moving across the tree. Quickly, she took another step.

Branch by branch, she made her way down, propelled by fear. A small branch broke under her foot, and she slipped, but grabbed onto another branch in time. She found her footing again and continued her descent.

She breathed relief when her feet hit the ground. Quietly, she crept to the edge of the ravine again. Should she slide down it, hoping the water was shallow, and scramble up the other side? Would that take her deeper into the woods, or out to the road again? Where were those houses she and Christy had talked about, anyway?

She decided to slide into the gully, since she had no intention of going back toward the shed. She looked around for something to sit on as she slid down, but there was nothing that would work. She sat down, scooted to the edge —

Two hands grabbed her from behind, and she let out a high-pitched scream.

"I've got you, you little brat!" Chamberlain said, lifting her and squeezing her under his arm. "I'll teach you to run away from me!"

She kept screaming until he clamped his hand over her mouth and stopped her. She bit him, and he jerked his hand away, allowing her to scream some more.

When his hand came back, he shoved a handkerchief into her mouth and clamped his hand over it again. This time she couldn't bite, and she could hardly breathe as his big hand pressed against her nostrils.

He ran through the trees with no regard

for the bushes and brambles tearing at her clothes and scratching her skin. When they came to the edge of the woods, she saw the shed and car, but there was no sign of Christy.

They reached the car, and he opened the trunk.

Christy sat up and looked around, eyes squinted, and started to scream. He pushed her back in, and threw Emily in on top of her. When he started to close it, Christy cried, "No, Mister! We'll be good. We promise. We won't run away again. Please don't put us in here!"

"Shut up!" he said through his teeth. "And if you make a sound as I drive through town, I'll pull over and kill you both. Do you believe me?"

Christy and Emily looked up at his searing blue eyes. "Yes," Emily whimpered, and Christy agreed.

"Lie down," he said, and they both did.

He slammed the trunk shut, and seconds later, started the car.

CHAPTER FORTY

Tony and Larry had just returned to Sharon's house when the phone rang. The two cops who'd been waiting beside all the equipment turned on the recorder and picked up their own phone to call for a trace, then nodded for Ben to answer.

"Hello?"

"I'm losing patience, and your girls are running out of time."

Ben closed his eyes and nodded to Sharon and Anne that it was him. They both ran into the other room to hear the conversation as it played across the recorder.

"Look, you obviously want a painting of some kind," Ben said. "I'll give you anything I have. Is it the Marazzio?"

The man laughed. "You're amazing."

"If that's it, Dubose took it. I don't know what he did with it."

"You have until 11:30 tonight, Robinson. I'll call you back later with details. Just be ready."

The phone clicked, and one of the officers cursed. "It wasn't enough time! He knows we're tracing him so he's keeping the conversations short."

Ben sank down at the kitchen table. "What am I gonna do?"

"Daddy, was that the kidnapper?"

It was Jenny, standing at the door in her robe, awake for the first time since she had been sedated. Her eyes were red and swollen, and she looked pale. She hadn't eaten in two days, and he doubted she could eat now. Ben stood up and drew her into a hug. "Yes, honey, it was."

"What did he say?" she asked, beginning to cry. "Is he bringing them back?"

"Maybe tonight," he said. He turned back to the cops, hovered around the recording equipment. "It has to be the Marazzio. What if we faked it again? What if I got another painting and pretended that was it? Last time, I didn't know what size or shape the bundle in the garment bag should be. But if it's the Marazzio, I know it was a roll about four feet long. Maybe we could make a switch for the children before he realized it wasn't the right one."

Tony looked at Larry. "It depends, Ben. On a lot of things. One of them is his delivery method. We'd have to make sure that he delivered the kids before he saw the fake, otherwise it could just make him mad enough to . . . retaliate. We don't know where he wants you to take it yet."

"But don't you see, I have no choice!" Ben insisted. "I have to do something. I don't have the painting he wants, so I have to come up with something else."

"He's right, Tony."

"All right," Tony said. "Let's find a painting and get it ready."

Jenny started to cry and threw her arms around her father. "Daddy, I've been praying for you."

"Don't pray for me," he said. "Pray for your sisters."

"I have, Daddy," she said. "I'm so sorry. This is all my fault."

"Honey, I told you. It isn't."

Sharon pulled Jenny away from her dad and held her while he prepared for the next phone call.

Later, Sharon slumped on the couch alone in her den, waiting, as everyone else in the house waited, for the phone to ring. Tony found her there and sat down next to her.

"You okay?" he asked.

"Yeah," she lied. "You?"

"Just getting psyched up for the big chase tonight. We'll get the girls back, Sharon. I know we will."

She let her eyes drift to some invisible spot across the room. "You have to."

He took her hand and fondled her fingers. "You're a strong lady, you know that?"

"What choice do I have?"

"You could fall apart. Believe me, it happens all the time. Most mothers would have passed hysteria by now."

"I'm glad you have a short memory," she said.

"Well, you've had your moments, but you might have had more." He gazed at her for a moment, noting how pretty she was. Her beauty was striking, but not in the way that he usually viewed beauty. There was an intelligence about her beauty, a dignity, and if he hadn't gotten to know her in such a vulnerable state, he probably would have been intimidated by her.

"Tell me about Christy," he said. "Is she smart? Is she athletic?"

"I think she's smart," she said. "She's only in first grade, but she's been reading since she was four."

"I mean, logic smart. Clear-headed smart."

"Yeah, she's got a lot of common sense. You could say she's even a little precocious. Jenny's always been an honor student, and I have a feeling that Christy will follow in her footsteps. She can count to fifteen in Spanish, to ten in French . . . and she knows all of the states in alphabetical order, because Jenny taught her a song about it. They're working on the presidents."

"Learning them?" Tony asked, amazed. "In the first grade, they learn all the presidents?"

"No," she said. "Jenny's teaching her. She's really good at memory work."

"She sounds like a kid who could take care of herself if she had to."

Sharon's eyes misted. "I think she could," she whispered. "She's strong. She climbs all the time, getting up to her tree house. She runs really fast, and she's a strong swimmer."

Tony smiled. "Good. That's what I wanted to hear. She sounds like a real interesting kid."

"She is. You'd really like her."

"Well, I hope after all this is over, and she's back safe and sound, that you'll give me the chance to get to know her."

"Of course. If you really want to."

"I do." He looked down at her hand, laced his fingers through hers.

She gazed up at him, her eyes serious, haunted. "Who are you, Tony Danks? Are you attached? Detached?"

He breathed a laugh. "None of the above."

"Why not? Why haven't you ever married?"

"Never found the right person," he said. "Besides, marriage hasn't had much appeal to me. Every cop I know who's gotten married has wound up divorced. With the exception of Larry, but he's a newlywed. Give him time."

"Uh-oh. A cynic."

"Not really," he said, hating that she saw him that way. "I'm a realist. I don't like to believe in things that can let me down."

"And here you are asking me to believe in you."

He grinned. "Well, that's because I won't let you down. You can put your faith in me and know I'll do my very best."

"But you can't control everything," she said, her face slackening again. "There are too many factors out of your control. So I can't put any real faith in you."

He looked hurt, but she persisted. "I can't put faith in anyone who's not in control."

"Well, no one is really in control here, except for the kidnapper."

"No. He just thinks he is."

"You *have* to believe in somebody."

"I believe in God. He knows where the children are."

He let that declaration hang in the air for a moment before asking, "Then how come you still don't have any peace?"

"Because I'm weak," she whispered.

Tony got up and walked to the window. He looked out on the news truck that waited outside for some sign of drama. "I'm not much of a believer in God, Sharon," he admitted. "I've had to do too many things on my own."

"You may have thought you were doing them on your own. But God was still God, whether you believed or not."

He turned back to her. "What if we don't find the girls, Sharon? What if this ends badly? Are you still going to believe that God was in control?"

He hadn't realized how biting that remark would be, but she looked up at him with horrified eyes. "It can't end badly, Tony. You see? Already you're giving up. And you expect me to believe in you."

"No, I'm not giving up. It won't end badly. I'm just trying to make a point. What about all the other parents who've lost children? Was God in control there, too?"

She wiped away a tear. "Yes, I believe he was."

"Was he in control when that man was luring your child into his car?"

It was almost as if he wanted her to break, to scream out that God wasn't in control, that the world had fallen out of God's grasp and chaos ruled.

"I don't know what you want me to say, Tony," she said in a shaky voice. "The fact that I'm a basket case doesn't take one iota away from God's power. It just proves how fragile my faith can be. It's an indictment of me, not God."

"Fragile faith?" he asked, his voice softening as he realized he was being too harsh. "Your faith isn't fragile. It's as strong as a rock."

"No," she whispered. "If it were, I'd be asking more directly for his will to be done. But I'm not sure I can do that yet, because I don't know what his will is." She began to cry harder and covered her mouth. "I'm just not to the point where I can trust God to take my child from me, even if there's a big, divine purpose. I don't want to lose my baby!"

He sat back down and pulled her against him, holding her while she wept. For the first time since he was a kid, he thought of praying. But then he wondered what he would say. *God, I don't even think I believe in you, but Sharon does, so if you're listening . . .*

Right. As if God would be open to listening to a prayer like that. But the feeling that his prayers were no good, that there was no way he could appeal to the Creator Sharon put all her faith in, made him feel too help-less.

He dropped his chin on the crown of her head as her tears soaked the front of his shirt, and feeling more humble the harder she cried, he closed his eyes. *Give us a miracle, Lord. Bring the children back. For Sharon.*

If there was a God, wouldn't he answer a prayer for Sharon, who believed so deeply in him?

But didn't bad things happen to Christians? Didn't tragedies befall them, just like everyone else? Weren't they frequent customers at hospitals and funeral homes, just like the regular joes were? Weren't some of their prayers not being answered?

He hated the thought that her faith might not make any difference. It would be nice if it did. After all these years of going it alone, he could use something to believe in. If he just had a sign . . .

But he couldn't rely on God to bring the children home. He could rely only on himself, and his experience, and the gun he carried in the holster under his arm. He could rely only on good luck and solid planning.

Sharon pulled herself back and wiped her eyes. "I never do this."

"Do what?"

"Cry. Openly, in front of a stranger, like I

have with you. It seems like every time I've been around you, I've broken down. I don't want you to think this is the real me."

"Isn't it?" he asked perceptively. "You're not really a sweet, loving, feminine beauty who loves her children more than she loves herself?"

She smiled through her tears. "You're good, you know that?" She sat up straight and shook her head. "I don't know why I feel comfortable enough with you to bare my soul like this."

"Because you have to be a tough guy for the others in the house," he said.

"Oh, is that it?" she asked, sniffing. "Why would that be?"

"Well, you can't be vulnerable around your ex-husband. That would be too painful, given your history. You have to keep that wall up, for your own protection, I would imagine."

She cocked her head and gave him a narrow look. "Is that right, Dr. Freud?"

"Yes," he said with certainty. "And you can't let your guard down around Anne, because you don't want to feel her pain. Then you'd have to be compassionate toward her, and you need to hold onto your bitterness. That's a defense mechanism, too."

She stood up. "Oh, that's ridiculous.

You're forgetting that my daughter is in the house, too. Do I have deep-seated bitterness about her, too?"

"No. But around her you have to be strong, so she doesn't shrivel. I've seen you come close to cracking with Lynda Barrett, but you held back. I think it may have been because Ben and Anne and everybody were around."

"So I picked you by default? I could have fallen apart with any cop, right? It could have been Larry?"

"I'm cuter," Tony said.

She couldn't help smiling. "While I find your whole scenario to be a lot of baloney, I think you're selling yourself a little short. The fact is that you have a way about you. I've felt I could be myself with you. You've understood."

"Some of it, maybe," he said. "But I'm glad you've felt comfortable with me. Sit down."

Slowly, she sank back down with a giant sigh. He began to massage her shoulders, working out the tension that had hardened itself in her neck and upper back. "There are some things a woman just shouldn't have to face alone," he whispered.

Her face sobered again, and tears pushed to her eyes once more as she relaxed against his ministrations. It felt so good to be pampered, she thought, to be touched with gentle hands, to be spoken to in soft, masculine tones. Part of her wanted to curl up in the warmth and comfort of it, to hide in the strength of it. But another part of her told her it was a fantasy, because he was not a believer. They had little in common.

Larry came into the room, and started at the sight of them. "Excuse me," he said. "I didn't mean to interrupt anything."

"I was just massaging her shoulders," Tony said, letting her go. "No big deal."

Larry glared at him for a moment. "Can I have a word with you, Tony? In the dining room?"

"Sure." Tony stood up and winked at Sharon as he followed Larry out of the room.

Larry was fuming by the time they reached the dining room. "What in the world do you think you're doing?"

Tony looked around innocently. "What are you talking about?"

"Sitting in there with her like that, rubbing her shoulders . . ."

"She's tense and upset. I was trying to help"

"You were trying to seduce her, Tony," Larry whispered. "And I think that's reprehensible. Her child has been kidnapped, and she's not thinking straight. How could you even think of taking advantage of a woman in that state of mind?"

Tony couldn't believe his ears. He gaped at his partner as his face reddened. "You've got a lot of nerve. If I remember correctly, you're the one who gets involved with victims, not me. Check out that ring on your finger if you've forgotten!"

"I've never taken advantage of anyone, Tony. I don't hit them when they're down."

"No, but you've sure offered your shoulder for them to cry on. How come when I do it it's womanizing? Did you ever think for a minute that I might feel genuine compassion for her? That I might have some of the same instincts you've had, to comfort someone who's at her wit's end?"

"Don't get involved with the victims, Tony. That's what you've always told me."

"Yeah, and when's the last time you listened?" Tony turned around to start out of the room, but stopped at the door and turned back. "You make me sick, you know that? You think just because you're some big Christian, that your motives are pure and mine aren't. You think that if *you* comfort someone, it's because you're a good Samaritan, but if I do it, I'm trying to get them into bed." Furious, he shoved a chair under the table, then lowered his voice to a harsh whisper and went on.

"Well, here's a news flash for you, pal. I can feel the same compassion you can! And my motives can be just as pure! That woman in there is broken and hurting, and anyone who took advantage of her right now would be the scum of the earth in my book. I'm not going to let your paranoias keep me from giving her a little comfort when she needs it. Look around and tell me if there's anyone else in this house who can give it to her!"

Larry only stood there, his hands in his pockets, staring at Tony. After a moment, he looked down at his sneaker-clad feet. "All right, maybe I jumped to conclusions. This case has me in knots."

"Think how *she* feels," Tony said, and headed back to the den to find Sharon.

CHAPTER FORTY-ONE

Emily was wailing, and Christy put her arms around her and pressed her sister's face against her chest. The car was going over something rough, like railroad tracks, Christy thought as they took the jarring jolts in the trunk.

"Shhh, Emily," Christy whispered. "He told us to be quiet. He'll kill us if we're not."

"He's gonna kill us anyway," Emily cried against Christy's shirt. "Christy, Daddy's not coming, is he?"

"Yes, he will," Christy said. "And if he doesn't, my mommy will. She won't let anything happen to us."

"But your mommy doesn't like me," Emily moaned.

"Who says?"

"My mom. She says your mommy hates us. That's why she didn't want me going to church with you."

"My mommy doesn't hate anybody!" Christy said.

The car came to a stop, and quickly, Christy put her hand over Emily's mouth. "He's stopping. Emily, if you get another chance, run again. We'll go in different directions. He can't come after both of us."

"But I'm scared!" she whimpered. "I want to get out of here. I want to go home."

The car started rolling again, this time on gravel, and Christy shook her sister's shoulder. "Hush! You sound like a baby!"

"But he hurt my arm when he grabbed me, and I can't move in this stupid place."

"Where did he hurt your arm? Show me."

Emily turned over on her back and, in the darkness, took Christy's hand and ran it along her arm.

"Where does it hurt?"

"All over," Emily said. "It hurts bad."

"It's probably bruised. When Daddy comes, he can look at it."

"He's not gonna come, Christy," Emily said, her panicked voice rising again. "He can't find us, anyway. Maybe he's not even looking." Her crying grew louder, and Christy searched her brain for something to quiet her sister.

"Hush," she said again. "Just listen. I'm gonna teach you a song. It's a real hard song, so you have to listen hard. And I have to whisper so he won't hear."

"I don't want to sing," Emily whined.

"You have to," Christy said. "It'll help you stop crying. Now, listen. It's a song about the states. It goes, 'Alabama, Alaska,

Arizona, Arkansas . . .' Now, sing it with me. Whisper. 'Alabama, Alaska, Arizona, Arkansas . . .' "

"I don't want to," said Emily.

"Do it!" Christy insisted. " 'Alabama, Alaska . . .' "

" 'Arizona, Arkansas,' " Emily finished on a whisper.

"Good!" Christy said. "The next part is 'California, Colorado . . .' "

Emily was listening, trying now to sing along. The effort of learning the song took her mind off of the cramped quarters of the trunk, the merciless way the wheels bounced on the gravel or over potholes, or the fear of what the man would do with them when they stopped.

They were up to the state of Hawaii before the car finally stopped. They heard the man slam his car door and start back to the trunk.

CHAPTER FORTY-TWO

The phone rang, and everyone sprang to attention. In the kitchen, Ben put his hand on the phone and looked into the dining room, waiting for the signal. Tony nodded.

Ben picked up the phone. "Hello?"

"May I speak to Detective Danks, please?"

Everyone in the house let out a weary breath as Tony picked up and Ben hung up. "It's for them," Ben told Anne, who had run into the room with Bobby on her hip.

"He's never gonna call!" Anne said, kicking the chair. "When's he gonna call?"

Leaning wearily against the kitchen wall, Sharon watched silently.

Tony was on his feet, reaching for his coat, as he hung up. "We've had a break!" he shouted. "They found the car the girls were abducted in. It was left back at the rental company with the keys in it last night. It was paid for in advance with a credit card. You'll never guess whose name it was in."

"Whose?" Larry asked.

"Ben Robinson."

"*What?*" Ben asked. "I never left the house last night! Everyone saw me!"

"Don't panic. The guy who checked the

car out to him gave us a description, and it matches the kidnapper, *sans* hat and glasses. He's talking our artist through a composite sketch right now." He stopped at the door and turned back. "If this pans out, Ben, then we know how he got a gun in your name."

"But none of my credit cards were stolen. He would have needed it days before the murder to get a gun."

"He probably had counterfeit IDs and credit cards made. It happens."

Sharon let out a long-held breath. "Thank goodness, we're getting somewhere."

Tony started out the door. "Larry'll stay here in case the kidnapper calls."

"I'm going with you," Ben said.

"No! You have to stay here in case he calls! As soon as we get a composite done, I'll bring it back to you."

"Fax it!" Sharon said. "Maybe Ben will recognize the guy!" She ran to grab a piece of paper and a pen. "Here's my fax number. It'll come straight into the house."

Tony grabbed the number. "I'll fax it as soon as it's done. Larry'll call me if you guys hear anything." Not waiting for an answer, Tony rushed out.

Albert Gates was a forty-two-year-old car rental agent who hadn't seen such excitement in years. He would never have dreamed that the polished gentleman who had come in here a week ago to rent a car would turn out to be a kidnapper. He couldn't wait to tell the boys at the pool hall.

Albert was suddenly important, someone whose words the cops were hanging on, someone who could make a difference, and he was enjoying every minute of it. Any minute now, the news teams would probably show up.

"The car was really dirty when we got it back," he was saying as the policemen took notes and the artist tried to sketch the description he'd already given. "It looked like he'd been driving on dirt roads. Red clay all over the fender."

The detective who'd just bolted in asked, "Is it still on the car?"

"No," Albert said apologetically. "I had it washed first thing. That's what I always do, to get it ready to go out again."

"Where is the car?" Tony asked. "I want to see it."

"It's the blue Taurus parked by the curb just outside the door."

Tony started back out of the room. "How long before that composite is ready?"

"We're almost there," the artist said, still sketching.

"All right. I'll be right back."

Tony went outside and looked the car over. Just as Albert said, the car had been washed clean. One officer was inside it, dusting for prints, so he leaned in the window. "Find anything?"

"Yeah, I'm getting some prints. But this car's been rented out four times already this month. Plus the agents here and their clean-up staff have all been through it. These prints could be anybody's."

Tony sighed and looked in the backseat. Nothing had been left. He reached through the driver's side window and punched the button to release the trunk. He walked back there and pulled the trunk open.

Nothing.

He stood back and tried to think. Dirt roads. Red clay. He got down on his knees and looked under the car. Just as he'd hoped, it was still dirty. Red clumps of clay still clung to the belly of the car. He reached under and scratched some off.

There were only a few rural places left in St. Clair. Like so much of the Tampa Bay area, it had been overbuilt. He got up and sat back on his heels, examining the red clay on his fingers.

It could be from a building site, he thought, but that was doubtful. Most of the building sites were too visible. Besides that, a single lot wouldn't be large enough to get that much mud caked on the car. It had to be a rural area.

He thought of the few farms still remaining on the east side of St. Clair, and the cover of woods that surrounded some of them. Maybe the kidnapper had taken the children there.

Dusting his hands off, he went back inside to ask about the mileage. Maybe it would give him some clue as to whether he'd left town.

"His eyes were a very pale blue," Arthur was saying. "He was a nice-looking man. And his nose was a little different than what you've done. . . ."

The artist followed the descriptions and made the necessary changes on the sketch.

"Yeah, that's real close. Only I think his lips were thinner. And his eyebrows were thicker."

Tony waited, watching, as the face emerged.

"That's it," the man said finally. "I'm sure. That's what he looked like. Isn't it amazing that you can do that just from my description? I've always wondered how that worked."

Tony leaned over the desk. "You're sure?

Absolutely positive?"

"Oh, yeah," he said. "It's him."

"All right." Tony held out a hand. "Let me have it. Where's your fax machine?"

"Over there," Albert said, getting more excited. "Who are you faxing it to?"

"Somebody I hope can identify him," Tony said. He took the sketch and pulled the number out of his pocket. Quickly, he dialed Sharon's fax number, and fed the picture through.

The moment the fax machine rang in Sharon's study, they all dashed for it.

They watched, breath held, as the face slowly emerged.

Ben waited until the machine had cut the page, then inverted it and studied it. "Oh, it can't be . . ."

"You know him?" Sharon asked.

Anne pushed closer to see the picture, and her face paled. "Ben, is that . . . ?"

"Nelson Chamberlain," Ben said, turning back to Larry, who stood behind him. "It can't be him! He was Louis's best friend. He's the one who posted my bond. Why would he help get me out of jail if he's the one setting me up?"

"Because you have something he wants," Larry said. "You obviously couldn't give it to him from a jail cell."

"But he's been in England. He couldn't be the one —" He blew out a helpless breath. "He knows Emily. She knows him —"

"That's why she went with him!" Anne cried. "Ben, don't you see?"

"But I trusted him." He studied the face again. "It just doesn't make sense. If he's the one who planted all that evidence against me, he was hoping I'd take the fall for the murder. Why'd he post my bond? He stood to lose that money."

Larry picked up the phone and dialed the car agency. "That was a small investment compared to what he stands to make. And it threw us off his scent for a while." The phone was answered, and he asked for Tony.

He waited until Tony picked up. "It's Nelson Chamberlain," Larry said. "One of the art dealers we've been trying to get in touch with. He's supposed to have been in England."

Weakly, Ben lowered into a chair.

"Red clay?" Larry asked. "What do you make of that?"

Sharon stepped closer, hoping they were on to something.

"Yeah, that wouldn't hurt. We need to search his house, and any other property he owns here. Maybe it'll lead us to them."

Tony was just coming in when Larry's number rang. He snapped it up. "Yeah? All right, shoot. Okay, I'm on my way. Get somebody over here to relieve us in case the guy calls."

He grabbed his windbreaker and jumped up as he hung up the phone. "They found some property Chamberlain owns on the east side of town. It's a few acres of wooded area. I'll go over there to see if there's a building anywhere around there where he could have the kids. Then I'll check his house."

"I'm going with you!" Sharon cried.

This time, Tony knew they couldn't stop her.

"What if he calls?" Ben asked, practically chasing them to the door.

"Hopefully we'll get him before he has the chance!" Tony called back. "But if he does, just get his instructions. Play along, like you have what he wants." He saw the police car already turning into their driveway. "They're here. They know what to do if he calls."

Sharon followed Tony at a trot, and Anne ran out behind them. "Tony, Larry! I'm coming, too."

"No, it's not a good idea," Larry said.

"But my little girl could be out there!" Anne cried. "I have to be there when you find her! She'll need me!"

Sharon looked beseechingly at Tony. This time, she said, "Let her come."

He shrugged and got into the car. "All right, get in."

The ride to the other side of town was fifteen minutes or so. Sharon and Anne sat in the backseat, watching out the window, both of them tense and hopeful.

"Turn left here," Larry said. "Yeah, that's it. I think this is the edge of his property."

In the distance, Sharon heard a police siren. "Won't he hear us coming? Shouldn't they turn off the siren?"

Almost as if in answer to that, the siren hushed.

They drove up a long dirt road, and Sharon scanned the trees for any sign of a structure where the children could be. There were no buildings, no houses, only this red dirt road and the dense forest beside it.

"What's that?" Larry asked as they followed the dirt road around a cluster of trees.

Tony leaned forward. "A shed," he said. "And there are fresh tire tracks. Bingo!"

Sharon felt the blood running out of her face. The children couldn't be in there. Not in a four-by-six dirt shack out in the middle of nowhere!

"Stay here!" Tony ordered. "It doesn't look like he's here, but he could be. We'll look first."

Sharon nodded. Anne sat paralyzed, staring toward the shed as the men got out, wielding their guns, and surrounded the little building.

The men shouted something, but there was no reply.

They heard the door being kicked in, and both women jumped.

After a moment, Tony came back around the building, shaking his head.

"They're not there," Anne said, and started to cry.

Sharon, too, covered her face and tried to cope with the horror of it. She got out of the car, not knowing which way to go. "But the fresh tire tracks. It's his property, isn't it?"

Tony looked down at the tire tracks. "Somebody was here, all right. Maybe even today."

Larry came out of the little shed. "Hey, Tony. Come look at this!"

They all rushed to the door. "McDonald's bags," Larry said. "Two cups."

"They were here!" Sharon cried. "He locked them in this dark place? They must have been terrified!"

"Where are they now?" Anne almost screamed.

"It looks like they dug a hole under the wall."

Tony went back out and checked the other side. "Look, footprints," he said. "It looks like one of the kids may have gotten away."

Anne and Sharon stared down at the beloved little footprint. "It's Emily," Anne cried. "She had on tennis shoes."

"She's right," Sharon confirmed. "Christy was wearing loafers."

By now, the other cops were following the prints, trying to trace the steps of the child and the bigger steps of the man who had taken them.

Anne turned back to the woods, the direction the footsteps led. "She ran in there! She's still in there! I know it." She ran into the woods, unstoppable, calling, "Emily! Emily, it's Mommy! Honey, don't be afraid. Just tell us where you are!"

Sharon followed behind her, praying that Christy was with her. But there were no footsteps for Christy.

Frantic, Anne came to the drop-off and looked down into the gully where a stream of water ran. Had Emily tried to cross it?

Had she fallen in?

She turned back, looking with horror at Sharon. "Where *is* she? Where *is* she?"

She was beginning to tremble from her head to her feet, and Sharon began to cry with her. They weren't here, and there were only two possibilities. They had either been caught by the kidnapper and taken somewhere else, or they were at the bottom of that gully somewhere, washed downstream.

"Emily!" Anne screamed. "Emily! WHERE ARE YOU?"

Feeling the same anguish Anne felt, Sharon stood motionless, fragmenting piece by piece until there was nothing left of her control.

"They're not here!" Anne screamed. "Sharon, they're not here!"

Sharon took a step toward her and put her arms around the weeping woman. Anne fell against her, heaving with sobs. "If we'd just come earlier. We could have saved them. We could have saved them."

Sharon wept, too, clinging to Anne like a sister, knowing that she was the only other woman on the face of the earth who knew exactly how Sharon felt.

Tony stood back, deeply frustrated that this lead had led nowhere. Yet this picture, of two enemies embracing, touched him in a place that he rarely visited.

Larry came up behind him and saw the women. When Tony looked up at him, Larry saw that his eyes were moist. Neither of the men wanted to look at the other.

"He must have rented another car," Larry said quietly. "I sent the others to check out all the cars that have been rented from other rental car agencies in town. We're getting the sketch printed up, so they'll be taking copies with them. Soon enough we'll know what he's driving."

Tony touched the shoulders of both women to coax them apart. "We'd better get back to Sharon's. He probably doesn't know we know who he is, so he'll be calling soon. Come on, we need to go," he said.

Sobbing, they separated and slowly made their way back to the car.

CHAPTER FORTY-THREE

Nelson Chamberlain drove the streets of St. Clair, desperately seeking someplace else to hide the children. He couldn't take them back to the shed, not after they'd escaped from there once. His home was out of the question, since he was supposed to be out of town. He hadn't gone near his own house since before the murder. He couldn't take them to his hotel, for there was no way to get them inside without their being seen. Their pictures were posted everywhere, and he had no doubt that the St. Clair police were searching everywhere for them and the kidnapper who had abducted them. He hadn't even tried to threaten the Robinsons against involving the police — that would have been a fantasy. The police always got involved, whether overtly or covertly. The fact that they'd been camped in Sharon Robinson's home since the children disappeared was something he could watch and stay on top of.

But where should he take the children now? He couldn't leave them in the trunk all day. The fact was, even though he needed them for leverage to make Ben Robinson act, they were really more trouble than they were worth. He had counted on keeping them in the little shed until their father capitulated and handed over the painting, but the little brats had ruined that.

He saw a pay phone at a convenience store, and inched the car as close as he could so that the cord would reach inside the car. Inserting a quarter, he dialed the phone number of the Biltmore.

He asked for Boudreaux's room. When the clerk responded that Boudreaux had checked out, Nelson's heart crashed. He couldn't have left! Not without the painting!

He searched his pockets for the number of Boudreaux's museum in France, and inserted a fistful of quarters. He thought briefly about using the cellular phone he carried in his briefcase, but quickly thought better of it. If his name did ever come up as a suspect, it wouldn't do to have records on his cellular phone bill that showed he had made calls to Boudreaux, Ben Robinson, or anyone else that could incriminate him. Especially not when he was still supposed to be in England. No, he'd just have to stick with the pay phones.

A French woman answered, and he said, "Excuse me. My name is John Lieber, and I'm a friend of Monsieur Boudreaux's. I was to meet him here in St. Clair, but I'm afraid

319

I missed him. Do you have any word on where he might be?"

"Oui, Monsieur," she said. "Monsieur Boudreaux has a message for you. He has moved to Holiday Inn downtown Tampa and is using the name Passons."

"Very good, very good," Nelson said, breathless. "Excellent. I'll call him right away."

He hung up and breathed out a gigantic sigh of relief, inserted some more quarters, and dialed information. He got the number, dialed it, then asked to be connected with Eric Passons's room.

He listened through two rings. "Hello?"

"Hello, Eric, how are you?" It was his most professional business voice, and he knew Eric recognized him immediately.

"Not well," the Frenchman said. "Very disappointed."

His temples were perspiring, and he pulled a handkerchief out of his coat pocket and dabbed at them. "Eric, has something happened?"

"Oui," the man said. "Some American phoned my secretary earlier asking where I was. I feared being drawn into this . . . uh . . . investigation. I changed my name and location."

"That was wise," Nelson said. "I'm glad

you left the information for me." He paused. "Look, Eric, I can promise you that I'll have the painting by tomorrow morning. Surely you can understand how the circumstances of Dubose's death have complicated things."

Eric laughed sardonically. "Complicated things? After all this time, you still do not have the painting?"

"I know precisely where it is," Nelson countered, his face reddening. "But I don't have to tell you how delicate these matters are. I have to be very careful how and when I retrieve it. And then there's the matter of transporting it."

"You understand, do you not, that I have a buyer for it? The longer I make him wait, the less likely he is to buy it. I really must not wait any longer."

Nelson sat back hard on his seat. He could hear low, muffled voices in the trunk. The children were singing something. He looked around to make sure no one was close enough to hear it.

"Will you give me until morning, Eric? We both know that the wait will be worth it in the long run."

"Not if I am . . . how you say . . . arrested? The picture would be taken from me. And with the murder, and now the kidnapping of Ben Robinson's children, I must tell you I have grave reservations. Perhaps later, in a year or two, after the suspicions have died down."

"In a year or two I can guarantee I'll have another buyer. One who might even pay more than you're offering. Your buyer could hide it for a period of time, until he's comfortable. But unless you act now, someone else will profit from it."

That did make the man hesitate. "Very well, Monsieur Lieber. If I wait until morning, and the picture is delivered, I will proceed with our bargain. But if I do not have it by noon, I will be on my way back to LeMans."

"You'll have it by morning." Nelson cleared his throat and wiped his perspiring face again. "You do understand, now, that there will be some restoration involved? The painting has been rolled up since its theft —"

"Which often means there are cracks in the paint. I understand that, Monsieur Lieber. My price has allowed for that. But if it is an authentic Marazzio, and you do indeed deliver it to me, I am certain that it can be restored to its previous condition. Now, about this investigation."

The singing had stopped, and he heard them talking. Didn't they ever shut up? He revved his engine, hoping the noise would overpower the voices.

"I am concerned in my mind as to who killed Dubose." He hesitated, as if choosing his words carefully. "It has occurred to me that you may have been involved."

Nelson laughed too loudly. "Me? Why on earth would I be the one?"

"The money we've agreed upon is quite a lot of motive, would you not agree? Perhaps you wished to dispose of Dubose so that the money would not be divided."

"That's ludicrous," Nelson bit out. "This is a clean, painless, harmless deal. People do not murder over art."

"*Pardon,* my friend," Boudreaux said. "But there have been many murders over the last decades, precisely over art. Money is a powerful motivator."

Nelson laughed again. "I assure you that Dubose's death was as much a surprise to me as it was to anyone. He was a dear friend of mine. I don't know what I'll do without him."

"Indeed," Eric said, not convinced. "My . . . what you say . . . instincts . . . warn me to return to France."

"Then your instincts are wrong. This whole endeavor will make you a richer man," Nelson said. "I'm not a fool, Eric. I'm well aware that you could sell the painting for a third more than what you're paying me. There are museums in Italy that would sell entire roomfuls of art to raise the funds for this one picture. As for the murder and the kidnapping, I can assure you that they have nothing to do with this transaction. My theory is that Ben Robinson was involved in drug trafficking, and he was probably the real target for the murder — that is, if he didn't do it himself. Robinson is a very complex, dubious man. Very dishonest. A marvelous painter, and quite a gifted restorer. What he had going on outside of the gallery, I don't know. But I feel sure it will all come to light very soon. You'll see. And you'll be very glad you didn't miss the opportunity to find the most important piece of lost art this century."

"Do you think Robinson has any knowledge of this painting?"

"No," Nelson said, as if with certainty. "Not at all. It was very carefully hidden."

When he'd finally convinced Boudreaux to wait, he hung up the telephone and rolled his window back up. The children had grown quieter now, and he racked his brain to think of the location of a pay phone where he could call Ben Robinson and let him talk to at least one of the girls. That might remind him of the urgency here. But all of the pay phones were too public, and someone might see the child. Not only that, but one of them might do something unpredictable to call attention to herself. He couldn't take that chance.

Once again he thought longingly of his cellular, but it just wasn't worth the risk. He would wait until dark, and then take one of the children with him to make the call.

Until then, he had to find some place to put them.

A thought occurred to him as he drove across the Spanish Trail Bridge, out to the eastern edge of St. Clair, where there were still a few small farms and some old dilapidated buildings that were boarded up. There was one in particular he remembered seeing a couple of days ago on the way to his own property. An old abandoned store. That was just the place, he thought, and headed toward it.

The car cut off, and Emily clung to Christy in fear. "We've stopped, Christy!"

"Shhh. Just be quiet."

They heard his car door slam, and braced themselves. In a moment, they heard keys jangling at the back of the trunk, and suddenly the trunk came open, letting in a harsh flood of light that made them squint.

The two grimy little girls sat up and looked fearfully at their kidnapper.

He grabbed them each by one arm and bent down close to their ears. "If either one of you so much as breathes hard while I'm moving you, I'll throw you off the St. Clair pier into the Gulf and your parents won't find you until you wash up on shore — after the sharks are through with you."

Both children trembled and allowed him to move them out of the car.

As he herded them from the car toward the dilapidated building, Christy searched frantically, though quietly, for someone who might see them. But there was no one anywhere around.

He opened the door. This building was much bigger than the last one, and it had a concrete floor. He acted like this was the first time he had been here, and he left the front door open, providing light as he dragged them in.

"No, not here!" Emily cried. "It might have rats! Please! Not here! I want to go home! I want my daddy!"

Nelson Chamberlain squatted down in front of her, his big, threatening finger pointing at her nose. "What did I tell you about making a sound?"

She tried to keep her lips shut, but she began to cry, and the sound wouldn't be muffled easily.

"Mister, we need to go to the bathroom," Christy whispered. "Is there a bathroom here?"

That seemed to give him an idea, and he got back up, still holding each of them by their upper arms. "Up those stairs, and we'll see," he told them. "Come on now."

Emily was crying harder, biting her lip and trembling as they took each step. Some light shone in through a window that had been shot out about fifteen feet up, but it cast only enough light to show the degree of dust and filth that had accumulated since this place was last inhabited. Dead hanging plants covered with spiderwebs dangled from slimy, fungus-covered macramé hangers. The place might have been pretty once, but now it was a study in filth and decomposition.

The man nodded toward a door in the back corner of the dusty room. "There."

"No!" Emily cried again, but he jerked them toward it.

The door opened into Emily's worst nightmare. There was a filthy, cracked commode with only half a seat on it; warped and rotting boards made up the floor. The sink had long ago been torn off the wall, leaving a gaping hole that revealed rusted plumbing

— the perfect place for rats to lurk. Above it all, at least ten feet up, was another broken-out window too high for them to reach, and a dozen or so dead hanging plants just like the ones on the other side, with long, brown vines laced with spiderwebs that seemed to reach down and grab for them.

"Mister, can't you leave us your flashlight?" Christy asked.

"No. The dark will keep you from trying to find some way out again."

"But . . ." Christy's voice broke, and she started to cry, but she tried to keep her voice steady. As her mother had told her more than once, whining got you nowhere. "Those dead plants have spiders, and there are rats in that wall, I can hear them. Can't you? If we're in the dark and we hear something or . . . feel something . . ." She sobbed and reached for Emily's hand. Her sister was trembling so hard she could hardly hold it still. "We might scream by accident . . . And somebody might hear us. If you want us to stay quiet, we promise we will if you'll just give us the flashlight."

The man was quiet for a moment. "All right," he said finally. "The batteries won't last long, anyway."

He handed Christy the small flashlight. "Now, go on. Get in there."

"It stinks," Emily squealed. "I'm scared."

"Mister, couldn't we stay out here, in this room?" Christy asked, crying fully now. "Please . . . We promise not to make any noise . . ."

He thrust them in and shut the door behind them.

Christy and Emily hunkered in a corner with the flashlight illuminating the nightmarish sights around them. Outside the door, they could hear him moving things to bar them in, since he didn't have a lock.

Emily buried her face against Christy's chest, and tried not to cry loudly. But Christy was having trouble herself. Her fingers, still filthy from digging, were hurting from where they'd blistered and bled as they'd dug. She knew that sores needed to be cleaned to keep them from getting infected, but she suspected that that was just one more thing she had to worry about now. She wondered what Jenny was doing. She wondered if Mommy was worried, if she and Anne were fighting. She wondered if Daddy was looking for them.

They heard something in the wall, and Emily's voice went an octave higher, though she kept her mouth muffled against Christy's shirt. Christy shone her light toward the sound, hoping to frighten whatever it was away, but she squeezed her eyes shut to keep from seeing it herself.

"Pray," she whimpered. "Pray hard. Now."

Emily only trembled, and Christy knew she couldn't count on her to pray. She'd have to do it herself. "Dear God," she squeaked. "We're so scared."

"It doesn't work!" Emily cried. "It doesn't work, Christy! We tried, remember?"

"It does work," Christy said. "It has to. Mommy said it works."

"Then why didn't it work before? Why didn't Daddy find us?"

"He will," Christy sobbed. "I know he will. We just have to pray harder. Now, either pray with me, or be quiet."

Emily chose to be quiet as Christy started praying again.

CHAPTER FORTY-FOUR

Nelson Chamberlain needed a drink. For a while, he drove around near the abandoned store, making sure there was no reason for anyone to get close to the building where he had hidden the children. They wouldn't be discovered there, he decided finally. The building was too old and dilapidated, and those who drove past it daily would never notice that anything was different about the old building. The girls were stuck there until he went back to get them. Now all he had to do was decide what his next step would be.

He drove into town to a trendy bar called Steppin' Out and pulled into the parking lot as it filled up with happy hour traffic. The bar was popular this time of day, he thought with relief. He could blend in, and no one would notice him. He walked into the noisy room decorated with twenties memorabilia, found a seat at the bar, and ordered a scotch. It calmed him as it went down, and he told himself that things were going to work out after all. Yes, a lot had to fall into place, but the more he drank, the more confident he became.

The music seemed to be growing louder,

an unidentifiable blend of guitars and drums, drowned out by the chatter of the after-work crowd. He looked around, through the haze of cigarette smoke, at the silk suits and designer dresses, the perfectly coifed locks of young professional women, the moussed hair of lawyers and accountants and consultants of every kind. He was comfortable here, as he was in bars like it all over the world. In ways, it was his sanctuary, the place where he knew he could come at any time for sustenance or comfort. Even now, as he nursed his scotch, he felt that comfort seeping through him.

It would all work out. It had to. So much was at stake. He had held onto the painting for over ten years now, after daring to take it himself from a museum in Palermo. In Italy, the statute of limitations for art theft was ten years, so he was out of the woods as far as prosecution there was concerned. He'd finally decided a few months ago that it was time to begin searching for a buyer.

But it wasn't his style to do it himself. He liked to stay detached from the particulars of such exchanges, so that if any of his deals went sour, they couldn't be traced back to him. Dubose had been the perfect liaison. With his contacts in the art world, and his legitimate role as owner of several small galleries, he was in a good position to find a buyer. Of all the art thefts Nelson Chamberlain had been involved in, this was by far of the greatest value. It was the *coup de grace*, the one that would make world news — though his name would never be mentioned in connection with it. The fact that it would make him a fortune was enough.

But once the contact had been established, Dubose had gotten greedy. He had demanded half of what Chamberlain would be paid for the painting, though Dubose had not been involved in the theft in any way. Because Dubose already had the painting and because he needed Dubose to make the exchange with the buyer, Nelson reluctantly agreed — until he realized that Dubose was not being honest with him about the price the dealer was willing to pay. He was getting more for it than he had reported to Chamberlain, and was keeping the bigger portion for himself.

That was bad enough, but when Ben Robinson discovered the canvas, Chamberlain's concerns had grown even more inflamed. What kind of fool hid something worth millions in a wooden compartment of a cold, damp attic, where anyone could stumble upon it? There was nothing to do, he thought, except to get the middleman out of the way, and handle things himself. He had to do away with Dubose to ensure that his own interests weren't violated. What a shock, he reminded himself ruefully, after he'd gotten rid of Dubose, to discover that the painting wasn't where it was supposed to be.

There was no doubt in his mind that Ben Robinson had it; Ben was the only other person who had known that it was there. What he couldn't understand was why the man hadn't agreed to turn it over to him after the first phone call. Maybe the police were trying to make him play cat-and-mouse games with him to draw him out. He only hoped that taking his children had made Ben think better of it.

He heard a loud round of cackling laughter, and looked up to see a woman dressed in a tight red sweater and tight black jeans with four-inch heels, flirting with a group of men half her age. She was obviously in her fifties, yet here she was competing with women in their twenties.

"You are just too much!" she was saying in a deep Texas drawl to one of the men standing beside her. Her voice carried over the crowd, as if to draw attention to herself. "For heaven's sake, you have to eat!"

Was she hitting on that man who was

young enough to be her son? Chamberlain wondered, amused. There was no telling, he thought. He watched her as she pretended to pout, then pranced over to the bar, pushing between two patrons, and got the bartender's attention. "Excuse me. You over there. Yes, you."

The bartender finished mixing the drinks he was mixing, and leaned toward her. "Can I help you?"

"Doris Stevens here," she said, holding out her hand with inch-long fake nails. The man shook halfheartedly. "I came in here to see if you'd let me put these posters up of those little kidnapped girls." As she spoke, she dug through her huge purse, and brought out a few copies of the posters. "Bless their hearts, they're friends of mine. Little Chrissy and Judy. The sweetest little girls you ever laid eyes on. And now somebody's kidnapped them, and well, I'm doing everything in my power to help find them."

The bartender took one of the posters. "A $25,000 reward, huh?"

Doris waved that off. "Their safe return would be payment enough."

"But the reward money wouldn't hurt, would it?"

She shrugged. "I guess I'd take it, if they insisted. Heck, if I find those kids, I'd deserve the money. And how much is that really, when you consider the value of these two beautiful little girls? Can I put 'em up or what?"

"Sure. Go ahead."

She took the posters back and clicked around the room, tacking and taping the posters, while simultaneously flirting with anyone nearby.

Chamberlain felt his body go tense as the faces of the girls stared out at him. Quickly, he turned away. No one suspected him. His plan was flawless. He was going to get the painting tonight, and he'd be out of town before anyone knew what had hit them. This was one crime the police would never solve.

But the painting was the key, and he had to have it tonight. There simply was no choice. If he didn't deliver it to Eric by tomorrow, he would have to wait another year or two before he could safely approach another buyer. This time he had no middleman. His own hands had gotten dirty for the first time, but it was worth it — as long as the deal went through.

Chamberlain downed his drink and ordered another.

A telephone rang somewhere close to him, and he watched as the man sitting on the stool next to his reached into his coat pocket and withdrew a small cellular flip phone. He answered it, and Chamberlain listened, half-interested, as the man took care of business from his bar stool.

When he hung the phone up, the man set it on the counter next to his drink, and resumed reading the stock market page of the newspaper.

The waiter brought Chamberlain his scotch, and he sipped it as he listened to conversations around him. The news was playing on a television screen up in the corner of the room, and he saw the pictures of the two Robinson girls flash across it. He tried to listen to what was being said, but it was difficult over the voices in the crowd. Nothing new, he surmised from what he could hear. They didn't have any leads yet.

He smiled. The Keystone Kops of St. Clair, Florida, were going to have to get their act together if they wanted to figure him out.

Feeling almost an ecstatic energy after his two doubles and the news report that said virtually nothing, he glanced at the pay phone on the wall and wondered if he dared call Ben Robinson from here. No, he thought, someone might overhear. And if they traced the call, he might not be able to get out of the parking lot fast enough before the cops showed up to find him.

Besides, he really needed to get one of the kids to talk to their father tonight, just to drive home his point that time was running out. Robinson needed to know that he wasn't playing games. Either he turned over the painting tonight, or the kids were history.

The cellular phone rang again, and the man next to him snapped it up and answered. As he spoke, three of his colleagues came in the door, and he waved toward them. They clustered behind his stool, crowding Chamberlain as well. The man took care of the call, then hung up and set the phone back on the bar. He turned his back to Chamberlain to talk to his friends in a conspiratorial huddle.

Nelson stared at the cellular phone, unattended on the bar. He couldn't use his own cellular phone, for fear that the call would be traced, but he could use someone else's!

He looked up at the television, pretending to be absorbed in the news, and quickly put his hand over the flip phone. In one swift motion, he slipped it into his pocket. Quickly, he dropped a couple of bills onto the counter and headed for the door.

He was out of the parking lot when the phone rang again, and Chamberlain began to laugh. He wondered if the man had even noticed yet that his phone was missing. He let it ring as he headed for the building where the children were. After a moment, it stopped.

Another perfect twist in a perfect crime, he thought. All he had to do now was figure out where to have Ben Robinson drop the painting.

He headed for the old abandoned store, but before he reached the road heading toward it, a train stopped him. It was slowing, and he watched as boxcar after boxcar passed, traveling no faster than twenty miles per hour. Slow enough to jump on, retrieve something, and get back off a few miles down the tracks.

Perfect. If Robinson put the painting on a boxcar when it was stopped, Chamberlain could be waiting a significant distance down the tracks, jump on, then jump off, and no one would ever be able to catch him.

He picked up the flip phone, called information, and asked for the number of the railroad office. Quickly, he dialed it and asked for information about when the next few trains would come through today. He was told that one was due to come through around ten o'clock. It would remain for two hours to reload, then would depart again at 12:30.

Elated and anxious, he drove the rest of

the way to the abandoned store, dropped the phone into his coat pocket, got out of the car, and reached down on the seat for his other flashlight. Then, treading warily, he went back into the dark, eerie building, and headed up the stairs for the children.

He heard their voices as he came inside and went up the creaky steps. Rodents scurried and scratched in the walls and in the dark corners of the room. He kept the flashlight circle in front of him, hoping the sound of his shoes would frighten them away.

The voices hushed as they heard him coming. He reached the bathroom. Grunting from the effort, he moved aside the steel drum, old machinery, and a long, heavy bench that he'd used to block them in.

The door creaked as he pushed it open.

His light shone around the filthy bathroom, until the circle spotlighted the children, hunkered so tightly together that it was difficult to even tell that there were two of them. They both looked up at him with their grimy faces, and he remembered that he hadn't fed them since morning. He'd have to take care of that later.

"Are you going to let us out of here now, Mister?" the older one asked him in a weak, raspy voice.

"No, not yet," he said, trying not to look

at them. He pulled the phone out of his pocket. "We're going to make a phone call, to your father. I want you both to talk to him, to let him know you're okay. If you do as I say, he'll come to get you tonight, and you can go home with him. But if you don't do as I say, you'll never see him again."

"We'll do what you say," the little one, the escape artist, said as her eyes got as round as quarters.

"First, you don't tell him who I am. If you do, you'll be dead in five minutes, do you understand me?"

The older one frowned. "I don't know who you are, anyway."

But the little one, Emily, piped up. "I do. You're Mr. Chamberlain. You come to the gallery sometimes and buy my daddy's paintings."

He knew that the minute she went back to her father, she'd be able to tell who he was. He couldn't let that happen. Somehow, the children would just have to disappear from the whole equation. But he needed them long enough to manipulate Ben.

"I'm going to talk to him for a minute," he said, "and I want absolute silence. When I tell you, you can say hello to your father, and that's it. You tell him that you want him to hurry and get you home, but you don't say anything about where you are, or who I am, do you understand?"

"Yes, sir."

"All right. Now, quiet. If you do this right, I'll bring you some food."

Both children sat in the corner, still huddled in fear, as he dialed the number.

CHAPTER FORTY-FIVE

The phone rang, and Ben bolted for it. He waited until Tony gave him the signal from the other room. Sharon, Anne, and Jenny hurried into the dining room where they could hear the conversation.

"Hello?"

"Are you ready, Ben?" the voice asked.

Ben hesitated. "Yes."

"Then tonight's the night."

In the dining room, Tony waited on the other line for the tracing to be completed.

"What have you done with my daughters?"

"They're fine, Robinson. You're lucky I haven't killed the sniveling little brats."

"How do I know you haven't?" Ben asked, his voice cracking.

"Well, you can find out for yourself. It might even give you a little more incentive. You see, if you don't deliver the painting when and where I tell you, or if you try something foolish, or if you pull what you pulled at the airport, you'll never see these girls again."

"So help me, if you hurt them, I'll find you. I'll track you down if it takes the rest of my life . . ."

Chamberlain laughed. "I'm trembling, Robinson. Say hello to your daughter."

There was a muffled sound, a shifting, and then Emily's weak, high voice on the line. "Daddy?"

Anne dropped to a seat at the table in front of the reel-to-reel tape recorder from which she could hear her child's voice. In the kitchen, Ben pressed his face against the wall. "Emily, honey, are you all right?"

"Daddy, I want to go home," she squeaked. "Please, Daddy —"

The phone was jerked from her, and then Christy was on the line. Her lower, raspy voice sounded breathy, weak. "Daddy?"

"Christy." He caught his breath on a sob. "We're looking for you, honey. We're trying to get you back. Can you tell me where you are? Any clue? Just a word?"

She hesitated. "Daddy, we're scared. It's dark and old and there are rats . . ."

He closed his eyes. "Honey, we're going to find you. We're doing everything we can to get you back tonight. Just hold on, okay? Take care of each other."

The man's voice interrupted. "It's your choice, Robinson. Either deliver, or say good-bye."

"I'll deliver," Ben said, glancing back at Larry who was watching him as he listened to the conversation. "Just tell me where."

"Midnight," the man said. "At the railroad station. There will be a train leaving at 12:30. I'll have a red handkerchief hanging in the opening of one of the boxcars between the Franklin Street and the Alethea Street intersections. Find it and put the painting in there."

"What about the children?"

"When I have the picture, I'll let you know where they are. And I'll know it when I see it. If you try to deceive me, Robinson, the children are dead."

Tony shook his head, signaling to Ben.

"No," Ben said. "You'll have to do better than that. Why should I trust you?"

"Because you have no choice. Midnight, Robinson. I wouldn't be late, if I were you. And I mean it. If you try to put a fake past me, you'll regret it. I'll know at first glance."

The phone went dead, and Ben stood holding it for a moment, frowning and looking bewildered and despondent. He looked into the dining room where the two cops were still trying to find the source of the call, and he saw his wife slumped down on the table, sobbing into the circle of her arms. He hung up the phone and went toward her. Sharon was sitting at the table, her face in her hands, weeping.

Ben went to Anne and touched her hair. She looked up at him and fell into his arms. He held her for a long time, crying with her.

Tony longed to reach out, to at least touch Sharon's hand, to comfort her as Ben was comforting Anne. But he held himself back, waiting for Larry to finish the trace.

Larry was on another line, frowning, as though things weren't working out. "What do you mean? Well, can you get the cellular phone's number? It's got to be Chamberlain's."

He waited several more moments, then wilted. "All right. So some guy named Stu Miegel owns that phone. Find him and question him. Maybe he's working with Chamberlain." His frown got deeper. "You're kidding. Well, that's just great."

He slammed down the phone. "You're not gonna believe this."

Tony had heard most of it. "It's not his phone. So whose is it?"

"Some guy who reported his phone stolen out of a bar about half an hour ago."

Tony rubbed his forehead. "What bar?"

"Your stomping ground. Steppin' Out. He said he set it on the bar, and the next thing he knew, it was gone."

"Did anybody show him a picture of Chamberlain?"

"He said he didn't recognize him. But that he hadn't looked around much, so anybody could have been there."

Tony was getting tired. He rubbed his eyes and looked at Ben, huddled with his wife, still in tears. "All right, Ben. Looks like we're going to have to deliver something. He's got to be bluffing about recognizing it at first glance."

"He's not," Ben said. "If I know him, he'd have memorized every stroke."

"We'll just have to take that chance. Is there any place we can quickly get a close reproduction?"

Ben thought for a moment. "What did he say, exactly? Could you rewind it and let me hear?"

"Sure." Larry flicked a knob, rewound the tape, then played it again.

Ben tried hard to focus his thoughts, though the despair over his terrified daughters lingered in his mind.

He groaned and flopped back. "I can't believe Dubose was involved with him, but he must have been. That's why he was so anxious to convince me it was a fake. Then he fired me because he thought I would ruin the deal, or give his secret away! We've got to find that painting. Maybe I can give him another painting of the same size . . . and just hope it's dark enough that he can't see it right away until they catch him."

"No!" Sharon cried. "You can't do that! He'll kill them. He said so. And what if the police don't catch him? What if he gets away?"

"Sharon, what choice do we have?" Tony asked.

"I don't know!" she shouted. "But you have to do better than that!"

"She's right," Anne said.

Larry began to pace, trying to think. "Dubose moves the painting after Ben discovers it — and when Chamberlain doesn't find the painting where it's supposed to be, he naturally assumes that Ben has it."

"We've looked all over that gallery and Dubose's house."

"Could he have given it to a friend? Sent it to someone?"

Ben stared at the wall for a moment, remembering that last day, before Dubose had fired him. He had been preoccupied, busy with something.

"I remember him getting a package ready to mail out," Ben said. "It was a cylinder, about four feet long. I never thought of it then, but it could have been the Marazzio. *The Multitude* was four feet by seven feet."

Tony was practically on top of the table as

he leaned over to prod Ben. "How did he mail it? U.S. Post Office, Fedex?"

"UPS," Ben said. "He always sent things UPS." His breath was short as he looked hopefully at both of them. "I know where he kept those receipts. It'll have the address he mailed it to."

Tony grabbed his sport coat. "Let's go."

Ben followed him to the door, but Sharon ran after them. "What can I do? I can't just sit here."

"Pray," Larry said over his shoulder. "Pray hard."

CHAPTER FORTY-SIX

"Why hasn't Daddy come yet?" Emily's voice was hoarse and raspy. Her lips were getting dry from thirst. She sat close to Christy, afraid to venture too far across the floor, for fear of what might lurk there.

"He will. Didn't you hear the man? He said tonight. Daddy will come tonight."

"What if he can't find us?"

"He will. I know he will."

Hearing a scratching sound in the wall, they tensed up and huddled closer. "What's that?" Christy asked.

Emily covered her face with both hands, but then dropped them, for they hurt too badly. The dirt from all the digging was still caked on them, but the sores they'd rubbed while digging were beginning to get infected. Christy had the same problem, except that she also had that cut on her head and the scrapes on her back from where she'd been jerked out from under the wall in the shed.

"It's a rat, isn't it?" Emily asked weakly.

Christy began to cry quietly. "Let's pray some more," she said. "We have to pray that God will keep the rats from coming in here.

We have to tell him how scared we are."

Emily bowed her head without protest.

"Dear God," Christy whispered, "could you please help us, please, and make those rats go away so we won't be so scared? We would appreciate it very much."

The scratching sounded again, and Christy stomped her foot on the floor and let out a loud yell, hoping to frighten whatever it was away. The sound grew quiet.

"I scared it," she whispered.

They heard a sound up above them, another scratching sound, but this one came from the window at the very top of the bathroom, probably fifteen feet up.

"What's that?" Christy asked.

Emily turned on the flashlight and shone it up. The light was weak because the battery was running out. The faint circle of light hit the window, and they saw something standing on the sill looking down at them.

"It's a —"

Before Emily could get the words out, it leaped from the windowsill to the floor.

Both girls screamed and backed further against the corner. Something furry grazed Christy's leg, and she screamed louder, harder. Then they heard a sound they hadn't expected.

"Meeeeooouw."

Emily caught her breath and shone the light on the animal. "Christy, it's a cat. Look!"

Christy opened her eyes and began to laugh with relief at the big yellow tomcat. "A cat? Come here, kitty. You scared me."

It was a good-natured cat, and it rubbed against Christy's leg and allowed her to pick it up. "Look, Emily. He's so sweet."

Emily giggled and petted him. "How did he get in? It's so high up."

"There must be a tree outside the window. See? I told you God would answer our prayer."

"What?" Emily asked. "We didn't ask for a cat."

"No, but he'll scare the rats off. And he'll keep us company, so we won't be scared."

Emily thought about that for a moment. "Yeah. Maybe he'll stay here until Daddy comes to get us."

"He'll have to," Christy said. "He can't get back out until someone opens the door."

"He's a good answer to our prayers," Emily giggled, rubbing her face in the purring cat's fur. "How did God know?"

"God knows what we need better than we do," Christy said matter-of-factly. "My mommy always says that."

"Has God ever sent *her* a cat?"

"Nope. Other things. It's always something different."

"So praying really works?"

"It worked this time, didn't it?"

Emily smiled as the cat curled up on her lap and lay down, purring.

CHAPTER FORTY-SEVEN

Nelson Chamberlain sat on a small hill near the train tracks, waiting for the 10:30 train to arrive. As he sat, he wove the red handkerchief through his fingers, in and out, until it ran out. Then, unwinding it, he looked up the tracks.

He could hear the sound of a distant train, and knew that it would be here any moment. He would be glad. He didn't like getting dirty, and it wasn't his style to sit on a heap of dirt waiting for a train to come by. His work was clean — never-get-your-hands-dirty work. But lately, he'd been getting his hands dirty more and more. It made him uncomfortable, but he supposed it would all be worth it when he had exchanged the painting with Boudreaux and was on his way to England.

The train grew closer, and he saw its headlight coming up the tracks. He watched as it slowed and passed him, and he counted one boxcar after another. The train slowed even more, until it finally came to a halt, creaking and crawling by in front of him.

He sat still until he was sure it had stopped, then waited another ten minutes before picking out the car where he wanted the painting delivered. There was one not far from where he'd been sitting that had an open door and nothing inside. If they set the painting at the back right corner of that one, as he'd told them to, it would be safe.

He got to his feet, dusted off his pants, and checked to make sure no one was around who would find him suspicious. The first car, where the engineer sat, was around a curve, and no one in it was able to see him. He slipped his handkerchief over the pipe that held the door in place, and tied it there. Then he checked it, made sure it was secure and could be seen.

Jumping off the car, he looked up the tracks. He was going to drive his car to a place about two miles from here, then walk back up the tracks for about a mile. When the train left at 12:30, after Ben had delivered *The Multitude*, he would watch for that car, jump on it while the train was still moving slowly, get the painting, then jump off near where his car was parked.

It was foolproof. They could, of course, station cops on the train when Ben put the painting on board. But they wouldn't dare try to grab him before he told them where the children were. Besides that, they wouldn't know where his car was parked, and once he jumped off the train and fled, they'd never be able to find or identify him. He would be home free after he got the painting and was back in his car on the way to the airport, where Boudreaux had agreed to meet him.

He laughed as he went back over the hill to his car, which was parked behind some trees so it couldn't be seen. Just a couple more hours of this nightmare, and he would finally be on his way to ending it.

CHAPTER FORTY-EIGHT

The UPS receipts were exactly where Ben thought they would be. Louis Dubose had been a master organizer. He kept his office immaculate and always filed away everything so it wouldn't clutter his desk.

The receipt they were looking for was at the front of the file. Victoriously, Ben pulled it out. "It's got the address as clear as day."

Tony looked it over. "Are you sure this is the right item?"

"Positive," Ben said. "Look, he mailed it out of town, but not too far away . . . in St. Petersburg. And it says it's a cylinder. It has to be it," Ben said. "Come on. We don't have much time if we're going to get it."

They flew across St. Clair and into St. Pete, checking their map to find the street the address was on. When they found it, they saw that it was a small shop called "Home Address." A sign in the window said, "Open till 10." "It's only 9:30," Tony said. "Somebody's on our side."

Tony, Larry, and Ben burst in. "Do you have mailboxes here, where people can send things?"

"Yes," the man said, gesturing toward an

entire wall of postal boxes. "Do you need one?"

"No." Tony took out his badge and flashed it to the man. "We're with the St. Clair PD. We need to confiscate the contents of Suite 320."

"It's over there. It's really a post office box, but we call them suites so it'll make people look like they have offices. Do you have a warrant?"

"No," Tony said. "But there are two children in trouble right now, and if we take the time to get one, they could wind up dead."

"But I can't hand over some other guy's mail to you."

"Look, all we want is a cylinder that's in there. It's going to save the lives of this man's two little girls, who've been kidnapped. Now, you can make me go get a warrant, but you're coming with me, got that? I'll take you in and question you for a couple of days on how you knew the guy who rented this box, and what your connection might be in his murder and the kidnapping of the two little girls."

The man looked a little stunned, then quickly reached behind the counter for the key. "All right. Open it."

Tony took the key and opened it. "It's a

cylinder all right. Return address . . . your gallery."

Ben breathed out a sigh of relief. "Open it. Let's make sure it's the right painting."

Carefully, Tony opened the box and laid it on the counter, while the manager watched with awe. He opened the cylinder and slid out the contents.

"See?" Ben said. "That's it, all right." He took it with careful hands and unrolled it partially. "That's *The Multitude.*"

"All right," Larry said. "We don't have any more time to waste. We have to go by the station to report to the captain before we make the drop. We'll need a lot of help on this one."

They thanked the tense manager, then rushed out with the package and drove as fast as they could drive back to St. Clair.

CHAPTER FORTY-NINE

Anne put Bobby to bed, then sat for a while in the rocking chair, thinking about her lost child. Where were Emily and Christy? Would they really get them back tonight?

Unable to sit still, she got up and walked through the house. She headed up the stairs, wanting to go into Christy's room, wanting to be among the things Emily had left there. She stepped into the doorway and saw Sharon and Jenny sitting on the bed, huddled together. They both looked up at her.

"Excuse me," she said, wiping her tears. "I didn't know you were in here." She backed away, but Sharon stopped her.

"Anne, wait."

Anne looked at her questioningly.

"We were praying for the girls, and for Ben. Would you come pray with us?"

Anne hesitated. "I'm not much of a prayer. If there's a God, I'm not sure he'd listen to a prayer that came from me."

"The fact that he ever listens to any of us is just evidence of his grace," Sharon said. "Come on."

Anne came into the room and sat down on the edge of the bed.

"Turn around, Anne," Jenny said. "Let's sit in a circle and hold hands. Jesus said that whenever two or more of us are gathered in his name, he would be among us."

"Really?" Anne asked. "He said that?"

"Yes," Sharon said. "We've got to pray for them."

"Okay," Anne whispered.

Sharon reached for Anne's left hand and held it tightly. Jenny took the other, as mother and daughter held hands, as well. And Sharon began to pray.

CHAPTER FIFTY

Across town, in Lynda Barrett's home, she and Jake sat on the couch in her living room, with fifteen other friends of Sharon's from their church. Sharon hadn't been told they were meeting, but it didn't matter if she knew or not. Lynda had called them right after she'd gotten the call from Sharon about an exchange being made that night. Lynda had known there was only one thing to do.

The fifteen held hands and prayed one by one, earnestly, deeply . . .

It was Jake's turn, and he grew emotional as he began to speak. "Lord, you said that you would intercede for us, with groanings too deep for words . . . when we don't even know how to pray. I don't know where those little girls are, Lord, or what they need, or what danger they're in, but you can see them. You know. Lord, please take care of them. Surround them with your presence. Don't let any harm come to them. They're so little . . . And Ben . . . he's out there looking for that painting . . . something he can give to the man who has them. Let him find it, Lord. And I pray for the kidnapper, that you'll work on him, as well. Foil him, Lord.

Get in his way. Convict him . . . I know you can answer this prayer, Lord. I've seen your answers before. But not our will, but thine. You know what's best . . ."

And so the prayers went on into the night as the group interceded for the family that was in such turmoil.

CHAPTER FIFTY-ONE

The girls fell asleep with the cat lying across their laps. They were so exhausted that they didn't wake when the cat sprang up after hearing a scratching on the wall. His night eyes spotted the small head jerking out of the hole in the wall where the sink had been. He hissed, but the rat wasn't daunted.

His ears stretched tightly back on his head, teeth bared, back hunched, until the rat had quietly made its way out of the hole and down the wall. It had scarcely hit the floor when the cat attacked.

In seconds, the rat was dead, and the cat dragged it to the corner of the room, behind the rusty, stinking toilet. There he left it, and went back to the girls. Neither of them had stirred.

Satisfied, he crawled back onto their laps, began to purr again, and went back to sleep.

CHAPTER FIFTY-TWO

"All right," the captain, Sam Richter, said as he paced in front of the roomful of cops waiting to spring into action. "We have men posted at the tracks already, trying to catch him when he hangs the handkerchief. If we don't get him then, we go ahead as planned. Everybody has their posts. You know what to do. The minute Chamberlain has the painting, apprehend him and bring him in."

"No!" Tony stood up and looked back at his partner for help. "Captain, that would be a mistake. We have to give him time to call about the kids."

"What if he doesn't?" Sam asked. "What if he heads straight for the airport and leaves on the next plane out?"

"He has no incentive to call," one of the cops said. "If he has the painting, he's not going to be worried about those kids."

"Maybe he'll worry because he's a human being," Tony said. "Maybe he'll keep his end of the bargain."

"The man is a criminal," Larry said. "He doesn't care about keeping his word."

Tony swung around, gaping at him. "Whose side are you on, anyway?"

"I'm on the kids' side," Larry said. "And if we go ahead and collar him, maybe we can make some kind of deal to get him to tell us where they are."

"There's one thing you're all forgetting," the captain said. "One of those little girls knows the kidnapper. He won't want her to identify him. So we face the danger of his going back to kill the kids if we don't find him right away. That is, if he hasn't already done it."

"He hasn't," Tony said. "And if he goes back, that's great. He's led us to them. We can collar him there before he has the chance to do anything. I'm not suggesting letting him go, Captain. Just give him some time after he gets the painting. Let's see if he leads us to them or calls the parents to tell them where to look."

The captain sat down on the table at the front of the room, a deep frown clefting his forehead. "All right, then what if he doesn't call or lead us to them? How far do we follow him before we take him?"

"As far as we need to."

"Even as far as the airport?"

"Yes!" Tony said. "Maybe he would call from there."

"What if he gets on a plane?" the captain asked. "Do we allow that?"

"Yes!" Tony said. "We go with him. We watch. We alert authorities at the destination to be prepared to apprehend him the minute he gets off."

The captain gave him a disbelieving look. "And what would that serve?"

"It would give him time, Captain," Tony said, his face reddening with the effort of persuasion. "Time to make a call from the plane. It might be the only place he feels safe doing it. Think about it. He'll think he got away without being followed, if we do our job right. Then when the plane takes off, he'll be breathing easier, thinking he made a clean escape. At that point, it would be logical that he would call the family from the phone on the plane."

"You have to have a credit card to make a call from the air. You really think he's going to mess up and use his own credit card to make a call, when he's gone to such lengths to keep from being traced?"

"He's resourceful. We already know he has cards in at least two other names. But if we grab him before he talks, he may never tell us where the girls are."

"Oh, he'll tell us," the captain assured him. "I'll see to that."

"What are you gonna do? Beat it out of him? Let him scream police brutality and get the whole case dropped for civil rights violations?" Tony dropped back into his chair. "Look, all I know is that there's a family out there who is sick with worry over their children. We're down to the wire now. Let's not mess it up."

The captain took a few deep breaths and checked his watch. It was 11:30. They would need to leave in just a few minutes to make the drop by midnight. He looked from Larry to Tony, then strolled to the window of the conference room. Outside, Ben Robinson was sitting at Larry's desk, calling his family to tell them they'd found the painting. He was crying quietly.

The captain turned back around. "All right, guys. Here's what we're gonna do. We're gonna let him get the painting, let him make his escape. Whoever gets close enough can follow him, but keep in close contact with me. If he heads for the airport, you follow him in."

Tony breathed a sigh of relief. "Thank you, Captain."

"Wait a minute. I didn't finish. Follow him in, but do not let him get on a plane. Do you hear me? Do not let him get on the plane."

"Captain, that's a mistake —"

"Apprehend him before he boards. That

will give him ample time to call the family. If he hasn't done it by then, we have to assume that he's not going to. We'll play heck getting the information out of him if he's apprehended in Atlanta — or, worse yet, in Mexico City or someplace like that. We need to find those kids tonight."

Tony slammed a fist on the table and got up. "Captain —"

"You've got my orders, Danks. Don't violate them."

"Fine!" he said through his teeth, heading for the door. "I just hope those orders don't ruin any chance we have of finding those girls."

CHAPTER FIFTY-THREE

It was nearing midnight when Tony, Larry, and Ben went back to Sharon's house, and Ben got into his own car with the painting. The cops stationed at the track had not spotted Chamberlain or the handkerchief yet, so Larry and Tony would follow Ben at a distance to the railroad tracks, and let him look for the marking and deliver the painting to the boxcar alone. Even if they spotted Chamberlain hanging the handkerchief, the cops watching for him had been instructed not to act until he had the painting in his hand.

There were no lights in the area of the railroad tracks that Chamberlain had designated, so it was difficult for Tony and Larry to see from where their car was hidden. They quietly got out of the car. Tony watched with night glasses as Ben walked along the tracks, the multimillion-dollar painting in its cylinder clamped beneath his arm, looking for the boxcar with the red handkerchief.

"Has he found it yet?" Larry asked Tony.

Tony shook his head. "No. And I don't see it. What if he hasn't marked it yet?"

His voice stopped cold when he saw Ben hesitate. There, above the door of one of the cars, was a handkerchief flapping in the wind. Ben glanced in both directions, then jumped into the car. Seconds later, he jumped out and headed back to his car.

"All right," Tony said, shoving the night glasses back into their pouch on his belt. "If we cross here, and come up behind the train, it should be dark enough that we won't be seen. The painting's hidden on the eighth car from here. You take the one before it, number seven, and I'll take the one after it. That way we can watch from both sides."

They crossed the tracks, stepping over a joint between two boxcars, and ran hunched over, counting cars. Larry jumped into the one directly behind the marked car, and Tony ran ahead and quietly climbed into the one in front of it.

Crossing the car, he sat by the opposite door, his body carefully hidden in the darkness so that he would have a clear view when Chamberlain came to get the painting. He knew that other plain-clothed officers circled the area, searching for the rental car they had discovered Chamberlain was using now. They had been told not to act if they found it. Just to stay in place so they could follow it when he made his escape.

Tony sat so still that his muscles ached, and he wondered if Sharon was holding up all right. She was at her wit's end. And he couldn't blame her. If they messed up tonight, if the children weren't found, or if they were found but they weren't alive . . .

His heart ached, and he told himself that they just had to be alive. He couldn't accept the possibility that they weren't. He couldn't stand the thought of telling her.

Time ticked slowly by, and no one came for the painting. He began to wonder if they had put it in the wrong car, or if this was all just some kind of hoax, if maybe he was a sitting duck for Chamberlain's warped sense of humor.

He looked up at the sky. Stars sparkled with an uncanny brilliance, like white paint splattered in fine drops on a black canvas. But he doubted even Marazzio could have duplicated it tonight. It was beautiful, and seemed to testify to such peace, that for a moment he found himself wondering if there really was someone up there beyond it, keeping the earth spinning on its axis, the moon circling the planet, the stars suspended where they were.

For the first time, the thought that there was seemed infinitely more comforting than what he had always chosen to believe. If there wasn't a creator, and the earth spun on its own, and the moon controlled its own destiny, and the stars were all there by coincidence — then the world truly was formed out of chaos, and nothing could be predictable, and he might be sitting here wasting his time while those children were in grave danger.

Maybe there was a God. And maybe he did answer prayers. Intelligent people prayed to him all the time. They seemed to think he answered. Even when things went bad, as they had with Jake Stevens and Lynda Barrett, they still seemed to believe that God was with them, working it all out.

He knew that two cars back, Larry was probably praying right now. They were probably all praying. Sharon, Jenny, Lynda, Jake . . . everybody. Heck, they probably had all their church friends praying on one of those prayer chains. Half the town of St. Clair, at least those who believed, were probably praying for him and for this whole operation right now. It was a little intimidating. And a little comforting.

He looked up at the stars again. *God, is it you?* he asked silently. *Are you really there? Or are they just talking to air? I've never been one to accept things on faith. That's for dreamers. I'm a realist.*

Then why was he talking to the sky? he asked himself wryly.

The car bumped, and he sprang to attention, ready for something to happen. He looked outside, but saw no one, then wondered if he'd missed it. Had Chamberlain gotten into the car behind his, jarring the car?

But then the car bumped again, and he realized this time that the train was moving. Slowly, inch by inch, it began to creep down the tracks. He checked his watch and pushed the indiglo button to light the digital readout. It was 12:30. Time for the train to leave.

It was all right, though. He had thought of this. He and Larry had agreed that Chamberlain might be waiting a little way down the tracks, prepared to jump on the car to get the painting, then off before the train picked up any speed. It would be the most foolproof way to keep from getting caught.

He braced himself as the train began to move, the noise of the wheels grinding on the tracks sending up a roar. Knowing he wouldn't be heard now, he pulled out his walkie-talkie and turned it on. "We're moving, guys," he told the other cops who were stationed at various intervals at the intersections down the tracks. "Keep your eyes peeled."

The train moved about fifteen miles per hour down the track, slow to someone waiting to cross the tracks, but too fast for someone inside waiting to catch a killer. He stayed in the shadows, watching, watching, as they passed intersection after intersection.

Where was he? Surely he didn't plan to wait until the train's next stop. He must know they'd have people waiting there, ready to catch him. No, the best bet would be to come onto the train from some unpredictable place — anywhere but a stopping point — and jump off before anyone could be the wiser.

"Bingo." It was Larry's voice, and Tony held the walkie-talkie close to his ear.

"What?" he asked.

"I see a guy with a flashlight checking the boxcars," he said. "I think we've got our man."

Tony turned off the walkie-talkie and set it back in his coat pocket. Suddenly he saw the flashlight beam searching the doorway of his boxcar. It moved onto the next, then the beam cut off — no doubt because Chamberlain had seen the handkerchief.

He watched, carefully, as a man ran alongside the tracks, right next to his own car, looking back behind him for the perfect moment to jump on board. He fell behind, in pace with the marked car, then disappeared.

"He's on," Tony whispered to himself. He inched closer to the door, and waited for him to jump back off. Nothing happened.

What was he doing? Was he checking the painting before he got off? Was he going to ride it to the next town?

Before he had time to panic, he saw the man jump back out and roll down the bank of grass. Time for action.

Tony watched him run toward a dark intersection, where a black car was parked off the street, near some trees. He let the train take him a couple hundred feet down the tracks, then jumped off himself. Larry followed.

Tony pulled the walkie-talkie back out and turned it on. "He's at the tracks at Gray Street, guys. The black Ford Tempo."

"We see him," one of the cops radioed back.

"Don't let him see you. And keep me posted. Somebody pick Larry and me up at the same intersection in about three minutes."

Larry was dusting himself off. "Are you all right?"

"Yeah, no problem. I'm just hoping this guy has an ounce of compassion inside him.

Maybe he doesn't want to abandon those kids."

"Let's hope so." They jogged back up the track to the intersection Chamberlain had left moments ago.

A car was waiting there for them, and they drove back to the car they had parked miles up the track.

CHAPTER FIFTY-FOUR

Ben walked into the quiet house, wondering where everyone was. His hands were shaking, and he went to the cabinets, searching for something strong to drink. Something that would calm him and make the wait less excruciating.

But he found nothing, and he realized idly that Sharon never kept alcohol in the house. If ever there was a need for some, it was now. How was she coping without it?

He sat down at the table and pressed his fist against his mouth as tears came to his eyes. What had happened after he left? Had they gotten Chamberlain? Had he told them where the kids were?

He couldn't sit still, so he jumped up again and went through the house looking for his wife or his daughter — or even his ex. They weren't downstairs.

Had something happened to them? Anxious, he ran up the stairs. The world had gone haywire, and someone had come in here and taken them, too —

And then he heard voices in Christy's bedroom.

He hurried to the door. Inside, he saw his

daughter Jenny, with both of the mothers of his children, sitting in a circle on Christy's bed, holding hands and praying.

He sucked in a sob, and they all looked up.

"Daddy!" Jenny lunged off the bed. "Daddy, did you see him? Did you find Christy and Emily?"

"Not yet," he said, wiping his eyes. She pulled him to the bed and he sat down next to Anne, who put her arms around him and dropped her forehead against his shoulder. "I delivered the painting. They . . . they told me to come home and wait for him to call and tell us where they are."

He felt himself losing control even as he spoke, and he collapsed against his wife and broke down completely. She got on her knees on the bed and held him, and Sharon sat back and watched her former adversary comfort the man who used to be her husband.

And it was all right.

"We were praying, Ben," Sharon whispered, reaching for his hand. "We have to keep praying. There's a phone in here. We'll hear if he calls."

He nodded, unable to speak, and kept leaning against his wife as they began to pray again.

CHAPTER FIFTY-FIVE

Nelson Chamberlain navigated the back roads of St. Clair, making his way to the interstate where he could head for the Tampa Airport. So far, he saw no one following him, and he laughed out loud. He had gotten away with it.

He patted the long cylinder on the seat next to him. He had already checked it, back in the boxcar by flashlight, so he knew that it was just what he'd expected — *The Multitude*, a priceless masterpiece by one of the greatest Italian painters who'd ever lived.

He reached into the box on the floor. There was a fake mustache and goatee, tinted glasses, and a black fedora. As he drove, he fit the mustache above his lip, pressed the adhesive tightly, then applied the goatee. He saved the glasses and hat until he was ready to get out. The garment bag sat in the backseat. When he got to the airport, where he'd told Boudreaux to meet him, all he would have to do is slip the long tube into the garment bag, make the exchange with Boudreaux, and get on the next flight to England. Boudreaux would head back to France. No one would find the children where he'd left them, and they would probably starve to death. But that was just as well. He couldn't risk having them identify him and ruin what was turning out to be the perfect crime.

CHAPTER FIFTY-SIX

"What have you got, guys? Anything yet?" Larry held the walkie-talkie close to his ear as Tony drove.

"Nothing," John Hampton answered. "He's headed for the airport so fast I'm afraid the Tampa police are gonna pull him over."

"All right. We're on our way there now. If he stops to make the call, don't let him see you."

He looked at Tony as he took the ramp onto the interstate. Tony looked as tense as he'd ever seen him. "What do you think? Will he call?"

"He has to," Tony said.

CHAPTER FIFTY-SEVEN

The pain in Christy's hands woke her, and she looked down at them, barely able to see them in the darkness. They were swollen and still grimy, and the open sores from where she'd rubbed the skin off were wet and painful. Besides that, she didn't feel good. She had a bad headache, and her back was aching. And her throat burned with thirst.

She moved the cat off her lap and got on all fours to crawl to the broken pipes where the sink had been. Maybe there was a leak there. Maybe something a little wet, that she could catch on her tongue . . .

Her hand grazed something hairy, and she jumped back with a scream.

Emily jumped up. "What is it? What's wrong, Christy?"

Christy pressed back against the wall and felt around for the flashlight. Her fingers were almost in too much pain to turn the switch on, but she managed. "Over there, in the corner," she cried. "I can't look! Look and see what it is."

Emily took the flashlight, wincing as she moved the circle of light slowly across the floor. When she saw the dead rat, she yelped.

"What?" Christy asked. "What is it?"

"A rat!" Emily cried.

The cat, awakened by all the commotion, pranced over to the rat and picked it up, demonstrating that it was dead. Then he dropped it back in the corner.

"He killed it! It's dead," Christy said, still crying.

"I don't want to look anymore," Emily said weakly. She shone the flashlight on her hands. Hers, too, were oozing and swollen and grimy. "My hands hurt."

"Mine, too."

"Are they 'fected? Mommy says if you don't clean a sore, it'll get 'fected."

"I think so," Christy said.

"What will happen? What does that mean?"

"I don't know," Christy said. "All I know is it hurts. I want to get out of here. I want to go home."

They started to cry harder. Finally, Emily asked, "When do you think Daddy will come? He said tonight. He promised."

"Maybe he couldn't keep his promise."

"But Mr. Chamberlain said he would kill us if Daddy didn't do what he wanted. Do you think he's gonna kill us tonight?"

Christy thought that over for a moment. Her first instinct was to say no, that he wasn't going to kill them, but then she realized that it could be likely. He hadn't fed them all day or brought them anything to drink. He had left them here with the rats. Why wouldn't a man like that kill them?

"I wish we had a phone," Emily said matter-of-factly. "I'd call 911."

"I wish we had a ladder," Christy said. "I'd climb out that window up there."

The cat purred and rubbed up against Christy. "Well, we have a cat. And we're together. When he put me in that trunk by myself when you ran away, I was scared I'd be alone."

Emily whimpered, laying her head against Christy's shoulder. "Do you think Mommy and Daddy know we haven't eaten? Do you think they know he might kill us?"

"They know," Christy whispered. "They just can't find us."

The cat purred and snuggled deeper into their laps.

"I wish I remembered that story," Emily whispered.

"What story?"

"The one your mom told us that night. About Beth."

"Beth and her tree cottage?" Christy

asked. "You don't have to remember. You just have to make it up. I'll tell it to you. You can help."

"Okay," Emily said.

"Once upon a time, a mean man came and stole Beth out of her tree house."

"And he put her in a dark, scary place," Emily added quietly.

"But Beth was very brave. And she was smart. Real smart."

"Could she read when she was four?" Emily asked on a weak whisper.

"Yes. And she knew that song with all the states."

"What happened to her?" Emily asked.

"Well, she watched and waited, and found a way to escape."

"What way?" Emily asked without much hope.

"There was a secret door in the dark place," Christy said. "A secret door that only the nice people could see. The bad man couldn't see it at all. And at first she didn't see it, because she was too upset."

"But then she saw it?" Emily whispered.

"Yes," Christy said. "And she tiptoed to it. But it needed a key to open it. And she didn't know where the key was."

"What did she do?"

Christy was getting sleepy even as she

spoke. She yawned. "I don't know. I need to think about it."

Emily didn't answer, and Christy saw that her eyes had closed. Christy rested her head against the wall and surrendered to sweet, merciful sleep. Her last thought before drifting off was, *God, please help Beth find the key.*

CHAPTER FIFTY-EIGHT

The portable light on their dashboard flashed as Tony drove at breakneck speed to the Tampa Airport. He didn't want to pass Chamberlain along the way, so he'd chosen an alternate route. Larry was on the radio with the cops who were tailing Chamberlain.

"Where are you now?"

"Nearing the airport exit," they said. "So far, nothing. There's no cellular antenna on his car. Could he be using a flip phone or something to call them?"

"No," Larry said. "I checked. They haven't heard anything yet. Just don't lose him, and don't let him see you. Let him think he's home free. Remember: There are two little girls whose lives depend on us."

CHAPTER FIFTY-NINE

Nelson Chamberlain pulled off the exit ramp of the interstate and headed toward the airport. Almost there.

He turned toward the rental car return. His first instinct, to abandon the car at the curb of the Delta terminal, had been a bad idea. As far as he knew, they hadn't yet traced this crime to him. Even though he'd rented this car under the name John Lieber, he didn't want any suspicions to arise that Lieber might not be who he said he was.

Someone met him at the parking lot as he pulled his car in. "Can I help you, sir?"

"Yeah," Chamberlain said, jumping out of the car and grabbing the garment bag. "I'm late for my flight. Could you take care of this?"

"No sir. You have to go inside."

"I can't!" He reached into his pocket and pulled out a hundred-dollar bill. "This should cover whatever I might still owe. Just take care of it, and you can keep the rest."

The man hesitated. "Well, all right. The shuttle to the terminal is right over there. It's almost ready to leave."

Chamberlain leaped onto the shuttle.

"Delta," he told the driver. "And hurry."

The other two passengers on the shuttle gave him indolent glances, then turned their gazes out the window. The shuttle started to leave.

"Wait!" Two men outside yelled at the bus driver, and he stopped.

They jumped on, breathless. "We almost missed you. Thanks for waiting."

One of them slid his duffel bag under the seat and sat next to Chamberlain as the shuttle started to leave; the other sat across from him, a garment bag slung over his shoulder.

Chamberlain dug his ticket out of his coat pocket and looked down to make sure that he wasn't late for his meeting with Boudreaux, and that he still had enough time to make the flight.

"What terminal?" the driver asked.

"Delta," Chamberlain said.

"Same here," one of the two men called out.

CHAPTER SIXTY

"So where is he now?" Larry asked via radio as he and Tony approached the airport and took the ramp heading for the terminals.

"On the rental car shuttle," a cop said. "Nick and John are on there with him. They're plain-clothed, so he won't know who they are."

"Good going," Larry said. "We're almost at the terminals now. Any idea which one he's headed for?"

"Not yet," the cop said. "But we'll have all of them covered. We have a couple of guys going over the rental car as we speak. Maybe we'll find some clues there."

Tony pulled over to wait for the rental car shuttle to come around. Moments later, it passed them and stopped at American. One passenger got off. Then it went a few feet to the TWA terminal. Another passenger got off.

"They're stopping at Delta," Larry said into the radio seconds later. "Three men are getting off. Yep. John and Nick are two of them. The other one doesn't look like him, but it's got to be. There's nobody else on the bus. He's wearing a black mustache and a goatee, a hat, and tinted glasses. Carrying a garment bag over his shoulder. Give him a chance to check in and make the call. He still might do it."

Abandoning their car, they both followed through the door where Chamberlain had gone. They saw the man up ahead, closely followed by the two cops.

"Come on," Tony whispered. "Go to the pay phone. Make the call."

But the man headed, instead, toward the gate where his plane would soon be boarding. He checked in at the desk, and they all waited from a distance to see if he'd still turn and make that call. Instead, he turned and, still carrying the garment bag over his shoulder, went into a bar several yards down. He hesitated at the doorway, looked around, then approached a well-dressed man sitting at the back in a booth by himself.

Larry and Tony watched as the other man stood up, and the two shook hands. Chamberlain slipped into the booth, and for a moment, they could only see the back of his head.

"All right," Tony told Larry. "This must be the buyer for the painting. Let's just hang back and take it easy. If we play our cards right, we'll kill two birds with one stone.

We'll get him *and* the buyer."

They waited as seconds ticked off, and as the time grew closer for Chamberlain's plane to take off.

CHAPTER SIXTY-ONE

In the booth at the back of the bar, where they were hidden by two half-walls with planters full of greenery, Chamberlain unzipped the bag, pulled out the cylinder, and handed the awkward package across the table to Boudreaux. The man's eyes were huge and awestruck as he carefully removed the contents. The canvas covered the width of the table; unrolled, it extended two feet beyond the edge. Chamberlain helped him hold it uncurled as Boudreaux gazed down at *The Multitude.*

"It's magnificent," Boudreaux said, breathless. "Just as I remember it." He was beginning to perspire, and he pulled a handkerchief out of his pocket and wiped his forehead.

"Where's the money?" Chamberlain asked.

"Fifteen million," Boudreaux told him. "It is safely in a bank account in Switzerland. The account was opened under the name John Lieber." He pulled an envelope out of his breast pocket. "All of the necessary documents are here. In fact, if you wish to call the bank to make sure the funds are there —" He checked his watch. "I believe you would have no problem."

Chamberlain pulled the documents out and studied them. "Yes, I would like to call."

"All right," Boudreaux said, carefully holding the rolled canvas. "Here is the security code for that account, as well as the account number. The telephone number is on the front of the document."

"Stay here," Chamberlain said. He got up and asked the bartender if he could use his phone to make a credit card call. The man slid the phone across the counter.

CHAPTER SIXTY-TWO

From outside the restaurant, Tony watched Chamberlain pick up the phone. "He's calling!"

"Maybe," Larry agreed. "But we can't apprehend him until we've confirmed it. I'll go call our guys over at the Robinson's and make sure that's who he's talking to."

"All right," Tony said. "Meanwhile, I'm going to get as close as I can. He doesn't know me. Let me know the second you have confirmation, and tell all the others to stand by."

Tony couldn't get close enough to hear the telephone conversation, but he found a place at a table that Chamberlain would have to pass on his way out of the bar. He sat down and strained to hear, but the classical music playing over the sound system was too loud, and Chamberlain was turned away from him.

Let him tell them, he prayed without even realizing it.

He was on the phone longer than Tony would have imagined, but Tony sat patiently, waiting for him to finish. He saw the man turn back toward the phone, as if preparing to hang up, and Tony slipped his hand under his sport coat, ready to draw his gun.

Chamberlain hung up and turned back to the table. The other man rose again, shook his hand, and slipped the painting back into the garment bag.

Tony began to sweat. Where was Larry? It was the perfect time, the perfect place to arrest both men without drawing undue attention. If they got out of the restaurant, it would make everything more difficult.

Chamberlain checked his watch. Then he paid his bill with the credit card that probably had Ben Robinson's or John Lieber's name on it so there would still be no trace that Chamberlain had ever returned from London.

Tony got up and glanced out into the corridor, where people hurried past. Sweat began to trickle down his temples.

And then he saw Larry rush up to the doorway of the place, shaking his head and mouthing, "No."

Tony gaped at him. "No?" he mouthed back.

Chamberlain started out of the restaurant, and Tony had no choice but to follow him. Other plain-clothed cops were coming in with their eyes on Boudreaux, prepared to arrest him and confiscate the painting as soon as Chamberlain was gone.

Tony followed him through the crowds, only feet behind him. Larry caught up with him.

"What's the story?" Tony demanded in a low voice.

"He didn't call. They haven't heard from him."

Tony let a curse fly under his breath. "I still say he's going to wait until he's on the plane."

"We've got to get him *before* he gets on the plane, Tony. We have no choice. You know our orders."

Tony saw Chamberlain heading for the Delta concourse, and he hurried to stay close behind him. Chamberlain was hurrying — almost running, and the faster he went, the more people seemed to gravitate between them. Tony broke into a run, bumped into a man, and almost knocked him down. He didn't stop, just kept pushing on, no longer depending on Larry or John or Nick or any of the others who waited for his signal.

As if he sensed he was being followed, Chamberlain zigzagged through people, trying to blend. At Gate 16, the flight was already boarding, and Chamberlain shot up to the flight attendant taking the tickets.

Tony bolted forward, grabbed the man, and flung him back against the wall. "Where are they? Where did you leave them?"

Chamberlain was visibly shocked. Had this guy really thought he'd get away with it? Tony wondered. "What?" Chamberlain asked.

"Where are they?" Tony screamed.

"I don't know what you're talking about," Chamberlain bit out.

"Where are the girls, Chamberlain?" Tony's eyes stung as he took the man by the collar and shoved him again. "The ones you kidnapped?"

"I didn't kidnap anyone."

Tony flung him into the wall, face first, then ripped his goatee off and threw it down. Getting a handful of his hair, he asked, *"Where are the children?"*

Chamberlain closed his eyes. "I don't know. I had nothing to do with any children."

Tony slammed Chamberlain's face into the wall again, then Larry pulled him off. "OK, Tony, get a grip!"

"Where are they?" Tony yelled. *"What did you do with them, slimeball!"*

But it was no use. Chamberlain wasn't talking.

"Read him his rights," Larry said to the other cops as he tried to calm Tony. "We're gonna go get some air. We'll meet you back at the station."

CHAPTER SIXTY-THREE

"Where are the children?" Tony Danks's question was posed with more calculated calmness now as he stood over the table where Nelson Chamberlain sat in the interrogation room of the St. Clair Police Department. But the look on his face belied that calm tone. He looked like a man who could rip Chamberlain's head off with his bare hands.

Larry sat across from Chamberlain, playing the good-guy to Tony's bad-guy routine. But tonight, Tony's behavior was no act. "Calm down, Tony," Larry said in a quieter voice. "Let the man talk."

But Chamberlain wasn't interested in talking. He studied his well-groomed fingernails, leaned back, crossed his ankle over his knee, and didn't say a word.

Larry tried again. "Look, it's not going to do you any good to leave those kids out there all alone. The jig's up, Chamberlain. You've been caught. Tell us where to find the kids, and the DA might show some leniency."

Chamberlain breathed a sardonic laugh. "I'm charged with murder, kidnapping, and theft. Do you honestly think they're just going to let me go if I talk? My reputation is already ruined. The way you Keystone Kops arrested me right in public in the airport, it's guaranteed to be all over the news by morning. It might even be grounds for a lawsuit after I'm acquitted. Defamation of character."

"You bet I'll defame your character," Tony bit out. "CNN has been following the kidnapping. They're right outside this office door as we speak, waiting to get a shot of the monster they've been speculating about."

Larry gestured for Tony to calm down again. "Why won't you tell us?" he asked. "Those kids are innocent. They haven't done anything."

"Why won't I talk?" Chamberlain asked flippantly. "Because I don't know anything about a kidnapping. This is all a very stupid mistake."

Tony kicked the chair next to Larry. The sound made Chamberlain jump, and when Tony grabbed Chamberlain's collar and pulled him face-to-face, he dropped his flippant look. "You had the painting, Chamberlain. The painting that you exchanged for information about the kids. We know you know where they are."

"I told you. I don't know anything."

All three men were starting to sweat. Tony

let the man go, and he jerked free and straightened his shirt, which was dirty from his roll down the hill after he jumped out of the train.

Larry leaned forward on the table and fixed his eyes on Chamberlain's. "Are they dead or alive?"

"I'm not saying anything else until I've got a lawyer sitting beside me."

Tony snapped. In one swift motion, he grabbed Chamberlain and threw him back against the wall, knocking his chair over.

"You're not in control here, Chamberlain! You got that? You're not calling the shots here. You have a choice. Either you talk, or I'll see to it that that well-groomed profile of yours is drastically altered. You like art, Chamberlain? You're gonna need an artist to repair your face when I get through with you."

"Where are the kids?" Larry asked again, louder.

Chamberlain closed his eyes but didn't answer. Tony flung him a few feet, letting him drop to the floor. "I've had it with this low-life. I'm throwing the book at him. And I'm locking him in the old wing. Let him sit in the dark, in the damp for a while, and see if he can remember where he put those kids."

Larry looked alarmed. "Tony, that wing is

condemned. It's infested with rats. Captain told us not to put any more prisoners there."

Chamberlain looked up at them, wide-eyed, from his position on the floor. "I want a lawyer. Now."

"You've already called one," Tony said. "It's not my fault he's out-of-pocket. Guess your luck is just going bad." He jerked him back up off the floor and pulled him toward the door. "I'll get him processed. That's when they strip you down, Nelson, old boy, and they search you real thoroughly. And then they give you some nice prison duds. You'll like them. 'Course that bright orange seems to attract the rats, rather than repel them. But you don't have a problem with that, do you?"

Chamberlain was sweating heavily now, and trembling slightly.

Larry stood up and stopped them at the door. "Tony, let me talk to him a minute. Just the two of us. You go outside and calm down."

Tony paused a moment, then finally agreed. He shoved Chamberlain back in, and slammed the door as he stormed out.

"Anything?" the captain asked, coming out of his office into the hallway.

"Nothing yet," Tony said. He rushed around to the two-way mirror and watched as Larry kindly told Chamberlain to sit back down. He asked him if he was thirsty, then poured him some water, and waited quietly while he drank.

The captain joined Tony at the window. "So you played the insane cop about to snap and tear into him?"

Tony nodded without taking his eyes off of the criminal. "Only it wasn't an act."

Chamberlain drooped over the table, raking his hands through his short-cropped hair. "Tony's a little high-strung," Larry said in a quiet, soothing voice. "He sometimes flies off the handle. I've seen him do worse than that to a suspect before. He just loses it, somehow, and he doesn't care what the rules are, or what kind of trouble he might get into. He has a one-track mind. I apologize for his behavior."

Tony couldn't help his slight grin as the captain chuckled.

"I'm not sure I can keep him from doing any of what he threatened, though, and just between you and me, he can be pretty tough. One suspect reported him from the hospital, and Internal Affairs got hold of it —"

"Hospital?" Chamberlain asked.

Larry paused and nodded. "Yeah. It was real ugly. Anyway, I'd hate to have you be another statistic, when all you'd have to do is just come clean. Keeping those kids' hiding place secret is not going to help you at all. It's only going to hurt you."

"I'm not going to prison for kidnapping."

"Even without the kidnapping, we have murder. It's a cut-and-dried case, Chamberlain. You could get the chair for that. But if you cooperate and let us know where Christy and Emily are, maybe the judge will go easier on you. Maybe he'd even let you out on bond."

"Where's the painting?" Chamberlain asked. "What did you do with it?"

"It's being tagged as evidence."

"It's priceless, you know. And I own it. When they find me innocent, it will be returned to me, won't it?"

"Certainly. As long as we can verify that it wasn't a stolen painting, and that you indeed have proof of ownership."

Chamberlain didn't answer.

"So tell us where they are, Chamberlain. Tell me where the kids are."

"I don't know where they are. I had nothing to do with their kidnapping."

"So you're not going to tell us? You're going to leave them there? Let them die before their parents can find them? What kind of man are you?"

Chamberlain was silent.

"Did you feed them, Chamberlain? Have you taken care of them? They're only five and six years old. Did you hurt them in any way?"

Chamberlain was mute as he stared back at Larry.

Tony moaned. They weren't getting anywhere with this guy. It was going to be a long night.

CHAPTER SIXTY-FOUR

It was almost morning when Tony made his way back to Sharon's house. There was no real need for him to be there anymore. They had their kidnapper, and didn't expect any more ransom calls. Larry had gone home to shower and have breakfast with his wife. But the fact that those children were still out there made it impossible for Tony to relax.

He knocked lightly on the door to the kitchen, and it was quickly opened. Lynda Barrett stood there, looking as tired as he did. "Tony. Any word?"

He shook his head. "He won't talk. I've tried everything. Boudreaux doesn't know anything about the kids. My gut tells me that Chamberlain acted alone, but he won't tell us a thing." She ushered him in. Jake was leaning against the counter next to Ben, and Sharon sat listlessly at the table, her eyes swollen from tears and exhaustion.

"He wouldn't tell you *anything?*" Sharon asked, looking up at him. "Are they alive? Are they with anyone? Are they being taken care of?"

"They said there were rats there and that it was dark!" Anne blurted from the doorway. "It didn't sound like anyone was with them. They're all alone, and he's going to let them die there!"

Sharon got up and set her hands on Tony's shoulders. "Tony, we've got to find them," she said, her voice pleading. "We can't just leave them there. You've got to help us."

He nodded. "I was thinking. Maybe it's time to call a press conference. We need to get the whole community involved. Maybe somebody knows something."

"Good idea," Lynda said. "I'll set it up right now."

Sharon looked hopeful. "You can use my office. There's a phone book in the bottom drawer."

Lynda and Jake went into the office.

Tony looked down at Sharon, wishing he had the magic that would bring her child back. "Sharon, you need to get some sleep. You haven't slept in days."

"Neither have you."

"That's not really true," he said. "I slept on your couch while I was here. You've got to rest. There's nothing you can do right now."

"You think they're dead, don't you?" Anne asked in a raspy, breathy voice.

He frowned and turned around. "No. I don't."

"But they could be. That may be why he won't tell you. There's no urgency, because they're dead, and —"

"They're *not* dead!" Sharon cried. "I know they're not. If Christy were dead, I'd know it. I'd feel it, somehow. But she's out there!"

Ben pushed off from the counter and faced Tony squarely. "I want to talk to him. Maybe he'd listen. Maybe he'd tell me."

"Ben, I'm telling you. I've worked on him all night. I've done everything short of beating it out of him."

"Well, *I* could beat it out of him!" Ben shouted.

"No, you couldn't. He's a stubborn man. It's only going to hurt him tomorrow at his arraignment, and I'm hoping the judge will put enough fear into him to make him talk, but we can't wait. I've got him in the worst holding cell the city owns," he told them. "Not a nice place. Then again, it's not nearly as bad as I'd like for it to be, but there are laws about cruel and unusual punishment."

"You ought to have him in a cage, chained to the bars," Ben grumbled.

Sharon shook her head and went to the stove. "I made breakfast for everybody, Tony," she whispered miserably. "But no one was very hungry. Do you want some? It's still hot."

He had to admit that he was hungry. "Yeah, I'll take some, if it's not too much trouble."

Sharon seemed relieved to have something to do. She dipped out some scrambled eggs and bacon and pulled some biscuits out of the oven. Tony watched as she poured him some orange juice and set it on the table. "This is Christy's favorite breakfast," she whispered. "We have it every Saturday morning. I made it thinking . . . hoping . . . that she'd be home to eat it."

Her voice cut off, and she covered her face.

"I was thinking," Tony said quietly. "When you have your press conference, maybe we could ask anyone who's willing to help look for the children to meet at, say, ten o'clock, and with some supervised effort, we could go over St. Clair with a fine-tooth comb. Search every abandoned building in town. Every hotel room. Knock on doors, ask questions . . ."

Sharon looked hopeful. "Do you think anyone would come?"

"Are you kidding? As bad as your church friends have wanted to do something, I'd say that we'll have so many people we won't know what to do with them. Until now, all they could do was pray. Now they can start doing something useful."

Sharon's expression didn't change as she watched him for a moment. "Prayer is useful, Tony," she said quietly. "It's the most useful thing they could do. Bar none."

He looked up from his plate. "Well, I know. I mean . . . you obviously believe that . . . but I just mean . . ."

"God's listening," Sharon said. "Whether we can see what he's doing about it or not. He is listening."

Anne and Ben were stone quiet as they all looked at her, wanting some of her reassurance, desperate for the faith that she still held.

Tony ate quietly for a moment, not sure what to say. Prayer had never seemed more useful to him than action. It was a foreign concept, even though Larry had told him many times how prayer had helped him with things that were out of his control. Sharon, like Larry, seemed too intelligent to fit Tony's preconceptions of the prayer-and-Bible-study crowd.

Lynda and Jake came back into the room in a few minutes. "All right, Sharon," she said. "The press conference is set for 9:00 A.M., on your front lawn. I called Paige, my secretary, and she's going to call all of the television stations in the Tampa Bay area, as well as the newspapers and radio news directors. This is big news, so I think there will be a phenomenal turnout."

Sharon looked up at the clock, then ran her fingers through her hair. "We're going to ask people to meet at ten o'clock to start an organized search."

"Good idea," Jake said. "I was thinking about going up in the plane again. I could direct people to sparsely populated rural areas from the air. It might help."

"Right now we're going to have some new posters made," Lynda said. "These will have the girls' pictures, as well as Chamberlain's. Maybe someone has seen him, and they'll remember. Every member of the media who shows up will want a picture, and we'll need to pass them out to everyone who helps. And we'll need a number people can call to report anything they know. Are your phones still hooked up here, Tony?"

"Yeah," he said. "We can get someone to man them."

"All right. Then we're in business." She started for the door, with Jake behind her.

Sharon sighed. "Thank you, Lynda. Thanks, Jake."

"We're gonna find your kids," Jake told the three forlorn parents in the room. "Hopefully before the sun goes down today."

While the others stacked flyers and planned what to say to the press, Tony hooked up a second VCR to the television and watched a video of the girls, looking for thirty-second clips of both girls to edit out for distribution to all of the television stations. They had already distributed photographs, but now it seemed that the public needed to see the children moving, laughing. Maybe it would pull their heartstrings, as it did his. He sat on a chair right in front of the television, his elbows propped on his knees, and his chin on his clamped fists as Christy and Emily climbed on a sliding board at a park, laughing and waving to the camera.

Their size startled him, and he told himself that he had seen them before they were kidnapped, and they hadn't seemed so tiny then. But now they were in such huge danger. He watched as little Christy slid down, then turned and walked back up the slide, all the while singing, "Zacchaeus was a wee little man, a wee little man was he . . ." She stood at the top of the slide, then took a leap, and fell into sand. She looked as if she'd hurt herself and quickly got up, dusted off her knee, and looked up at the camera as though she wished her father would cut it off.

"I don't feel like performing right now,"

she said, lips trembling. "Turn it off."

He did, and it quickly flashed to another scene, where she was "performing," both she and Emily decked out in Anne's clothes, high heels, and jewelry as they sang a song they had made up, complete with bad choreography.

Christy seemed to be singing, or imagining, or laughing in every frame, and he sat helpless for a moment as tears sprang to his eyes. Was she singing or imagining or laughing now? What must be going through those little girls' minds?

The thought that they could already be dead hit him like a sledgehammer between the eyes, and he shook his head and swallowed hard. They couldn't be. They had to be alive. If he was any kind of cop, he'd find them.

The scene switched to a Christmas shot, when they were both sitting on the floor opening presents, with Jenny behind them. It must have been a Christmas that Sharon had spent alone. He wondered how she had filled it, and wished he had been there to help. He had been lonely last Christmas, too.

The perfect shot of the girls came when they were outside on Christmas morning, both donning their new roller blades, and trying to stand straight without falling as they wrapped their arms around each other and smiled at the camera. He pressed "pause" and froze the scene, and for a moment, just stared at those two little happy, innocent faces.

It was almost more than he could bear, and he sat still, fighting the tears in his eyes, fighting the fears in his heart.

Just hang on a little longer, girls, he told them silently. *I'm gonna find you real soon.*

Then, trying to pull himself together, he quickly turned on the second VCR and copied the scene to be splashed across television screens, both locally and nationally, until they were able to find the children.

CHAPTER SIXTY-FIVE

Both children were getting weaker, and Christy could feel Emily's fever as she leaned her head against her. Christy, herself, was having chills, even though the cat was helping her to battle them.

Her lips felt like scabs, and she saw as the light came through the window overhead that Emily's were cracked. The five-year-old looked deathly pale. Her eyes seemed sunken in.

What had happened to Daddy? Why hadn't the man come back?

She looked around the filthy bathroom and saw the dead rat that the cat had killed last night. She turned her eyes away from it, unwilling to look at it any longer. The cat purred on her lap, and she stroked him. "You did good," she whispered weakly.

She looked up at the broken window through which the cat had come, and wished she could climb up there. She was a good climber, she thought. But both of their hands were so tender, and they didn't have much energy.

The cat meowed and looked up at the window, as if wishing he could get out.

"It's too far, boy," Christy said, though she didn't know what gender the cat was. "You can get down from there, but not back up."

But the cat got off her lap and sat back on its haunches, as if readying itself to pounce. It leaped onto the commode tank, and from there fixed its eyes on the closest plant a few feet up. He pounced, then bobbed in the hanging pot of dried leaves and dirt for a moment, shook off a spiderweb, then looked up, evaluating its next move.

It leaped again to the next plant, sending it swinging, then to the next higher one, and the one above that. In moments, the cat had reached the window.

Christy's eyes widened. She sat up, and shook Emily. "Emily, wake up."

Emily stirred slightly, but was too lethargic. "Emily! I have to show you something!"

Emily opened her eyes. "What?"

"The cat. It climbed back up and got out the window. Maybe we could climb, too." She stood up and, feeling dizzy, leaned back against the commode. After a moment, she recovered her balance and took a step toward the wall where the cat had found the first foothold. "I think I can do it. I'm a good climber. You are, too, Emily."

Emily surveyed the wide space between

the plants. "I'm not that good. That's high, Christy. Besides, we're too heavy. What if they won't hold us?"

"They will," Christy said. "They have to. I can do it, and if I make it, I can come around and get you out. Or go for help."

"No," Emily whined. "Don't leave me here by myself. I'm scared."

"I promise I won't leave you," Christy said.

"But what if you can't move the stuff in front of the door?"

"I will," Christy said. "I'm strong. Daddy always says so."

"But if you get out, and you can't move the stuff, you won't be able to get back in. I'll be all by myself."

"You're what they call a pestimist," Christy said.

"I am not! What is that, anyway?"

"It's somebody who thinks of so many bad things that they become a pest."

"I am not a pest! I'm just scared!"

"Yeah, well, you're a scaredy-cat, too."

Emily started to cry, and Christy was instantly filled with remorse. She went and sat back down beside her, and put her arm around her. Emily was burning with fever. "I'm a scaredy-cat, too," she admitted. "That's why I want out. But don't worry. I won't go. I'll stay here with you."

Emily rubbed the tears from her eyes and looked up at the window. "I wish the cat could talk, and he could tell somebody we were here."

"I wish he could bring us some food and something to drink."

"I wish he would come back and keep me warm. I'm so cold."

"I wish he would come back and keep you company while I climb out."

"Maybe he will come back," Emily whispered weakly. "Maybe he just had to go to the bathroom. You promise you won't leave me?"

The conversation was exhausting Christy. Looking at the window, she wondered if she could make it even if she wanted to. "I promise not to do it right now."

Emily didn't need more. She just laid her head against her sister's shoulder, and waited. . . .

CHAPTER SIXTY-SIX

Sharon couldn't believe the number of people that had convened on her front lawn in less than an hour. Through her living-room window she saw television vans, setting up local, live broadcasts. A conglomeration of cords all led to a cluster of microphones on the front steps of her home. She turned back to Anne and Ben.

"This is a little unnerving," she said quietly. "But the publicity has to help."

"It will," Ben assured her. "Somebody has seen something. If we can just get the word out, we'll find them. I know we will."

"I guess we can each say a few words. Which one of us should go first?"

"You go first," Anne said quickly. Tears came to her eyes, and she pinched the bridge of her nose. "I don't think I can get anything out. You're the professional. You're so good at talking to people . . . you'll say the right thing."

Sharon looked at Ben. "But Ben, you'll speak, won't you?"

He nodded. "Yeah. You go first."

Lynda came in the side door. "Are you ready?"

"Yes," Sharon said. "Are they?"

"It looks like it. One of the stations told me they're doing a feed to CNN. This is going to be national news."

"Really?" Sharon asked. "Why?"

"Look at it from a news directors' point of view. A kidnapper is caught before he tells where the kids are. Every heart in America will be wrenched over this, and someone will be able to tell us something. Let's get to it."

Sharon sighed and almost wished she had changed clothes and put on some makeup, but she just wasn't up to it. She called into the other room. "Jenny? Are you ready?"

Jenny came in carrying Bobby. "Mom, do we have to go out there? There are so many of them."

"Yes," Sharon said. "The whole family's doing this. We're in this together."

Sharon took a breath, bracing herself, and opened the front door. The crowd began to hush as she walked up to the cluster of microphones. Slowly, Anne and Ben came out behind her, then Jenny and Bobby, then Lynda.

Sharon stepped up to the mikes and cleared her throat. "We called you all to come here today, because . . ." She stopped, cleared her throat again. "Because our children, Christy and Emily Robinson, have been kidnapped. As you know, their kidnapper was apprehended early this morning. But he has yet to reveal the location or the condition of our little girls."

Her voice cracked, but she struggled on. "We have every reason to believe they're alive . . . and we need the help of the community to find them. If you've seen anything, please call 555–3367 and report it. If you know of any place in your area that might be a good hiding place, please call. We're depending on this community to get our little girls back. They've been missing for days now, and we don't know if they've eaten, or if they're being taken care of. But we do know that the person we believe to be the sole kidnapper is not taking care of them anymore. Time could be running out . . ." She stopped, braced herself, and got too emotional to go on.

Ben stepped up to the microphones and touched her shoulder gently as she turned away. "I'm Ben Robinson, the father of Christy and Emily. We're asking anyone who can take the time today to please meet at Roosevelt Park at 10 A.M. We're going to start a citywide search for the girls. And girls, if you can hear me, please know that Daddy is looking for you. We're going to find you . . ."

His voice broke, and he stepped back and hugged Anne, who was beside herself already.

Questions broke out from the crowd. "Mr. Robinson, does this kidnapping have anything to do with the murder charges that have been filed against you?"

"I'll take that." Tony came out of the crowd and trotted up the steps. "I'm Tony Danks with the St. Clair PD, and I can tell you that the charges against Mr. Robinson have been officially dropped as of this morning. The kidnapper is our primary suspect in this murder, and if you'll read the statement that I passed out to you, you'll see what the ransom demand was and how it fits into this kidnapping. Again, we will begin a citywide search at 10:00 A.M. this morning, at Roosevelt Park. We need everyone who can come to help us find these children."

He stepped back, and Lynda Barrett took his place. "As an added note, I've been asked to speak for the family to tell you that the $25,000 reward is still being offered to the person who finds and returns these children."

"Are you still trying to get the information out of the kidnapper?" someone asked.

"Yes, of course," Tony said. "He just isn't being very forthcoming."

"Mr. Robinson, is it true that these children are half-sisters?"

Ben stepped forward. "Yes. Christy is my daughter with Sharon. Emily is my daughter with Anne. But they're only a year apart in age. They're very close."

Sharon looked at him and saw the shame, the remorse, on his face at having to admit that their family was such a tangled web. She, too, hated the way it looked. Instantly, they would be labeled a "dysfunctional family." It was a term she hated even more than the word "divorce."

They stood there for a few moments longer as questions were fired at them from the crowd. Enlarged photographs of the girls were passed out to everyone, videos were copied and distributed to the television stations, and finally, the family went back in as Lynda and Tony fielded the rest of the questions.

Two hours later, as Larry and Jenny and Lynda manned the phone lines, Sharon, Anne, and Ben joined Tony and what looked like the rest of the town of St. Clair at Roosevelt Park. Hundreds of people had turned out to search for the children, and a mob of reporters, even more than she'd met on the front lawn of her house, recorded the event.

Sharon was so moved as they drove up that she couldn't speak. Tony saw the emotion on her face, and reached for her hand. "Are you all right?"

"Yes," she whispered. "I'm just surprised."

"St. Clair has a great community spirit," he said. "I knew they'd come."

Anne and Ben got out of the car, but Sharon held back.

"Are you sure you're all right, Sharon?" Tony asked her.

She sat there for a moment, not answering, just staring at the mob of people waiting to find her child. "I guess that . . . I'm just afraid . . . of what they might find." She wiped her tears away.

Tony scooted closer to her on the seat and wiped a tear rolling down her cheek. "Sharon, last night you said that they weren't dead. You said you would have known it. You trusted. Don't you still feel that?"

"Yes," she cried. "But maybe that's just what I *want* to feel. What if they're dead? I just don't want to know."

"They're not dead," Tony whispered. "Chamberlain is a high-brow art dealer. It would go against his nature to kill two little girls."

"It was in his nature to kill Dubose."

"But this is different. He would have no reason to kill them."

"When he left them, he knew they could identify him. He may have wanted to make sure that they didn't."

Tony grew quiet for a moment. He'd thought of that himself. "Sharon, those children need you right now. They need your faith. Now, I'm not even sure I believe in the same things you do, but I've got to tell you. Your faith has been a comfort to me during this whole thing. I may not believe in God, but I believe in your faith in God. What was it you said just yesterday, about God knowing where they are?"

She leaned her head back on the seat and closed her eyes as more tears poured out. "They're in the palm of his hand."

"Maybe he'll show us where they are," Tony whispered. "Now, come on."

They got out of the car and pushed through the crowd to the raised platform where Anne and Ben were already standing.

Jake Stevens was in the crowd, passing out flyers and pictures of the girls. His mother, Doris Stevens, who'd developed a reputation around town for being a Porsche-driving-teenager-in-a-fifty-five-year-old-woman's-body, was standing in a crowd of people telling the tidbits she knew that no one else knew.

"Jake, my boy, is good friends with the parents, ya see, and he says that the daddy and his family moved in with wife number one on account of that bum murder rap they pinned on him, so the girls were together with their older sister when she went to the grocery store . . . You know, this was all over a painting, and that man, Somebody Nelson, the kidnapper, he killed that Dupuis fella who ran the art gallery . . ."

Tony couldn't help grinning slightly, but Sharon was too focused on starting the hunt.

She stepped up on the platform, and looked at Ben. "Who's gonna do the talking?"

"I will," Ben said.

He stepped up to the microphone and tapped it. There was instant feedback, and someone adjusted it as the crowd got quiet.

"I really appreciate you all coming here today," he said, his voice wobbling. "Some pictures of my girls, Christy and Emily, are being passed out right now, along with the phone number to call if you see anything or think of anything that might help us. Uh . . ." He stopped, cleared his throat. "Christy's six, and she's real bright and real strong. And Emily is five . . . not as athletic as Christy, or as daring. But they're survivors.

We . . . uh. . . . don't know how long since they've eaten. And the weather's been getting colder . . . they didn't have their coats . . ." His voice broke and he stepped back, unable to go on.

Tony gave them a few more instructions, organized the groups into sections of the city to cover, then escorted them all back to the car.

"I think the three of you should go home now," he said. "Let these people look for them."

"No," Sharon said. "I'm going to look, too. I can't sit in that house any longer doing nothing."

"But what if someone finds them? You'll need to be home."

"I can take my cellular phone with me. I'm going, Tony. Don't even try to talk me out of it."

"Take us home," Ben said. "We're going, too, but we'll take our own car."

"All right," Tony said, and headed back to Sharon's.

CHAPTER SIXTY-SEVEN

They searched the town high and low, from abandoned buildings to hotel rooms. Tony spent five more hours trying to intimidate the information out of Chamberlain, but to no avail. Even at his arraignment, when the judge ordered him to tell where the children were or be held in the same cell until the Grand Jury investigation, Chamberlain maintained that he knew nothing about them.

Sharon searched in the most destitute part of town, where crack dealers and druggies and prostitutes loitered on the streets. She searched the buildings there with a vengeance, calling out the girls' names at the top of her lungs, until she was too hoarse to be heard any longer.

She had no luck, and her cellular phone never rang. Hourly, she checked at home to see if anyone had given them any leads at all, but any that had been given had already been checked out.

Finally, she drove to the beach, to her favorite spot where she often took the girls, and sat in the car, staring out across the sand and the blue waters of the Gulf.

Why aren't you answering, God? Why have you turned away?

The mighty pounding of the waves were her answer, each white-topped crest tipping toward her like an indictment. For a long while she sat, staring at those angry waves, searching her own heart and mind for the answers she needed.

She had come close to admitting the problem with Ben once, when they'd stood out on that porch and she'd told him of her ulterior motives in inviting him to live in her home. She had confessed, partially, to him, though it hadn't been a confession that sought forgiveness. It had been merely a statement, without heart, without much remorse. It had even been flung out in anger.

Now she wondered if it had been enough. God was dealing with her, she thought. He had something to teach her about her own faults, her own shortcomings, her own sins.

"Oh, God, help me to see what you see," she whispered. "I really want to be pleasing to you."

And then she knew.

She started the car and headed home. Maybe if she got her heart right, once and for all, she could pray effectively, she told herself. Maybe then she wouldn't feel this wall between herself and her Savior.

It was late afternoon when she finally returned home, not ready to give up, but desperately needing some cleansing.

The house was quiet — the phone wasn't ringing. Jenny's eyes were swollen as she sat in front of the telephone, waiting for something, anything, to happen. Lynda was studying a map of the town, trying to figure out any places that had yet to be searched.

"Have Larry or Tony called in?" Sharon asked.

"No," Lynda said. "They're apparently not having any luck with Chamberlain."

Her eyes filled with tears. "I wish they would let me at him. I'd get the information out of him!"

Sobbing quietly, Jenny lowered her face into the circle of her arms. Sharon softened and went to hug her. "Honey, have you eaten?"

"No," she said. "But neither have you. And neither have they . . . at least not since Chamberlain was found." She looked up at her mother. "Mom, why didn't he get me, too? Why didn't he just take me with them? Then I could be there taking care of them, making sure they were all right."

"You are taking care of them," Sharon said. "You're here, doing everything you can."

"Mom, I'm so afraid they're dead!" she said in a high-pitched voice. She fell into her mother's arms, and they clung to each other for a moment.

The phone rang, and Jenny jumped for it.

"I'll get it," Lynda said, but Jenny jerked it up. "Hello?"

She wilted as the caller spoke, then said, "Okay. I'll tell them."

She hung up. "It was Tony. He wanted to check on you. He said he's on his way over."

Sharon went cold. "Does he have news?"

"No," Jenny said. "He said he didn't. But they're still looking."

Sharon leaned heavily back against the wall. "Where are your father and Anne?"

"They got back about half an hour ago. Anne's taking care of Bobby, and Daddy's out on the back porch."

Sharon glanced through the den and to the back door. Sighing, she said, "I need to go talk to him."

She left them there and headed back through her house, to the back porch where Ben stood against the screen, gazing out at the tree house where he had sat with his little girls just days ago.

He heard her coming out and turned his head. She came to stand beside him and looked at it, too. "We were going to paint

433

the tree house," he said quietly. "Since I wasn't here for the building of it, I thought I could at least do that. They wanted to paint a mural."

Sharon swallowed. "God willing, you'll still have the chance."

"Well, that's just it," Ben said. "I don't know if God is willing. I haven't done much for him."

She looked down at the tiles beneath her feet.

"You have, though," he whispered. "I guess I'm counting on him listening to you. You always did the praying for both of us."

Sharon shook her head. "It's occurred to me that maybe my prayers are worthless," she whispered on the edge of tears.

Now he looked fully at her. "Worthless? Why?"

"Because I'm still holding so much against you."

He breathed a mirthless laugh. "Yeah, well, I guess you deserve to." He turned away from the screen and went to sit down on one of the cushioned patio chairs. "You know, it's strange, looking back on what I did to you. It didn't seem so bad at the time."

Sharon couldn't look at him. She kept her eyes on the floor.

"You were doing so great professionally, and I was struggling. You weren't that naive little woman who used to look up at me like I was the one who hung the moon."

"I found out you weren't," she admitted.

"I missed having someone to look up to me," he said. "And when I met Anne —"

Sharon shook her head, unable to bear the explanation again. "Don't, Ben. You don't have to do this."

"Yes, I do," he said.

"Why? I didn't bring it up so we could salt old wounds. I came out here to forgive you."

"Is it really forgiveness, Sharon, when you can't even discuss it?" He rubbed his face and looked at her over his fingertips. "I really need to say these things to you."

She glanced at the door back into the house and wondered if she could make a clean exit. But he was right. That was no kind of forgiveness.

"My children live in two different families because of what I did, Sharon. Two of them I only get to see on weekends. Moving in here and seeing how unnatural everything is . . . well, it started me thinking about how drastically I've altered all of our lives." He looked up at her, struggling with the words. "Sharon, I never meant to hurt you. But even worse, I never meant to hurt Jenny or

Christy. When I think of leaving you when she was just a little baby . . . giving up that daily experience of watching her grow . . ."

"You were the one you hurt," she whispered.

He nodded, as if he knew that was true. "I told myself that you were strong. And you prospered so over the years. I mean, look at this house. You did it yourself."

"I didn't do it myself," she whispered. "I leaned on God, and he took care of me. He does that. He makes provision."

"There have been times, over the years, when I looked back on my affair with Anne, and I realized how I deceived myself, and you, and her. There were really no winners. Everybody had to pay."

"That's divorce," Sharon said.

A long moment of silence stretched between them, and she looked down at her former husband, collapsed on the chair, in turmoil over the present, and in just as much turmoil over the past.

"I'm gonna say something that isn't easy for me," she said, sitting down opposite him and leaning her elbows on her knees as she knitted her fingers together.

"What?" he asked.

"It wasn't just you. I had a part in ending our marriage."

Wind whipped through the screen, ruffling his long hair. "How do you figure that?" he asked. "You were faithful."

"That's true. I never cheated on you. Not with a person. But with my work. And with my affections. Maybe it was my job to keep looking at you the way I had in the beginning. Maybe I set myself up for an Anne to come along." She swallowed, and made herself look at him. "All those times you wanted affection, and I was distant, cold . . . I told myself you were just a passionate artist, that your feelings didn't have to be taken seriously."

His face changed as he gazed at her. "I never in a million years thought I'd hear you say this."

"I should have said it a long time ago, Ben. Yes, you hurt our family when you left. But I hurt them, too. Maybe I left the marriage long before you did."

He struggled with the emotion twisting his face.

"I forgive you, Ben," she whispered. "I hope you can forgive me."

"I do." They were the words he'd spoken on the day they'd exchanged vows, and now they were spoken to heal them of their broken vows. He got up and hugged her, tightly, desperately, then quickly let her go.

"Now maybe God will listen to me," she whispered. "Maybe he had to bring us through this to get us to this point. Come in with me. We'll get Anne and Jenny, and start praying again."

He rubbed his red eyes and followed her in.

CHAPTER SIXTY-EIGHT

Tony pulled into Sharon's driveway and sat for a moment in his car, wishing with all his heart that he had some good news for her. He hated to go in there empty-handed again, but he felt a compulsion to be here with her, as though he had some part in this loss they shared.

He got out of the car and walked to the door, but before knocking, decided to walk back to the gate that led into the backyard. He opened it and went through, and looked around the yard at all the signs of the little girl who lived here. Her Barbie bike with glittery iridescent ribbons streaming from the handlebars stood on the patio next to a little toy stroller. Across the yard, her tire swing sat motionless, empty. He walked across the lawn to the tree house, and looked up. Something drew him up there, so he shrugged off his sport coat, dropped it on the ground, and began to climb the ladder.

He opened the hatch at the top of the ladder and went in to the little room where she'd stored so many treasures. Milk cartons and shoe boxes and rolls of string and glue . . .

He could just imagine the little rascals up here playing to their hearts' content, never worried that some stranger might come along and rock their world.

Unable to handle the emotions suddenly coursing through him, he slipped out the hatch and climbed back down. He grabbed his coat and hurried across the yard.

When he knocked on the door, Lynda let him in. "Any word?" she asked hopefully.

Tony shook his head and sighed. "No. Chamberlain's not saying a word. And now he's got this bigshot lawyer with him trying to strike a deal."

"What kind of deal?"

"Well, it's real nebulous, since the man is swearing he had nothing to do with the kidnapping, but what I'm gathering is that if we give him clemency, he might tell us where they are. But remember, all of this is being conveyed through hints — he still claims to be innocent. The DA says he's going to go for the death penalty, and the judge has done everything but torture him to make him talk. Still nothing."

She groaned.

"Where's Sharon?" he asked.

"Upstairs in Christy's room. She's a wreck. They all are."

"I'll go talk to her before I get back to the

hunt," he whispered.

He went up the stairs quietly, since the house seemed so still. It felt strange disturbing it. He saw the pink walls in the room down the hall, and assumed that was Christy's room. Quietly, he went to the door.

There were Sharon, Jenny, Ben, and Anne, huddled on the bed with their arms around each other and their heads bowed, praying out loud for God's help in delivering those kids.

Something about the scene touched his heart . . . *broke* his heart. They were enemies . . . adversaries . . . Their pasts had shipwrecked their futures. Yet here they were, bound by their love for those little girls, acting as a family under the eyes of God.

Tears came to his eyes, and he stumbled backward, quietly, because he didn't want them to hear him. What if they looked up and invited him to join them? He hadn't really prayed since his "Now I lay me down to sleep" days as a boy . . . and he wasn't ready to do it now.

He rushed back down the stairs, feeling like a coward — the big, bad cop who could put the fear into everyone but Nelson Chamberlain, the one who was afraid of nothing — running from the idea of getting caught in a prayer.

He slipped out the door before Lynda could see him and got quickly into his car. He'd cranked the engine and pulled out of the driveway before the first tears stung his eyes.

He had never felt more helpless in his life. Two children were out there who he was powerless to help, and a man sat in jail who wasn't afraid enough of him to talk. Always before, there had been some way of working toward a solution. This time, however, everything seemed out of his hands.

Was Sharon right? Was God really in control? Was there even a God at all?

He drove until it began to get dark, and the stars began to appear, revealing the majesty of the Creator who was artist, astronomer, and physicist. To Sharon, he was a comforter. He was in control. He knew where those children were.

He pulled his car off the road, looked up at the dark sky, and asked himself for the first time in a very long time if he really believed. He wasn't sure. But Sharon's faith, her graciousness with her ex-husband and his wife, sure seemed real. And she was an intelligent woman, not some superstitious soul who would fall for anything. She'd been through fires and come out of them still believing.

His eyes were full of tears as he looked up through his dirty windshield. "If you're up there, God, I don't know why you'd waste any time on me," he whispered. "I'm not exactly what they call worthy. And I haven't given you more than a passing thought in about the last ten years, except when Larry has hassled me about you. You know Larry — yeah, what am I saying, of course you do."

He didn't know why he was crying. It was crazy. None of this made any sense, but as he spoke, a sense of tremendous waste, monumental loss, overtook him. "I can't believe you can even hear me, if you're there, but I figure it's worth a try, anyway. There's probably nothing that could have made me come to you, God, except maybe two little girls out there alone . . . and their grieving mother who believes in you."

He rubbed his eyes, angry at himself for losing control like this. "God, you've gotta help us. You've gotta help them. Not for me . . . not because of anything I've done . . . but do it for them. Those helpless little —"

He sobbed into his hand, then tried to pull himself together again. "I'll make a deal with you, God. If you bring them back safely to their parents . . . I'm yours. I'll be the best believer you've ever seen. I'll do anything you say . . . I'll even pray and read the Bible, even though what I've seen of it I've never understood. But I'll take classes and learn. I'll do all the stuff Larry does, and more. I'll even start being one of those people who gives money to poor people, and visits prisoners, and God, that's a big promise, because I don't have much compassion for the people I lock up . . ."

He sighed and wiped his face. "I think if you could work enough miracles to get Sharon and Ben and Anne praying together, then you can give me that kind of compassion. And you can help us find those kids."

He didn't quite know how to sign off. "Amen" seemed so trite, but "Bye" sounded too silly. So he let it hang there . . . wondering if anyone had heard.

Peace gradually washed over him as he pulled back out onto the street and started searching for the children again.

CHAPTER SIXTY-NINE

Emily wasn't acting right. Since the afternoon, all she had wanted to do was sleep. Her lips were cracked and bloody from thirst, and her eyes were sunken deeper into her face, casting dark circles under them. Christy had tried to wake her up, mostly from fear since darkness was beginning to close in again, but she barely stirred.

She had to get help, Christy thought, looking at the window again. She had to make her way out.

She got up and steadied herself as a wave of dizziness washed over her. After a moment, she recovered her equilibrium, and she stepped up on the rim of the commode and climbed to the broken lid. She looked up and found the plant where the cat had first jumped on its way out. The spider had repaired its web, but she shoved that thought out of her mind.

"Help me climb like a cat, God," she whispered. "Help me climb like a cat."

She was a good climber, she reminded herself. It was her favorite thing to do. She could do this, even if it was hard.

She judged the distance between where

she stood and the plant, and reached out her foot. It reached, but just barely, and she pressed one hand against the wall and reached for the grimy macramé with the other. She tested her weight on it, felt the stake in the wall give slightly, but she didn't let it stop her. Quickly, she pulled her other foot up. The plant swung from its hanger, creaking with her weight, so she quickly stepped up to the next one.

Her hands throbbed and bled as she clawed at the wall for a hold, measuring her next step. When she'd gotten both feet on the next hanging pot, she began to get dizzy again.

Hold on, she told herself. *Just wait a minute.*

She waited, swinging slightly, until the dizziness passed, then looked up the wall for the next foothold.

She pulled her body up, and looked up at the window again. It was still so far up there, but she could make it, she thought. She just had to take it easy, go slowly, be careful.

Her arms were getting tired, something that never happened, and she told herself it was weakness since she hadn't eaten. She would only get weaker if she didn't find help. She had to get out somehow.

She clawed at the bricks with each foothold, and winced at the pain in her fingers.

She was hot, but she wasn't sweating, and her throat felt as if it was on fire. If she only had some water, she thought. Just a drop . . .

She looked down, and saw her sister lying limply on the floor. She was burning with fever, and looked so weak. What if she died?

She couldn't give up now. She had to make it up.

The next plant was too high, so she grabbed its pot with her hands and tried to climb the bricks, toe hitting grout, one brick at a time, until she was able to step up to the next plant. She grabbed on to the bricks with one aching, infected hand, and held the macramé for dear life with the other.

Just above her was a wooden planter bolted to the wall, and she reached up and grabbed it. She pushed up until she was able to get her weight over it. Once she got her feet on it, she rested and looked up. The window was only a few feet away. She could make it.

She took a deep breath and calculated that three more plants would get her to the window, and she stretched her leg with all her might to reach the next one, then the next one, until finally she could reach the windowsill.

With all her strength, she pulled herself up, but the window wasn't open. The cat had come in through a broken hole in the glass. But she was too big to fit through it.

She tried to plant her feet on the window-sill, and held on to the top casing with one hand while she struggled to raise the window with the other. It was stuck.

She looked down at her sister still lying on the floor. The room was growing darker, but outside it was only dusk. She could see the big tree beside the window, the tree the cat must have climbed to get in. The branches reaching to the window were small, but she could make it, she told herself, if she could just get the window open.

Holding the casing as tightly as she could with her infected hands, she kicked at the glass. Shards fell out and crashed to the dirt outside. She looked down to see if the noise had disturbed Emily, but her sister still lay there, deep in sleep.

The hole looked big enough to get through, so she ducked through it, kicked the broken glass off of the ledge, and carefully sat down to get her bearings. The cool air against her face made her feel stronger. She tried to find a branch big enough to hold her. None of them looked secure. She grabbed the closest one and straddled it with both arms and legs, sliding toward the center.

It swayed downward as if it might break with her weight, but she grabbed the bigger one beneath her, and climbed down to it. It was stronger, and she slid in toward the trunk, then found another, stronger one, and another, until she felt secure.

It was a massive tree, a perfect climbing tree, but it didn't give her the pleasure that climbing usually did. Her hands were bleeding and sore, and she was shaking. She made her way down, one branch at a time.

When she'd made it to the bottom branch, she looked down. It was at least a six-foot jump to the ground from here, and she wasn't sure if she could manage it. But she had no choice. Emily was still in there, all alone, and she had to hurry.

She judged the distance, as the cat had done, then held her breath and leapt. She made a perfect landing.

Now what? she asked, looking around. There were no buildings, no houses, anywhere in sight. Only this lonely road with a ditch on either side, and thick woods.

She went to the road, looked up and down it, but saw nothing. No cars, no people, no houses.

She would have to get Emily out, she

thought, and then they could run away as far as they needed to find help. And she had to hurry, in case the man came back.

She ran back to the front door of the dilapidated structure and pushed it open.

The building was getting dark, full of monstrous shadows and scratching noises and creaks that terrified her. But she couldn't be afraid, she told herself. Emily needed her.

She ran up the stairs, careful to avoid the holes in them, and found the bathroom. The man had slid a huge bench against the door and piled a steel drum and other pieces of rusted machinery on it to weigh it down. She tried to slide it back, but it wouldn't budge.

Christy climbed on top of it, and turned backward, pushing her back against the wall and using the force of her legs to try to slide the bench away. But she just wasn't strong enough. It was jammed tightly against the door, and there was no way she would ever get it open.

She thought of calling out to Emily, trying to wake her again, but then she realized that her sister probably needed the blessing of sleep. If she woke to find herself alone, she would fall apart. Until Christy got her help, she didn't want to wake her.

She was trembling now, both from fear

and courage, both from despair and hope.

"God, you can help us," she whispered weakly. "You helped me climb like a cat. Please send somebody now."

CHAPTER SEVENTY

Doris Stevens had been dead-set on winning that $25,000 reward money when she'd set out to look for the kidnapped children that day, but after an all-day search, she was getting discouraged. St. Clair was no huge metropolis, but it was bigger than Slapout, Texas. If she had looked for two lost children in Slapout, she could have turned the whole town upside down in two hours flat, and she would have found what she was looking for.

Now she had less than an hour to shower and change for her shift at the diner where she worked, and she wound her Porsche through the backstreets on the outskirts of St. Clair, heading for her trailer, which was parked on the only piece of land she could afford on her salary. It was far out, yes, but it was home. She'd been urged to sell the Porsche and buy a house or a condo, but she couldn't bring herself to do it. She loved that car. It was the only thing of any value she'd ever had.

It was getting dark, so she turned on her headlights and wove around the curves, ignoring the speed limit, since she rarely encountered other cars this far out. Maybe, if she was lucky, the kids wouldn't be found today, and she'd still have a shot at the grand prize tomorrow.

She turned up the radio on her favorite cry-in-your-beer country tune, something about being cheated on in the worst kind of way, something she could relate to many times over. She began to sing along in her nasal, twangy voice, as loud as the speakers blaring in her car. She had always thought she could have made it as a country singer.

A cat dashed across the road in front of her, and she barely missed hitting it, swerving only slightly to avoid losing control. Suddenly alert, she cursed and reached for her cigarette box, shook one out, pressed in the lighter, and stuck the cigarette in her mouth. She waited until the lighter was ready, then reached to get it out to light her cigarette.

From the corner of her eye, she saw something up ahead, and she dropped the lighter on the floor and looked up.

A child stood in the middle of the road, waving her down.

She swerved, slammed on brakes, lost control. The car skidded to the right, into the ditch, kept sliding several hundred feet further, then slammed full force against a tree.

She sat still for a moment, trying to decide

if anything was broken. Nothing but the car, she thought in misery. Then she screamed a curse, and slammed her hand against the steering wheel.

She saw movement outside her window and looked up, and saw that child again. Furious, she flung open the door. "You almost got me killed! What in the world were you doin' standin' out in the middle of the street? Where's your mama? I'm gonna march you right home to her and tell her what you did!" She got out and looked at her crumpled Porsche, and stamped one high-heeled foot. "Look what you did! It's ruined! The only thing decent I ever had, and you ruined it!"

The little girl looked like she'd just lost a fight, and she was shivering. "I'm sorry," she said in a hoarse, raspy voice. "But I . . . I need help. My sister's locked in that old building up the road, and I have to get her out 'cause she's sick. Please. Will you help us?"

Doris looked down at the little girl and could tell that she wasn't doing so hot herself. She had a nasty cut on her forehead, and dried blood matted her bangs. The child looked familiar, except for the dark circles beneath her eyes, the ghost-like pallor to her skin, the blistered lips. "Honey, what's your name?"

"Christy Robinson," the child said.

Doris caught her breath. "Oh, my word! You're the kidnapped kid! You're the one we've been lookin' for!"

"You have?" Christy asked.

"Yes!" Doris shouted. "And I found you! Twenty-five grand is mine! I'm goin' to Atlantic City, that's what I'm gonna do! I'm gonna get me a fancy dress and stay in some fancy room with a hot tub —"

The little girl seemed to be dizzy, and she leaned against the car to steady herself. Doris instantly shut up. "Okay, kiddo. First things first. If only I had a car phone. I mean, there's one in the car, but I couldn't afford to pay for it, so I disconnected it. Heck, I can barely afford to put gas in it, but it doesn't matter now, does it? It's gone. Well, at least it does have insurance. That's somethin'." She saw the half-bottle of Coke sitting in the drink holder, undisturbed even though the front of the car was smashed in. "Honey, you look thirsty. You want this?"

Christy's eyes widened and she took the Coke and finished most of it off in one gulp. She probably hadn't had anything to drink in a while, Doris assumed.

She stopped when there was about two inches left in the bottle. "My sister needs the rest of this," she said. "We have to hurry.

The man might come back, and if he finds me gone, he might hurt Emily."

"The man?" Doris asked. "That Nelson Chamberlain fella? Oh, no. He's not comin' back. He's in jail."

Christy looked up at her with those dull, lethargic eyes. "Really?"

"That's right, and honey, your parents are sick with worry over you. They've been lookin' everywhere. Come on, let's go get your little sister."

"Do you have a flashlight?" Christy asked. "We might need it. She has one, but she's not awake. And she's locked in a bathroom, and there's all this stuff shoved in front of it, only it's too heavy and I can't move it. I climbed out the window, but Emily's not as good a climber, and she won't wake up."

"Oh, blazes," Doris said, realizing the urgency of the situation. She went to her trunk, opened it, and found the flashlight and hydraulic jack that Jake had put there. She took them both out, thinking that she might need the jack if the door was barricaded as thoroughly as Christy said.

Christy led her back up the road to the building that was encased in darkness now. It was the old country store that she passed every day. Why she hadn't thought to look there earlier, she didn't know. But the front door was always open, and windows were broken out, and she had just assumed that if anyone were hidden there, the door wouldn't be open.

She shivered at the thought of going in there, and turned on the flashlight. It lit up the downstairs. "I gotta tell you, kiddo. I ain't much of one for bravery. This ain't the kind of place I like to go."

"Me, either," Christy said. "But it's okay. Come on. We have to get to Emily."

Every muscle in her body was rigid with tension as she made her way up the creaky stairs and saw the door barricaded with that big bench, a steel drum, and some other equipment.

She set down the jack and tried to pull the bench away, but she wasn't strong enough. "All right," she said, grabbing the jack. "Never fear. This'll move it right out of the way." She wedged it the best she could between one of the pieces of machinery and the wall, then began to pump it. It immediately began to expand, pushing the bench inch by inch back from the door.

"That's good! I can open it now," Christy said. She slipped between the bench and the door, and opened it.

Emily was still sleeping deeply on the

floor. "There she is!" Christy said. "I think she's sick."

Doris slipped into the filthy place and knelt next to the tiny child. She touched her head. "She's burning up with fever," she said. "Poor little thing." She picked her up in her arms, and handed the flashlight to Christy. "Here, I'll carry her, and you lead us back out with the light."

Emily didn't stir as they hurried out of the building.

"Where will we go?" Christy asked.

"My place," Doris said. "It's only about a mile up the road. I can call your mama and daddy from there, and get you somethin' to eat. Give me that Coke, will ya?"

Christy handed it to her, and watched as she poured a couple of drops on Emily's lips, then a couple more. She saw Emily swallow. "Come on, darlin'," Doris said. "Drink some of this, for Doris. It'll make you feel better."

Slowly, Emily's eyes began to open, and she raised her head enough to drink. When the bottle was empty, Doris said, "Okay, let's go."

They walked for what seemed an eternity, and her high heels began to cut into her feet, rubbing blisters and making her ankles ache. But she had the kids, she thought. That was the main thing. That and the money.

"Did that man hurt you, honey?" she asked as they trudged along.

Christy shrugged. "He locked us up."

"But did he . . . *do* anything? Are you all right?"

"I'm hungry," Christy whispered. "And my hands hurt. And I'm cold."

Emily stirred in Doris's arms. "Christy?" she whispered.

Christy looked over at Emily. "Yeah."

"Did God answer our prayers with her?" she whispered weakly.

Christy smiled. "Yeah, he did."

Doris didn't know quite what to say to that. She'd never been the answer to a prayer before.

"Is Daddy coming to get us?" Emily asked.

"You bet he is, darlin'," Doris said. "As soon as I can get us to a phone. Look. See right up there? That's my trailer."

Christy looked so relieved that she stopped for a moment and just took in the sight, before pushing herself on.

CHAPTER SEVENTY-ONE

Tony went back to the house, unable to rest or go home until he'd found the children. Lynda had already left, and Sharon, Jenny, Anne, and Ben all sat around the kitchen table, waiting that excruciating wait that seemed almost pointless.

He joined them at the table, feeling so helpless, so ineffective as a police officer, so inept as a human being.

And then the phone rang. Jenny sprang for it. "Hello?"

"Yes . . . uh . . . is this the Robinson's residence?" a woman with a deep southern drawl asked.

"Yes, it is."

"Well, this is Doris Stevens — Jake Stevens' mama? You know my boy, don't you?"

"Yes," Jenny said.

"I've got some good news for you, honey."

"What?" Jenny asked cautiously.

"I've found your kids."

Jenny sprang out of her seat and grabbed her father's arm. "Are . . . are you sure? Christy and Emily? You have them?"

Everyone sprang up from the table, and

Ben grabbed the phone away from her. "This is Ben Robinson. You've found my girls?"

"Sure have," Doris said. "Here's Christy. She can tell you for herself."

He waited a moment, then heard Christy's hoarse, weak voice. "Daddy?"

"Honey!" He burst into tears. "Where are you?"

"With Miss Doris. Daddy, will you come get us now? I want to go home."

"Of course!" he shouted. "Are you all right?"

"I don't feel good, Daddy," Christy said. "And Emily's real sick. She has fever."

"Put the lady back on."

Doris took the phone back. "Hello? I can give you directions if you've got a pencil. I'd bring 'em to you, but I'm afraid I wrecked my car to keep from hittin' your daughter."

He jotted down the directions, and they all jumped into the car.

CHAPTER SEVENTY-TWO

Christy ate a piece of cold chicken and watched out Doris's window for any sign of her father, but it had only been a few minutes since she'd talked to him. Doris said it would be at least fifteen before he'd be here.

Doris was holding Emily like a baby and coaxing her to drink. The child's fever was too high, and she hoped with all her heart that they'd be able to stop it in time. "Come on, honey. Drink some more for Doris. You don't want your daddy to be all worried about you, do you? He's on his way, you know."

Emily's eyes fluttered open, and she drank a little more.

"My heavens, look at these hands," Doris said. "Honey, you need to go back to that pan of water and soak your hands," she told Christy. "Get some of that dirt off. They're all infected. And this child's whole hands are swollen. I'm gonna have to let the doctor clean hers. I can't bear to hurt her when she's this sick. You know, you're a hero."

"Me?" Christy asked, turning around. "What did I do?"

"You may have saved your baby sister's life."

"You did that," Christy said. "I prayed that God would send help. He sent you."

"Oh, now, I don't know about none of that superstitious stuff. I prob'ly woulda seen you anyway."

Christy smiled knowingly and shook her head. "Nope. He sent you."

"Wouldn't I know it if God had sent me?"

"Maybe not," Christy said. "But he sent you just like he sent the cat."

"What cat?"

"The cat who protected us from the rats."

Doris shivered. What had these poor children endured for the last few days? Her heart ached as she looked down at the pale, weak child in her arms. No baby should have to go through such things.

"I hope they sling that man up by his toenails and make him eat mud," she muttered. "Treatin' two beautiful little girls like this. It just breaks my heart." She dabbed at the tears in her eyes.

Christy saw headlights, and began to jump up and down. "They're here! They're here!"

Doris peered out the window and saw the station wagon, followed by two or three other cars, some of them police squad cars and a television news van. "Blazes," she muttered. "Wish I'd had time to wash my hair. Go let your daddy in, honey."

Christy ran to the door and down the steps, and straight into Ben's arms as he bolted out of the car. Then Sharon took her from him, and the child clung to her mother.

Anne ran past them and into the house, and found Emily lying weak and feverish in Doris's arms. Sobbing, Anne took her quickly from the woman, kissed the child's face, and began whispering to her.

Tony's eyes were red with emotion as he stepped into the trailer, followed by Ben and Christy and Sharon. Doris wiped her eyes at the reunion as the mothers cried over their children.

"She's burning up," Anne shouted up to Ben.

"Her hands are infected, too," Doris pointed out. "And she ain't eaten a bite. I tried to feed her, but all she'd do was drink a little."

"Christy's feverish, too," Sharon said. "We've got to get them to the hospital."

"The squad car will escort you," Tony said. "Go ahead and take them."

Photographers were gathering and cameras rolled as the children were rushed out to the car and driven away with a flashing escort. Doris ran out and grabbed Tony as he

started to get in his car, ignoring the reporters who were trying to get her to stop and
give them an interview about how she'd
found the children. "Can you drive me to
the hospital?" she asked. "I really want to
know how the little things are."

Tony looked surprised. "Sure. We're going to need a statement from you, anyway.
How did you find them?"

Doris started to say that it was a fluke, that
the child had just appeared in her headlights.
But then she thought better of it. "Well,
accordin' to that little Christy, God sent me
to 'em. She swears up-an'-down that I'm an
answered prayer."

Tony's eyes welled with tears, and he
smiled. "You know what, Doris? Christy's
absolutely right."

CHAPTER SEVENTY-THREE

The children were kept overnight in the hospital, with IVs to battle their dehydration, and antibiotics to fight the infections originating in their hands. Both girls had their hands bandaged, and Christy had a bandage over her forehead.

Anne and Sharon requested that they be allowed to share a room, so that Ben could see both children at once. Jenny came in as soon as someone from their church had come to relieve her from taking care of Bobby, and tears sprang into her eyes at the sight of her two sleeping sisters. "Oh, Mom . . . Anne . . . I'm so sorry for letting this happen to them."

Sharon pulled her older daughter into a hug. "Honey, it's not your fault. And they're going to be fine."

"Really? Are you sure?"

"Yes."

"Were they . . . abused in any way? Molested, I mean?"

"No," Sharon said with certainty. It was one of the first things the doctor had looked for.

She walked Jenny back out of the room,

knowing that Anne would keep an eye on Christy if she woke. "Honey, I know you're still blaming yourself for all this, but I want you to know that some good did come out of it."

"What?" she asked. "How?"

"God used it, to make me confront the fact that I'd never really forgiven your father. Or Anne. In my heart, I think I really hated them."

"You couldn't have hated them, Mom. You let them move in with us."

"Well, I had several different motives for that. One of them was to look good to you. The more generous I looked, the worse they looked. But there sure wasn't any love involved."

"What about now?"

She glanced back in the room. "Anne's a mother, just like me. She loves her kids every bit as much. And she's been a good stepmother to you and Christy. I haven't made it easy for her. And your father . . . he's not a bad man. He made some mistakes, and his mistakes hurt me, and you, too. But I was far from perfect myself, Jenny."

Jenny wiped her eyes. "Me, too."

"God forgives our mistakes," Sharon said.

"He's awesome," Jenny whispered. "So awesome."

Sharon hugged her daughter again, and saw Tony standing across the hall. He'd heard everything. "Tell you what," she told Jenny. "Why don't you stay with Christy for a while, and I'll go get something to eat. I haven't had much in the last few days, myself, and I'm starting to feel a little hungry."

"Okay," Jenny whispered, and went back into the room.

Sharon went out of the room and looked up at Tony — who looked as tired and relieved as she did. "You've been great, Tony. Really great."

He seemed to struggle with emotion as he looked down at his feet. Unable to say what was on his mind, he nodded toward the waiting room. "Doris is the real hero. She's in the waiting room."

Sharon took his hand and they went to the waiting room. Doris was in there with Jake and Lynda, chattering ninety-to-nothing about how she'd found the girls. When she saw Sharon, she sprang to her feet. "How are they, hon?" she asked.

"They're great," Sharon said, hugging the woman who'd saved her daughter. "They'll both get to go home tomorrow. I just don't know how to thank you enough. The reward doesn't even begin to cover it." She wiped her eyes. "I'll write you a check tonight before you leave."

Doris glanced at Lynda and Jake, then let out a heavy sigh. "Oh, heck, I can't take your money. At first, when I was lookin' for 'em, I thought I could. I mean, they were just pictures on a flyer, ya know? But now that I know 'em, and I seen what they've been goin' through . . . well, I can't take money for it. It just doesn't seem right. Not when Christy's so sure that God was usin' me to find 'em. I can't imagine why. Not like he's ever been able to use me before! Out of the mouths of babes. Who am I to dispute it? But no money."

"But your car," Sharon said. "It's totaled. Let me at least help you . . ."

Doris raised her hand to stem the woman's offer. "My insurance will pay for the car. It was fun while it lasted, sure. But I think I'm gonna take the insurance money and get me a little second-hand car of some kind, and use the rest of the money for a down payment on a nicer place to live. That trailer's too far out. It's time I did that, anyway."

Jake hugged his mother. "Mama got a call from Oprah Winfrey a few minutes ago," he said with a grin. "She's going on her show next week."

Sharon laughed. "Really?"

"Yeah," Doris said, waving a hand as if it meant nothing. "Somethin' about modern-day heroes. Can you imagine?"

A flock of reporters rushed to the door of the waiting room and descended on Sharon, but she pointed them to Doris. "She's the one who found the children," she said. "Sacrificed her Porsche to do it."

They all surrounded her as Sharon and Tony slipped out of the room.

Downstairs, Sharon and Tony sat sipping coffee over empty plates. Neither of them had realized how ravished they had been after not eating much for several days. A feeling of utmost peace seemed to fill Tony in a way that he'd never before experienced.

"Something weird happened to me today," he said, not able to look at Sharon as he spoke.

"What?" she asked.

He shrugged. "Well, I don't know. I was . . . sort of . . . under the fig tree."

Her eyebrows shot up. "You prayed?"

He couldn't meet her eyes. "I sort of made a deal with God."

"Uh-oh," Sharon said. "You're not supposed to bargain with God."

He smiled. "He took me up on it. I told him that if he brought the girls home safely, that I'd be a believer, and that I'd be the best Christian he had ever seen."

Sharon couldn't believe her ears. "And?"

"And I'm keeping my end of the bargain," he said. "He did it, didn't he? He really answered." He swallowed and looked up at her. "See, I've been struggling with this. Some voice in my head keeps saying, well, he may have answered, but why'd he let it happen in the first place? And then I heard you and Jenny talking, and I realized that he really may have created good out of it. In a lot of ways. For one, I never dreamed Doris Stevens would turn down the money. That's a miracle in itself. And this afternoon . . ." He wiped his eyes. "I saw you and Ben and Anne praying together . . . you had just put away your problems, your differences, all that baggage . . . and you went to God. That was good, wasn't it?"

She smiled. "Yeah. It was good."

"And it worked." He propped his chin on his hand and looked at her with probing eyes. "God may not have caused the kidnapping. I don't know. But I do know that he used it to knock me in the head. He used it for a lot of things."

She smiled as tears formed in her eyes. "Then it was worth it."

Gently, he took her hand. "Sharon, would

you consider going out with me when all this is over? We were supposed to have had dinner. We never got to."

She smiled poignantly. "A real date?"

He nodded, feeling like that awkward teenager again. "I would consider it an honor to spend as much time with you as you're willing to spend with me."

"I would love to," she said, squeezing his hand. "As a matter of fact, why don't you come to church with me Sunday?"

He nodded. "This time, there's nothing I'd like more."

AFTERWORD

Recently, when I was reading the book of Zechariah, something jumped out at me that I had not understood before. It was in chapter 7, when the people came to the prophet and asked him to inquire of God whether they should continue observing the fast to commemorate the destruction of Jerusalem, since Jerusalem was now being rebuilt. God answered their question with a question. He asked them if they were fasting for him, or for themselves. And then he added something that seemed unrelated to their question. "Administer true justice; show mercy and compassion to one another. Do not oppress the widow or the fatherless, the alien or the poor. In your hearts do not think evil of each other." The people must have frowned at one another and thought, "Did God misunderstand the question? We asked about fasting on a particular day, and he answers us with all this stuff about justice, compassion, and our hearts."

I've read that before and it has gone right over my head, but this time, it shone in my face like a beacon illuminating my own sins. I go to God expecting a pat on the back for

473

all the good deeds I've done, all the people I've helped, all the enemies I've forgiven, all the worship I've sacrificed my time to offer. And God says, "Get real, Terri. Who were you doing those things for? Me or yourself?"

It's as if I look up at God and say, "Well, if that's not enough, what do you want?"

And he replies, "I want your heart pure. Your good deeds amount to nothing but filthy rags if your heart isn't pure. If worshiping me is a sacrifice, and if your good deeds are nothing more than markings on the scoresheet of your life, then you still don't get it."

Like the chicken-and-the-egg question, I guess it all comes down to the question we Christians continually have to ask ourselves. Which came first, the righteous heart or the good works? Do good works give us a righteous heart, or does our righteous heart lead us to do good works? Which would God rather see?

I know the answer, and most of you do, as well. God doesn't ask for a scoresheet or a legalistic report card. He's already done all the work to save us. He sent his Son to die on the cross for all of our sins and to demonstrate our inheritance in his Resurrection. All he asks is that we give him our hearts. All of our hearts.

So many times I've run myself ragged trying to do things that I believe are pleasing to God, only to realize sometime later that I've neglected my prayer life and my Bible study — in fact, I've left God out of it entirely. "Was it really for me you fasted?" God asked. Interesting question. And a painful one, as well.

And God sits quietly, watching and shaking his head, wondering when we will learn.

Thank God that he doesn't wash his hands of us. Thank God that he asks those probing, painful questions that remind us what is important. Thank God that he never stops teaching us.

May our hearts be so pure, so full of his righteousness, so Christlike, that our good deeds burst forth as acts of worship, rather than sacrifice.

And may God never stop working on me.

God bless you all,

Terri Blackstock

ABOUT THE AUTHOR

Terri Blackstock is an award-winning novelist who has written for several major publishers including HarperCollins, Dell, Harlequin, and Silhouette. Her books have sold over 3.5 million copies worldwide over the last twelve years, under two pseudonyms.

With her success in secular publishing at its peak, Blackstock had what she calls "a spiritual awakening." A Christian since the age of fourteen, she realized she had not been using her gift as God intended. It was at that point that she recommitted her life to Christ, gave up her secular career, and made the decision to write only books that would point her readers to him.

"I wanted to be able to tell the truth in my stories," she said, "and not just be politically correct. It doesn't matter how many readers I have if I can't tell them what I know about the roots of their problems and the solutions that have literally saved my own life."

Her books are about flawed Christians in crisis and God's provisions for their mistakes and wrong choices. She claims to be extremely qualified to write such books, since she's had years of personal experience.

A native of nowhere, since she was raised in the Air Force, Blackstock makes Clinton, Mississippi, her home. She and her husband are the parents of three children — a blended family which she considers one more of God's provisions.

The employees of Thorndike Press hope you have enjoyed this Large Print book. All our Large Print titles are designed for easy reading, and all our books are made to last. Other Thorndike Press Large Print books are available at your library, through selected bookstores, or directly from us.

For information about titles, please call:

(800) 257-5157
To share your comments, please write:

Publisher
Thorndike Press
P.O. Box 159
Thorndike, Maine 04986